BLACK SUN

Black Sun

Chronicles of Jeremy Nash
Book 3

Frank F. Fiore

WordCrafts

Black Sun, although based on actual events, is a work of fiction. The author has endeavored to be respectful to all persons, places, and events presented in this novel, and attempted to be as accurate as possible where historical and scientific issues are concerned. Still, this is a novel, and all references to persons, places, and events are fictitious or used fictitiously.

Black Sun
Copyright ©2012
Frank F. Fiore

ISBN: 978-1-962218-75-7

Cover concept and design by Mike Parker.

Published by WordCrafts Press
Cody, Wyoming 82414
www.wordcrafts.net

Author's Note

Crypto-history is the historical revision or reinterpretation of history surrounding past events. Over the years, Nazi Germany has become a prime source of theories and reinterpreted events in its history. Indiana Jones as an example. Other examples abound—stories of secret Nazi bases connected with hollow earth theories, U-boat convoys to Antarctica, Nazi super weapons, both fact and fantasy, esoteric and occult energy sources like zero point energy, and the list goes on and on.

It seems that crypto-historians have been able to weave any kind of conspiracy theory into Nazi crypto-history. Even German mysticism and the occult have been made part and parcel of Nazi crypto-history.

Nanotechnology and genetic research have the power to transform the world—for better or worse. Genetically enhanced foods combined with nanotechnology have the power to improve life or the power to destroy it. Chemical nano-capsules placed in the human body will someday have the power to heal—or kill—creating a frightening new form of targeted biological weapons. My novel CYBERKILL is an example.

Finally, the promise of self-replicating, nano-factory technology, if left unmonitored and uncontrolled, could unleash a plague that could wipe out any and all carbon-based life on earth.

Prologue

Time is running out, shuddered Professor Alfred Tillman as he nervously made his way through the damp night towards his flat in Kreuzberg.

Kreuzberg, near the old American Checkpoint Charlie crossing point into East Berlin, was a neighborhood suspended between two worlds. A ghetto slum for immigrants, it also served as a criminal haven for drug dealers. Tillman knew the neighborhood wasn't safe during the best of times, let alone the dark of night.

He picked up his pace.

Shortly, he rounded a corner and found himself on an even bleaker street. Trash cans everywhere. Open sewage in the streets. Tillman wrinkled his nose and ducked into a dilapidated four-story apartment building. He paused at the name registry, found the one he was looking for, and rang the bell.

"Who is this?" asked a suspicious voice on the other end of the intercom.

"Alfred Tillman. I need to speak with you. It's important."

The voice turned affable. "Oh, yes, professor. Please come up."

The door buzzed open. Tillman was just stepping through the entrance when he heard the sounds of footsteps on the sidewalk. A man was turning the corner outside, walking casually toward him, smoking a cigarette.

Tillman quickly and silently closed the door behind him.

A moment later the aged professor arrived at Evrin Ibrahim's flat. The room was wildly decorated in Turkish motifs. Intricate hand-made mohair carpets lined the floor. Delicate vases stood on rosewood pedestals surrounded by hanging oil lamps and ornate hand-carved furniture. Such unexpected luxury and refinement was a shocking contrast to the squalor of the miserable neighborhood and apartment buildings.

"Would you like some hot tea, my friend?"

Tillman nodded.

Ibrahim disappeared into the kitchen. As Tillman lowered himself to a couch, he heard a siren approaching from outside, growing louder in the still night—*is it an ambulance?* He felt a panic. Ibrahim returned to the living room with two cups of tea.

"Cream and sugar?" he asked.

"Yes, both please," Tillman replied.

"What are you doing out on a night like this, my friend?" Ibrahim asked, carefully handing the steaming cup to Tillman. Nearly as old as the professor, Ibrahim was a Turkish immigrant whose kind face belied his troubled past.

"I need a favor."

The Turk sat on the edge of his couch sipping from his delicate cup. "And what favor would this be?"

Tillman reached into his pocket and handed Ibrahim what looked like a small receipt.

His Turkish friend examined it. "What's this?"

"It's a valet stub where I parked my car."

Ibrahim inspected the small piece of paper. "This is a valet receipt in old East Berlin. What are you doing with a car there?"

Tillman stepped over to the dark window and slowly moved the curtain aside. The wet street below was alive with flashing lights. "It doesn't matter. What does matter is that you give it to my daughter as soon as you can." He turned and reached into his satchel, pulling free a sealed envelope. "And give her this, too."

"I don't understand," Ibrahim replied.

"Tell her this is as far as I could go."

"Why not give it to her yourself?"

He knows something is wrong, thought Tillman. *Perhaps I should just tell him—no. Better to not involve Ibrahim. Already I could have made a grave error by coming here tonight.*

"She's out of town tonight, and I..." He stopped talking and let his voice trail off. Tillman was never a very good liar, and his friend deserved better. He stepped away from the window and held the envelope out to Ibrahim. "Will you do this for me, my friend?"

"Of course, Alfred. As soon as she returns."

"Thank you. Now I must go."

The Turk stood suddenly. "Why not stay and talk some more?"

Trust me, my friend, Tillman thought. *I would not leave the warmth of your home if I didn't have to.*

Instead, he said, "No, thank you. Not tonight. I—" But he was interrupted by an unusual, muffled sound coming from the hallway.

Immediately, Tillman's heart thumped once. Hard. From somewhere in his throat.

Are they here?

Ibrahim frowned and headed for the door. Tillman almost stopped him but decided against the act. After all, if the noise was nothing, he would have alarmed his friend for no reason. And Tillman was not in the mood to answer questions.

But are you in the mood for dying?

Ibrahim opened the door, and Tillman, prepared for anything, was mildly surprised to see two paramedics carrying what appeared to be a man and a woman down the hallway on stretchers.

"My God," exclaimed Ibrahim. "That's the Kleinman couple. They live in the apartment next to me."

The paramedics moved hurriedly down the hallway toward the elevators, ministering to the couple as they went.

Ibrahim shut the door and folded his arms across his narrow chest. "First the Romanoffs, now them."

Tillman had other issues to contend with—life-threatening issues, in fact—but nevertheless his old curiosity got the better of him. "What do you mean?" he queried.

"Last night, a couple down the hall, the Romanoffs, were rushed to the hospital."

"Both of them?"

"Yes."

"And what was wrong with them?"

"Food poisoning."

"Ah," said Tillman, smiling gently. "Perhaps it's good that you didn't offer me any food then, my friend."

Ibrahim smiled weakly, but Tillman saw that the man was clearly troubled. Tillman placed a hand on the Turk's shoulder. "I must go now. Be careful what you eat."

"Only halal for me," said Ibrahim, chuckling hollowly. "And only kosher for you. Are you sure that you do not want to stay?"

"I must be going, my old friend. Duty awaits. *Osher uvreéut.* To your health."

And with that, feeling less courageous than he sounded, Tillman left.

The rain was coming down harder now as Tillman made his way to the rear of his run-down apartment building. The air was chillingly cold, and a stiff wind found every hole and loose stitch in his clothing. Tillman shivered and looked over his shoulder again. He was alone.

Thank God.

At the back entrance to the building, as he paused under a sagging overhang to search his threadbare pant pockets for his keys, he heard a noise.

A rustling, in fact.

His heart immediately slammed in his chest. Tillman spun, ready to defend himself, but there was no one there.

He took in some breath, holding his chest. *My God,* he nearly had a heart attack.

I'm too old for this, he thought.

He was about to turn around when the sound came again.

From the nearby trash cans. He leaned forward, peering through the dark and wetness, suddenly feeling foolish. A small, furry thing—just as scared as he—dashed across the alley and through a broken wooden fence. Some homeless, hungry alley creature.

Finally exhaling, he fingered his key, found the keyhole, and opened the door into his apartment's back hallway.

Almost immediately he felt a presence.

Tillman choked back a gasp. A man was there, standing back in the shadows, near the trash chute. Tillman nearly turned and fled but forced himself to remain calm.

Just another resident heading out the back door, right?

Tillman thought he knew all the residents in his small apartment building, but sometimes people came and went, friends and guests and various workers.

It was nearly midnight.

He shouldn't be here, thought Tillman. *He's waiting for me.*

Fear raged through him. *Calm down. Deep breaths. It's going to be okay.*

Heart pounding, sweat breaking out along the sweep of his forehead, Tillman took in some air, summoned his courage, and stepped forward.

"Excuse me," he said, and made a move to pass the shadowy figure coming toward him in the hallway.

Immediately a hand, thick as a bear paw, dropped down to block his path. Like a drawbridge. Like a trap. A squeaky noise escaped Tillman's lips.

"Good evening, Professor Tillman," said the man in German.

"Who-who are you?"

No answer. The big hand matched an equally powerful forearm roped with muscle and covered in thick blond hair—a sailor's arm, a weightlifter's arm. But what Tillman saw on the inside of that forearm sent a cold chill down his spine—

A black, stylized swastika tattooed in the shape of a twelve spoke sun wheel.

"The Black Sun!" Tillman gasped, hardly breathing the words.

This can't be happening.

Tillman backed into the now closed exterior door. The man stepped forward, into the murky light cast by the dusty overhead bulb. The man had dead eyes, soulless eyes. He also had starkly blond hair, cut military short, almost a caricature of a Nazi eugenics experiment.

Caricature or not, the man towered over Tillman, and the old Jew knew this was not good. Not good at all.

Tillman reached blindly behind him, his hand groping, fumbling. Before him, the blond stranger stepped forward, and there seemed to be something new in those blank eyes. Tillman recognized it immediately, and it sent another chill coursing through him.

It was pleasure.

My God, he's enjoying this.

Tillman's searching hand found the doorknob, and just as he turned it and pushed, just as a cool breeze and some rain found him from outside, the tall German pounced.

Tillman screamed, as loud as he possibly could, anything to wake the neighbors, but the man clamped his vice-like hand around Tillman's throat. The professor's agonized scream turned into a strangled gurgle.

Tillman vainly fought for air. Almost immediately blackness encroached along the periphery of his vision. And as a strange lightness in his head set in, Tillman realized that death wasn't so bad after all.

That was his last thought as he died looking into those dead eyes.

The Set Up

Siegfried Stobl was the seed of a new pure progeny and a Knight of the Holy Lance of the Black Sun Society—a Nazi Society that was outlawed after World War Two. The Black Sun members were the elite of the Thule Society, a secret international organization of old whose goal was to defend the world against Jewish domination.

For Stobl, killing those unworthy to be called the Master Race was not only a duty, but his pastime hobby as well.

It was also, in fact, damn fun. One of Stobl's few real pleasures in life.

Unfortunately, the Jew had screamed, and loudly. Now Stobl had to move quickly. He easily hefted Tillman over his shoulder and carried him swiftly down the first floor hallway to Tillman's bare apartment. Stobl had already jimmied the lock.

Once inside, the German closed the door and carried the body into the living room, where he dumped it unceremoniously across a worn rug.

But Stobl wasn't done yet.

He took full and determined breaths that filled his nostrils with the old and musky smell of the apartment as he went to Tillman's file cabinet against the far wall. He rifled through it until he found what he was looking for. It was a large folder labeled *Volks-Agrarindustrie*. He removed the contents from the file folder, rolled them up, and shoved them deep into his jacketed pocket.

Next, he moved to Tillman's computer and booted it up. As it hummed and groaned, he withdrew a memory stick from his pocket and inserted it. In a short while he had uploaded the entire contents. That done, he launched an email application and watched as a series of emails quickly appeared in Tillman's inbox.

Finished, he searched the hard drive for anything referencing *Volks-Agrarindustrie* and then deleted it.

Only one thing left to do.

Stobl systematically walked around the living room, knocking over furniture here and there, emptying drawers and tossing their contents on the floor, making enough noise to guarantee the attention of neighbors.

He quickly exited the apartment and disappeared into the night.

The Hotel

*P**oor, crazy bastard!*

Jeremy Nash was flushed by applause and adrenalin. After his much-publicized lecture at Germany's famed Des Liein Skeptics Club in Humboldt University, he decided to take a walk through Berlin to the Brandenburg Gate before returning to his hotel.

His thoughts, predictably, were on Alfred Tillman, the Jewish scholar and professor.

Or, as Nash had previously preferred to categorize him—*the nut job.*

Immediately, he regretted his choice of words. After all, Nash had just been informed by one of his colleagues that Tillman, a crypto-historian who had been hounding Nash for years about various Nazi conspiracies, had been found murdered just that evening.

What did you get yourself into, old man, you crazy bastard?

It had stopped raining, and Nash could see a hint of the moon behind the retreating clouds as the celestial body cast an eerie silver glow on the wet streets.

As an expert debunker and bestselling author of conspiracy theories, myths, and legends, Nash had often been confronted with kooks before. It came with the territory; all his adult life contained a neverending supply of those who aggressively confronted Nash on his skeptical inquiries into those shady untruths waiting to be exposed. But this Tillman guy took the cake. As a well-known crypto-historian, the man's delusions of German conspiracies to push forward the master race—dating back to World War Two— bordered on the paranoid.

He should have been committed.

Nash paused, lifted his face to the cool wind, and hoped the insane professor was finally at peace.

He also, briefly, wondered who had killed him.

He turned back at the Brandenburg Gate, back to where he was staying. Later, deep in thought, he almost missed the entrance to his glitzy hotel. Too flashy for him, but the Skeptics Club had paid his way, and who was Nash to say no to complimentary champagne and fresh berries in his hotel refrigerator?

Nash stepped into the brightly lit foyer. It was late, and the lobby was mostly empty. Nash had traveled alone and planned to spend the next day perusing the various sights and sounds of Berlin before heading back to his home in Roswell, New Mexico. Roswell—an ironic home base for one of the world's foremost skeptics. Nash liked the juxtaposition. He thought of himself as bringing balance to an otherwise delusional town.

He was seriously looking forward to settling in with his laptop, finally getting around to working on his long-delayed book, *A Taste of the Apocalypse*, and uncorking that free bottle of champagne. Which was why, when a rotund, red-faced man hurried up to him, Nash inwardly groaned.

The man thrust a police badge in Nash's face. "Herr Nash?" he asked in English with a heavy German accent. "Jeremy Nash?"

Nash noticed two other figures approaching—two other imposing figures. Nash frowned. "I'm Jeremy Nash. What can I do for you, officer?"

"Herr Nash, you are under arrest."

In Custody

Two hours later, after being booked and fingerprinted, Nash found himself sitting in a small interrogation room opposite a stocky detective.

The officer lit a cigarette and offered one to Nash. Nash declined. He sat forward, leaning his elbows along the scarred table.

"Look here, I have a right to know why I was arrested."

The detective exhaled a billowing plume of smoke. "Rights? Who do you think you are? A German citizen? You come here and break our laws, and now you expect to have rights?"

"What the devil are you talking about?"

The detective didn't speak. Nash looked at him, then around the room. There was a large mirror spanning the length of the wall facing him.

"I demand to know why I'm—"

"You demand nothing, Herr Nash," said a female voice as the door to the interrogation door opened and a striking woman slipped in.

She was tall, nearly six feet, with medium length blonde hair tied back in a professional manner. Deep blue eyes complemented her tastefully cut turquoise blazer and black slacks. Her Prada boots completed the image of a capable, self-assured, and stylish woman. She sat next to the detective, across from Nash.

"I don't understand," exclaimed Nash. He felt confused and completely stunned.

The squat detective spoke. "Herr Nash. I'm detective Bruno Schmidt. This is frauline Kara Ackerman. She's the defense attorney assigned to your case."

"Case? What case?" asked Nash, sharply. What could the Berlin police possibly want him for? Was it the stop light he blew through on his way to the lecture?

"Murder," said Schmidt curtly.

"I'm being accused of murder?" Nash blurted out. He found that he was standing.

"Please sit, Mr. Nash. Thank you. And, yes, the murder of Alfred Tillman."

Tillman? Nash blinked, completely confounded, searching for words and when they finally came, all he could say was, "But that's preposterous."

Schmidt pulled out a single sheet of paper from a file folder in front of him. He passed the paper over to Nash. "Is this not an email from you to Herr Tillman a month ago threatening him bodily harm if he attempted to see you?"

Nash quickly scanned the piece of paper. Remarkably, it was a printed copy of an email sent by him to Tillman the month before. But it wasn't an email he had ever sent.

"I didn't write this," Nash denied vehemently. "This is a fake. Where did you get it?"

Schmidt and Kara glanced at each other. Both raised their eyebrows. Schmidt might have smirked.

"We found that, and these, on Herr Tillman's computer." The older detective removed several more pieces of paper from the folder, passing them all to Nash. He continued, "There is a pattern of your belligerence towards Tillman over the last year."

Nash looked at Kara. She watched him quietly. Nash sensed she was studying his every move, perhaps even his every expression.

If she's supposed to represent me, thought Nash, *then why doesn't she say something?*

Nash took in a long breath. "Look, detective. I didn't write these emails. I have not been in contact with Herr Tillman for over two years."

Schmidt ignored Nash's comments. "When did you arrive in Berlin?"

"Last night."

"What time?"

"That's all verifiable, detective," said Nash. "You need only check the flight's manifest. I arrived at six p.m. Berlin time."

"What did you do after your arrival?"

"I took a taxi to my hotel where I checked in."

"Then what did you do?"

"I gave my speech at the Des Liein Skeptics Club, then took a short walk."

Schmidt's blue eyes never wavered or, as far as Nash could tell, blinked.

"You traveled alone, Herr Nash?"

"Yes."

"So, no one can give you an alibi after your speech?"

"Well. Uh, no."

Schmidt grinned, and the look was wolfish. Nash felt something sink inside him. He had a very bad feeling he knew what the detective was going to say next.

He was right.

"According to the hotel workers, you left thirty minutes before Herr Tillman's official time of death."

Schmidt continued. "Herr Tillman was murdered in his apartment. He was suffocated. He fought back but not hard enough. The neighbors heard the scuffle in his apartment, came in, found him dead, and called the police."

"It wasn't me," Nash said weakly, shaking his head.

Schmidt closed the file folder with determination. "Herr Nash, you have been charged. Counselor Ackerman will represent you. If you wish to retain your own legal counsel, you are free to do so."

The detective turned to the female attorney. "Counselor, you may speak with your client now."

Schmidt stood and left the room.

In Deep

Kara Ackerman glanced down at her watch.

Great, thought Nash. *I'm keeping her from something more important.*

She looked at him and drummed her fingers idly on the table for a moment.

"I usually prosecute cases," she said in a non-emotional tone.

"Good for you," offered Nash. "I did not kill Tillman."

She studied him some more. "So you say." She opened her briefcase and removed a packet of cigarettes. She offered Nash one. He declined. "Do you mind?" she asked.

Nash had more things to worry about than secondhand smoke. He shook his head sharply.

She snapped open a silver lighter and quickly lit the tip. She sucked hard on the filtered end and exhaled a curling plume of smoke. Throughout the whole process, she never took her gaze off him.

"I specifically asked for your case," she said, squinting through the smoke.

"And why would you do that?"

She looked at the glowing tip of the cigarette. "Because Alfred Tillman was my father."

His stomach sunk and Nash stared at her a moment as her words hung in the air. "I'm sorry," he finally said.

"So am I."

"But your name is Ackerman," Nash said.

"That's my stepfather's name. My father, Alfred Tillman, divorced my mother when I was just a child."

"Well, Fraulein, it was nice meeting you, but I want another counselor."

"No, you *don't*," she exclaimed sternly. "Whoever set you up went to great lengths to implicate you, Mr. Nash. As it stands, there is enough evidence to keep you behind bars for a very long time."

She withdrew a piece of paper from her jacket pocket and pushed it in front of him.

"What's this?" he asked.

"It's a note from my father. A close friend of his gave it to me just this evening. His friend told me my father said to tell me, *this was as far as he could go.* I could only assume he wanted me to pursue this further—she narrowed her eyes—with you."

Nash was now confused *and* dazed. "What's in it?"

She pulled the paper away. "We can talk about that later. What's important is that my father wanted me to find you should anything happen to him."

"So he knew his life was in danger?"

"Apparently."

"In danger from whom?" asked Nash.

"That's where I need your help," said Kara. "Obviously, his killers went to great lengths to frame you."

"I don't understand," said Nash. "Your father knew he could be murdered, and he wanted you to find me if that happened?"

"So far, that seems to be the case."

"Then let's show the note to the police. That could help prove my innocence."

"Not necessarily," she corrected him. "In the note, my father states he feared for his life. Unfortunately, he doesn't say who he feared it from. Your name, unfortunately, is mentioned in the note. The police could use this information to further support their case. In the very least, it'll strengthen their will to keep you under arrest for further questioning while the real murderer goes free."

Kara sat forward in her chair; her cigarette forgotten. "This is Europe, Herr Nash. Not the United States. The police can hold you for weeks, months."

Nash saw her point. "May I read the note?"

She nodded and handed it to him. He scanned the writing scribbled on the back of a four-color handbill and saw that she was telling the truth. The letter could be interpreted in a variety of ways.

"Fine," he said, sitting back and away from her stinging cigarette smoke. "As my counselor, what do you suggest?"

"I want you to help me find who killed my father."

"How can you be so sure it wasn't me?"

She studied him long and hard, finally crushing her cigarette in an overflowing ashtray. Apparently, smoking laws were nonexistent in German interrogation rooms.

"My father trusted you," she finally replied. "And I believe you. Furthermore, you don't look like a murderer."

Relieved, Nash sighed, "Your father was a pain in my ass for many years, fraulein."

"My father was a pain in many people's asses," she quipped. "Now, we must go. We need to prove your innocence."

"How?" asked Nash.

She pulled out a small yellow card from her purse. "I believe we can find the answer with this."

"What is it?"

"A valet parking receipt."

Nash blinked, thoroughly confused. *Jesus, she's as crazy as her father.*

She lowered her voice and covered her hand with her mouth. "But first, we need to get you out of here."

"What do you mean?"

"Just follow my lead."

Fugitive

Kara opened the door of the interrogation room and a tall, twentyish officer with cropped, dark brown hair snapped to attention. Nash was close enough to the door to overhear their conversation. His German, although anything but proficient, was certainly serviceable.

"Are you finished, counselor?" asked the officer in German.

"Yes."

"Good," he said. "I'll tell detective Schmidt."

"That won't be necessary," she replied. "I'll escort the suspect to the holding cells myself."

The policeman didn't immediately respond, and Nash was suddenly certain he was going to spend a long time in jail. He was very much regretting his decision to speak to the Berlin Skeptics Club when a clipped answer broke the silence. "That should be fine. You don't need any help?"

Nash nearly cheered.

Still a long way to go before you're free. And even then, won't you be a fugitive? Jesus, this is insane.

Kara answered, "No, that won't be necessary. After all, where can he go?"

Don't push it, thought Nash.

The guard must have consented because Kara ducked her head back in the interrogation room and motioned for him.

A very small voice in his head told him to stay where he was and trust the German legal system. And then he reminded himself he had no idea how the German legal system worked—or if it was even considered fair.

How did I get into this position?

He didn't know, but someone had set him up. And if there was a chance to prove his innocence outside of jail, he was going to take it.

Knowing full well his life was about to forever change—going from a free man to a fugitive—Nash slowly rose from the table and followed Kara into the hallway.

Her plan has to work first. And if it doesn't?

Nash didn't want to think about that.

Heart pounding, Nash walked as casually as he could next to Kara, perfectly aware that she was, in fact, perfect in almost every physical sense.

How did that crazy bastard have such a beautiful daughter? Think about it later, Jeremy.

The two walked side by side down a brightly lit hallway that was adorned with exactly—nothing. The depressing passageway led directly to the lobby of the police station. Beyond the lobby was the entrance door to the holding cells. Nash knew that once he passed through those doors, there was no hope of escape.

"So, um, what's your plan?" he asked.

"Working on it," she replied.

Oh, great!

Once in the lobby, Nash saw the guard at the holding cell reach into his pocket and take out a string of keys, searching through them.

Time was running out.

He broke out in a cold sweat. He could feel it trickling down the center of his spine. He knew he was breathing harder, too. Glancing at his attorney, he could see she looked as cool as a cucumber.

Or is it a gherkin in German? Focus, Jeremy!

Halfway through the station lobby the front doors burst open and a young woman, cursing in German, exploded through the doors with two officers manhandling her into the station. Behind her was a clatter of men with cameras, all shuffling for position, taking pictures and screaming at the frauline to look at them.

"Who the hell is that?" whispered Nash.

"Elsa Witt. Our version of your Lindsay Lohan."

"What's she yelling about?" asked Nash. He had a serviceable grasp of German, but her drunken screeching and bellowing was beyond his comprehension.

"She's cursing out the officers. Something about being arrested, not her fault...probably picked up at some night club."

Nash noticed the attention of everyone in the lobby, including the officers on duty, was focused on the inebriated celebrity...and not on Kara and himself.

Kara, apparently, was one step ahead of him.

She pulled Nash towards the lobby entrance and into the rabid pack of paparazzi. Nash immediately found himself in a churning sea of yelling, screaming, and pushing.

Worse yet, he was being pushed back into the station—pushed, in fact, right into Elsa Witt.

When Nash and Kara were within a few feet of her, the German pop icon did the unexpected. At least, unexpected to Nash.

She projectile vomited!

The crowd groaned and recoiled. Her vomit splashed across the tiled floor. Worse, some of the paparazzi got nailed by the stuff. Nash, who thanked his lucky stars, had dodged the puke, pulling Kara with him.

Kara, to his amazement, swiped a camera from the open bag of one of the paparazzi. She shoved it into Nash's hands. "Start taking pictures," she ordered, pulling him down and speaking directly into his ear.

"What?"

"You're a paparazzi, you dummkopf! Start taking pictures!"

Nash fumbled with the unfamiliar camera until he realized he didn't need to actually take pictures. He brought the camera

up to his face and pointed it in Witt's direction as the paparazzi were now being shoved out the front door by the police officers.

Nash, to his astonishment, was shoved out along with them. Once on the sidewalk, Nash dropped the camera and walked swiftly down the street. To his further surprise, Kara took his hand. To anyone watching them, they looked like a happy couple going for a nighttime stroll.

They reached a corner, and Kara pulled him down a side street. A few blocks from the police station and a few minutes later, they approached a light rail station.

"We're taking a train?" Nash asked bewildered.

"Yes. It's the fastest way out of the area."

"Then where?"

"A hotel. Haven't thought that far ahead yet."

Nash was mildly surprised and pleased that she continued holding his hand as she led the way to the station.

Interpol

Detective Schmidt was certain he was close to having a stroke, and the dull throbbing in his temple only seemed to be getting worse. The news he just received was utterly, inconceivably flabbergasting. He stared blankly at the tall officer in front of him.

"They're gone?" he asked with anger in his voice.

"Yes, sir."

"Where did they go?"

"We don't know, sir."

"How did they escape?"

"There was some confusion, sir, with the appearance of Elsa Witt—"

"This isn't happening. I want an AP on them throughout the city. Set up—"

Schmidt was cut off in mid-sentence. "Negative, detective."

He turned and saw a well-dressed, stocky German in his mid-fifties with a closely cropped salt-and-pepper beard. The man, who was about sixty pounds overweight for his six-foot three-inch frame, supported himself on an ornate steel cane.

"Who are you?" demanded Schmidt.

"My name is Klaus Heinrich." The man pulled out a small wallet and flipped it open.

Schmidt read the badge and ID. "Interpol? What's your business here?"

"Jeremy Nash is our business. This investigation is now Interpol's."

"Nash is accused of murder, Herr Heinrich. In my city. That makes him my concern."

"We have intel on a possible terrorist plot here in Germany. Nash is implicated," said Heinrich.

"I don't understand."

"Then let me explain it to you, Herr Schmidt. Nash is an international terrorist. He's been involved in an attack on the Dome of the Rock in Jerusalem." Heinrich snapped his wallet shut. "That makes him my concern."

Orders

Adrian Adler sipped his champagne as he listened half-heartedly to a short, overweight French businessman droll on about genetically enhanced food products. These annual social gatherings, always held at a swank Berlin resort, were more business than pleasure and bored Adler to tears. The fact that Adler's own company threw the party made little difference.

As the Frenchman continued, and as Adler occasionally nodded in the appropriate spots, he found himself paying closer attention to the businessman's stunning female escort who, in turn, seemed to be just as interested in him. He always liked it when that happened.

Adler was the CEO and Chairman of the Board of Volks-Agrarindustrie, Inc, a conglomerate of companies that ruled over an immense agri-business empire. This empire not only grew, packaged, and distributed food to countries throughout Europe, but had a lucrative research and development arm creating genetically modified foods.

What the fashionable guests did not know was that Adler was something else. Something secretive—and illegal.

We all have our secrets, he thought, and smiled again at the young lady. She smiled back, coiling a lock of hair around an index finger.

As the excited Frenchman now argued against one of Volks-Agrarindustrie's recent bio-technical breakthroughs in nano-agriculture, Adler found himself openly flirting with the man's date. They both smiled at each other from over their drinks. And the Frenchman had just caught wind that perhaps he did not have all of Adler's attention when the CEO's cellphone vibrated.

Adler nodded at the businessman, smiled at the blonde beauty, and politely excused himself, making a mental note to look her up later.

Adler was a direct descendant of Heinrich Himmler's Knights of the Round Table. More important, at least to him, he was the head of the newly formed Black Sun Society—a society whose goal, among other things, was to realize the Nazi dream that was destroyed over half a century ago.

And nothing was going to prevent it this time. Not even the unsettling information he had just received on the phone call.

"He escaped?"

"Yes. With a woman," Stobl replied. "I watched them leave the police station."

"Are you still with them?" asked Adler.

"Yes, sir."

"Have they seen you?"

"No, sir."

Of course not.

Stobl was good at what he did. Yes, Adler was certain that Nash and this woman were completely unaware that they were being watched.

"Who's the woman?"

"I don't know."

"Find out."

"Yes, sir."

Adler nodded. He liked that about Stobl. No questions asked. Willing to follow orders. Of course, Stobl's genetic background would permit no other behavior. Stobl, Adler knew, was proud of his racial purity. His father was, in fact, a result of the Himmler's Aryan breeding program—Lebensborn.

"His escape poses a problem, but I'm sure you will find a solution, Herr Stobl."

"I fix problems," Stobl replied without emotion.

Adler leaned back in his black leather chair and grinned. "Good—fix both of them."

He clicked off, stood, and straightened his tie. Now, it was time to find that blonde.

Flight

"How much longer?" asked Nash as the train pulled into an empty station.

"Next stop," Kara replied.

Nash noticed several passengers board, including a Middle Eastern woman wearing a traditional *jilbab*—a black dress that covered her from the neck down to her feet—and a *niqab* which left only a small slit for her eyes. She sat down opposite Kara and Nash.

As the train was about to pull away from the station, two young men with heads completely shaved and wearing grungy t-shirts and baggy jeans stumbled into the car. They were immediately boisterous and to Nash seemed either drunk or high.

He watched as they made a beeline for the woman garbed in black, sitting on either side of her. The crude remarks started immediately, as they bantered back and forth with the woman in-between. Some of the nearby passengers got up and moved to another car. The woman, for her part, stared rigidly ahead, completely ignoring the two loudmouths.

One of them pulled at her plastic grocery bag, trying to get a peek inside. The woman slapped his hand away, which enraged the punk. As he grabbed at her bag, Nash began to stand and was taken aback when Kara pulled him down into his seat.

"You're the last one to bring attention to yourself. I'll handle it."

With open-mouthed surprise, Nash watched as she stood casually and walked straight over to the two men harassing the woman.

"Having fun, gentlemen?" she asked.

"Piss off," said one of the thugs in German, without bothering to look at Kara. He had a scar under his left eye and yellow teeth. Nash waited on the edge of his seat, ready to jump in at a moment's notice.

"Why don't you leave the woman alone," said Kara easily, smiling.

"What part of piss off didn't—" but then the thug stopped short when he got a look of Kara, no doubt stunned by the beautiful woman standing boldly in front of him. "Then again, maybe you'd make better entertainment." He smirked and suddenly stood up, grabbing the back of Kara's neck and pulling her towards him.

Nash was on his feet, but before he could move an inch, Kara had already kneed the punk in the groin. The kid collapsed back into his seat, holding his crotch. And as his companion reached for her, Kara whirred around and kicked him straight in the face. As the punk's head snapped back, she withdrew something from her purse. Nash saw that it was a can of pepper spray. She pointed it at the first skinhead who, Nash saw, was reaching for something in his belt. To Nash, it looked like the handle to a knife. A long knife.

A stream of the burning liquid from the can changed his mind.

"Get the hell out of here," she ordered.

The moaning punk slid out of his seat, grabbed his friend—who was clawing at his burning eyes—and they hurried, with whatever dignity they had left, out of the car.

When those creeps were gone, a few people clapped, and Kara, to Nash's amazement, actually turned beet red. She slid in the seat next to him.

"That was impressive," complimented Nash.

"Police self-defense course," she whispered, returning the pepper spray to her handbag. "As a prosecutor I put a lot of *schwein* like them in prison." She smiled. "A girl needs to protect herself."

"From what I saw," said Nash. "Those two were the ones who needed protection."

She grinned, but then turned somber. "I'm afraid for my country, Mr. Nash."

"What do you mean?"

"We have an immigration problem. A big one. There are those in my country, hell, in all of Europe, who believe the best way to deal with this problem is through intimidation and violence. Chase them back to where they came from."

"You mean the neo-fascists."

"Yes," she said. "If the politicians can't solve the unbridled immigration into Europe, the fascists will—and then we're right back in the nineteen thirties."

"And what side do you fall on?" Nash inquired, as the train pulled into the next station.

"I fall on the side of the law," she replied, standing. "This is our stop. Let's go."

Nash followed her off the train and through the station. She moved quickly, her long legs covering a lot of ground. Normally, under different circumstances, Nash would have been endlessly fascinated by such long legs. Instead, he found that it was all he could do to keep up. He checked once to see if the skinheads followed but only spotted a tall blond man far behind them.

A block away, Kara led him to the *Hotel Adlon Kempinski* on the *Unter den Linden.*

"I've heard about this place," said Nash. "It was one of few buildings spared during the bombings in World War Two."

"You know your history," she said.

"Some. My side interest in college was the Second World War."

"Did you also know that during the Cold War the hotel sat right on the edge of no man's land between East and West Berlin?

"No. But it's sort of like us," Nash added, "now."

Kara gave him an odd look.

"No man's land. Us. Our situation. You know?"

She shrugged her shoulders. "An analogy, huh? Well, just remember, though it was spared during the Second World War, three days after the war ended, it burned down."

Bad omen, Nash thought.

A few minutes later they entered the hotel lobby, and Kara

walked over to the bellman's desk. A stern looking Hun with an aged face eyed Nash and Kara as they approached.

"May I help you?" he inquired.

Kara removed the valet receipt from her pocket and gave it to the man. "Would someone retrieve our car, please?"

The bellman took the receipt and tapped a small bell on his desk. A few moments later, a dark-skinned young man appeared, dressed in white slacks and a yellow golf shirt.

The bellman actually turned his nose up at the valet. "Retrieve this car, boy. Hurry along." The young man nodded and hurried away as the bellman watched him disapprovingly, shaking his head. He then turned to Kara and smiled broadly. "You can pick up your vehicle at the front entrance."

They thanked him and walked out of the lobby. As they exited into the night, Kara looked sideways at Nash. "See what I mean?"

"I do," said Nash, who had seen it all. "The detestable look the Bell Captain gave that young man."

"Racism is rampant."

A classic old BMW coupe pulled up in front of them. Nash thought it looked like it hadn't been washed in months. Dirty or not, it was stunning. He nearly whistled.

The young man exited the BMW and opened the door for Kara. She casually handed the valet a five euro note and got behind the steering wheel. Nash, his heart hammering, climbed into the passenger side while Kara adjusted the side and rear-view mirrors.

She reached to turn the key in the ignition, then hesitated. Nash saw she was studying a small octangular-shaped stone with a reverse number seven on it, hanging from the key ring.

"Everything okay?" he asked.

She nodded. "I thought this was lost."

"What is it?"

"It's a runic stone. My father gave it to me several years ago. Then somehow, well, it was gone." She paused a moment, deep in thought, and Nash was struck with the realization that the crazy

old bastard who had stalked him for years had a daughter who still cared for him. She continued, "When he gave it to me, he was so excited about his latest research. The hollow earth theory, I think it was."

"It's not a theory," Nash heard himself saying. "It's a fantasy."

She chuckled quietly to herself. "Yes, that would be father. Sometimes I wonder if he ever truly lived in this world. I think, perhaps, he would have preferred fantasy." She turned the stone in her hands, letting some of the ambient light catch it. "Father said it would bring me luck."

"Good," said Nash. "Because we need it."

She finally turned the key and the old car thundered to life. "We need to go."

"Where are we going?" asked Nash.

"Someplace quiet and out of the way. My guess is that my father left something for me in this car."

To Nash, someplace quiet sounded like heaven. He sat back, closed his eyes, and tried to forget that he was a fugitive from the law.

As the BMW drove off, a cab eased away from the hotel driveway and slipped behind them. Stobl, with fresh blood splattered over his clothing, ignored the dead cab driver lying in the front seat next to him, his throat cleanly cut.

Threat

As Kara drove, Nash noticed she kept looking into the rearview mirror.

"Everything okay?" he asked. It suddenly occurred to him that his whole life, literally, was in the hands of the daughter of one of the biggest kooks he had the misfortune to meet.

"There's a cab following us."

Nash slowly turned his head, shifting his gaze to the rearview mirror. He didn't like what he saw. There was indeed a yellow cab back there, and as it passed beneath a pool of lamplight, Nash saw a hulking blond-haired man behind the wheel. The cab was coming up on them fast. Too fast.

"Jesus, he's going to hit us!" shouted Nash. "Hang on."

The jolt from the impact shot them forward into traffic, and Kara, miraculously, just managed to miss a dump truck in front of them. She regained control and aimed the BMW down the far-right lane of the busy street.

Nash looked back. The cab was right behind them, close enough to make out the blond driver's grim expression.

"I take it this has something to do with your dad?" asked Nash, aware that Kara had picked up an alarming amount of speed. Cars in other lanes blurred past. If they should come across a cop...

Nash didn't want to think about it.

"No idea," said Kara, whipping around a slow-moving city bus. "But probably."

"What did your father get himself into?"

"How about we discuss this later," she quickly retorted, and hung a death defying right turn that nearly rolled the car.

Nash looked back. The cab, amazingly, was still behind them, having just completed the same turn. Even worse, the man behind the wheel had just stuck his arm out the window. He was holding something. A gun.

"Duck!" yelled Nash.

He reached to her side and shoved Kara's head down just as the back window exploded. The same bullet ripped through the front window as well. Right where Kara's head had been.

Kara had briefly lost control of the vehicle, but now they were speeding straight down a side street and quickly putting some distance between them and the cab.

"Thanks," breathed Kara.

Nash nodded, briefly marveling at the blond man's amazing aim. Or had it been a lucky shot?

Nash's side view mirror suddenly exploded. The sudden impact caused Kara to swerve violently to the right. She regained control, just prior to hitting the curb, and they both slumped further down in their seats. Heart hammering, Nash stared at the empty spot where the missing mirror had been. *This is impossible*, he thought. If anything, the man was even further behind. How could he drive and squeeze off accurate shots at a tiny BMW a hundred yards ahead of him?

Nash didn't know, but he didn't like what he had seen. He didn't like anything about this.

Trip from hell, he thought.

"We're going to attract the police," Kara calmly announced—surprisingly—considering they had what appeared to be a madman on their tail. "That is, if someone hasn't called them already."

"Then we should get off the streets."

"And give him an easier target?"

"Good point," realized Nash.

"I know," said Kara, and suddenly hung another right, the tires squealing as the vehicle briefly hovered on two wheels. But the nimble BMW continued to respond nicely and shot forward once again, speeding down a narrow street that just as easily could have been called a back alley.

"Where are we going?" asked Nash. He glanced back to see the cab reverse past the narrow opening and then turn into the street. He heard it pick up speed, growling behind them.

"Kreuzberg. It's a no-go zone. Police stay out of that neighborhood. We'll try to lose him there."

"How?"

"I know the neighborhood. My father lived there."

They whipped past decrepit apartment buildings and shoddy retail stores. They passed a bum or two, and the air stank of garbage.

They were pulling away from the cab, but to do so, Kara had to drive recklessly through the darkness. There were few lights, and what little there were offered little visibility. Nash turned his attention from the cab behind them, deciding to help her see the road.

And just as he did so, a delivery truck pulled out in front of them. As the BMW's headlights flashed across the truck, Nash had a brief glimpse of the driver's terrified face just before Kara yelled "Hang on!" and wrenched the steering wheel hard.

Nash heard himself scream.

A Dangerous Chase

They slammed hard into the side of the panel truck.

Nash was thrown against the passenger side door, his head cracking the window. Blood instantly flowed down his scalp and into his shirt.

Light flashed through the driver's side window.

The cab was coming. Fast. It was going to hit.

Dizzy and disorientated, he grabbed Kara's limp arm and pulled her toward him as the cab, tires squealing, plowed directly into the driver's side door.

Nash lay still for a moment with Kara on top of him and tried to regain his wits as he surveyed the situation. They were alive, but Kara seemed unconscious. His head was bleeding. Somewhere out there was a man—a man wanting to kill them. And now he smelled smoke.

He turned the handle of his door, but it was stuck. He slammed his shoulder into it and it finally gave. As he reached for Kara, she moaned, looked at him, and then her eyes suddenly widened.

"You hurt?" he asked.

She looked back at the driver side door, seeing that it was, in fact, crumpled all the way into the front seat.

"No, I'm, uh, I'm OK," she stammered. "You saved my life."

"Never mind that," he said. "Something's on fire. Get out!"

He pulled Kara out of the vehicle, and as she stumbled to her feet, she looked at him with alarm. "You're bleeding bad."

Nash glanced at the cab, which was on its side nearby, its tires wobbling. The driver was gone.

Nash quickly scanned the surroundings. He was nowhere in sight.

"It's nothing. We need to get out of here."

Just as he said that, flames appeared on the BMW's dashboard, and spread quickly through the cab. Nash had just begun to tug at Kara, with no idea where they were going—just anywhere but there—when Kara did something inexplicable.

She dashed back to the BMW and dove inside, disappearing into the flames and smoke. He ran after her and was about to yank her kicking feet out when she reappeared, coughing and wiping tears from her eyes. How she wasn't on fire, Nash couldn't imagine.

He pulled her away from the burning wreckage. "Jesus, what the hell were you thinking?"

She sucked in wind, still coughing. "I...I needed to get this." She held up the car keys with the attached runic stone.

"Well, you got it," said Nash. "Now we need to get out of here before the police show up, or before our mad cab driver makes another appearance."

As Nash spoke those words, he scanned the area. He saw someone who was clearly dead propped inside the cab. Definitely not the blond driver who had been shooting at them. Nash caught something else, too. Something odd about the truck they had hit. Although there was a picture of bread baking in an oven on the side of it, it had a myriad of radio equipment attached to the roof.

Then it hit him. The bodies. People lying around on the street. Quiet and still.

Drunk, asleep—or dead?

He had no time to analyze the strange scene when Kara took his hand and raced him down a narrow side alley.

"Where we going?" asked Nash.

"A friend's," she answered.

When Stobl opened his eyes, he found himself surrounded by

garbage bags. He sat up and briefly surveyed his wounds. A dozen or so scrapes along his face and neck and shoulders from being ejected through the side window—no problem. He looked at a long scrape along his arm—already it was scabbing over and healing. No broken bones. He felt no pain, only a sense of failure.

Both vehicles were on fire now, and a crowd was gathering in the shadows. There was no sign of his targets.

Time to abort his mission. He checked his inside coat pocket. His revolver was there. His cell was still in the front pocket of his jeans. Whether it worked or not, he didn't know. Either way, there was nothing to link him to the dead cab driver.

Stobl stood and walked away, brushing refuse from his leather jacket, as the bum who sat nearby watched him in open-mouthed astonishment.

Stobl removed his revolver, turned, and—from the shadows—put a silenced shot between the bum's eyes.

No witnesses.

Old Scrolls

To say that Raymond Thomas—Professor of Near Eastern Languages and Cultures at UCLA—was disappointed was an understatement.

"I'm sorry, Raymond," said Abraham Lieter. His colleague from Cairo University, Lieter had invited him to the Cairo conference on Proto-Indo-European language, where a collection of rare and recently discovered scrolls had been unveiled. "The scrolls looked so promising."

"They still are," asserted Thomas, gathering his papers. He had photographs of every scroll, and he planned on studying them in detail. Hell, he planned on making them his life's work. This had been a major find. Major...and incomplete. "Of course, if we just had those missing pieces..."

"Yes, my friend, if only—" finished Lieter, patting his friend on the shoulder.

Thomas had been so confident that these scrolls were the key, especially when he had received word of their recent discovery by a docent in the Cairo Museum. Today had been the grand unveiling, attracting scholars from around the world. An unveiling that had been as disappointing as it had been exciting.

Proving Proto-Indo-European language was the common ancestor of the Indo-European language was the Holy Grail of linguistic research, at least in Thomas's field of paleo-linguistics. Unfortunately, the scrolls, although an incredible find, had been incomplete, with obvious and frustrating gaps.

"Take heart, my friend," said Lieter. "Who knows what will be found in the future, eh? So will you be staying long in Cairo?"

Thomas carefully slipped the last of his papers into his brief-case. He shook his head. "I'm heading back tonight. In fact, in a few hours."

"Can I drive you to the airport?"

"No, and thank you," he uttered, shaking his head. "I'll catch a cab. We'll talk soon."

The two men said their goodbyes, and Thomas left the university conference center. Outside, a hot wind kicked up sand and debris. Sweat instantly formed on his brow. Although Thomas loved his linguistics research, which sent him to a variety of locations around the globe, the desert environments were not his favorite. He missed the temperate climate—the perfection of the beaches of southern California.

As he stood outside the conference center and looked for a passing cab, a tall sun-bronzed, buff looking character in a safari jacket, a brown fedora, and pilot sunglasses exited a black Mercedes and walked straight toward him.

"Professor Thomas?" asked the man in a New York accent.

Thomas eyed him suspiciously. "Do I know you?"

"My name is Jake Stone. Do you have a minute?"

"Actually, no. I'm catching a plane soon."

"Have a cup of coffee with me, professor," said Stone, smiling. "I promise I'll make it worth your while."

"What's this about?"

"It's about the scrolls," said the American. "In particular, the missing pieces."

The Offer

They walked into a nearby air-cooled Kahwas, or, as Thomas thought of them, the Egyptian version of Starbucks.

Minus the cute girls, he observed, frowning as he took in the surroundings.

"This is a traditional Kahwas," explained Stone as they were seated in a far corner, away from other patrons. "Meaning, no women."

"Perhaps we should have gone to an untraditional one," quipped the professor.

Stone laughed and ordered them two coffees. Thomas, familiar with the strong Egyptian coffees, ordered his with plenty of sugar and cream. Around them, young men and old played board games; backgammon, chess, and dominoes.

"So what's this all about?" he asked when the waiter had departed.

Stone leaned back in his chair and pulled a pack of American cigarettes from his jacket. He offered one to Thomas.

The linguist shook his head and instead removed a pipe from inside his jacket.

Stone tossed him his matches. "A pipe man, I see. A man of refinement and taste. I would expect no less from you, Professor Thomas."

"How do you know so much about me?"

"I've done my research, professor," said Stone, exhaling a plume of smoke and taking the coffee out of the waiter's hand.

"Why?" he asked.

"I like to know who I'm hiring."

Before Thomas could respond, the American continued, "I understand your conference was a bust."

Thomas hesitated, trying to choose how to proceed. "What is your interest in the conference? And how did you know it was, as you put it, *a bust?*"

"I pay a lot of money, professor, to know what I know. In your case what I know about you comes from a young investigative journalist named Albert Marsh." The American sipped his coffee. "And I know the scrolls are incomplete."

Thomas, usually eloquent in both simple conversations and speeches, found himself stumbling over his tongue.

Stone leaned forward, an obvious gleam in his eye. "Tell me, professor, have you ever heard of the Fuhrer Convoy?"

Thomas got hold of himself. "I demand to know—"

"Please, professor. Humor me. Soon, I'll tell you anything you need to know."

The linguist sat back and took a pull on his pipe, running one hand through his grey-flecked hair. He really should be at the airport now. In fact—he checked his watch—it would be boarding in about an hour. He could still make it if he left now...but the American, admittedly, intrigued him.

I will give him ten more minutes, he thought.

"The Fuhrer Convoy?" Thomas said at last. "No, I haven't."

"Do you have time for a little story, professor?"

"Actually, I have a plane—"

Stone slid an envelope across the table.

"What's this?" asked Thomas.

"It is a plane ticket to the States for a flight tonight. First class, of course. So, professor, you have nothing to lose. All I ask is that you hear me out."

"Who *are* you?"

"Soon, professor. All will be revealed soon. May I tell you the story of the Fuhrer Convoy?"

Thomas opened the envelope. Indeed, a first-class British

Airways ticket to LAX. He shrugged and slipped the envelope inside his jacket pocket.

"Okay, Mr. Stone. You seem to have thought about everything. I'm listening."

Stone smiled and motioned for the waiter to bring another round of coffees. "In the final days of World War Two, a convoy of U-Boats left Germany for a secret location. That convoy carried a very valuable cargo. In fact, it carried much of the spoils of the Third Reich. Along with advanced technology, there were treasures plundered from Nazi occupied lands, ancient artifacts—and gold. Lots and lots of gold."

"And what has that got to do with the language scrolls that were found?"

"Good question. Do you know where the scrolls originated?"

"Not yet. But I hope to soon."

"Then let me help you. They're from Tibet."

"How do you know this?"

"Because they're from the Himmler expedition, professor. In nineteen thirty-five, the Reichsführer, SS Heinrich Himmler, founded an organization called the Ahnenerbe to uncover the hidden past of the Aryan race. This included racial studies of the Tibetans and the claim that northern India and Tibet are the ancestral home of the mythical Aryans."

Stone dashed out his cigarette and focused his attention on the coffee. "Various artifacts were brought back by the SS explorers to prove the Nazi theory of the Master Race. Some of those artifacts—your scrolls included—ended up here, in Egypt, and much was abandoned when the Nazis were pushed out of North Africa. The rest were taken to Germany and then put on the Führer Convoy to another location."

"What location?" asked Thomas, now hanging on Stone's every word.

"Nazi Antarctica," Stone replied. "*Neuschwabenland. Agartha—* the inner earth under the ice."

"You're talking about the Hollow Earth Theory, aren't you?"

Stone smiled. "I see you do read things other than your dusty tomes. But did you know that between December of thirty-eight and April of thirty-nine, the Nazis mapped extensive areas of Antarctica?"

Thomas shook his head.

"The first charting of its kind, really." He paused. "They even dropped thousands of metal balls with swastika flags attached to poles from the air to give the German claim to that portion of Antarctica some physical sign—an area of two hundred and fifty square kilometers, to be exact."

"I still don't see how any of this—"

"Patience, professor. Now, let's skip forward to nineteen sixty-nine. An ailing Rudolph Hess in Spandau Prison in Berlin gets a package from a Colonel Maximilian Hartmann, who had command the U-211, the Germans' advanced technology prototype submarine. If the reports can be believed, it was decades ahead of its time, with the potential to change the outcome of the war. As it turns out, Hartmann was tasked by Hitler himself to lead the Fuhrer Convoy." Stone casually lit another cigarette. "You see, in the final hours of the war, Hitler sent his most prized possessions to Antarctica via the U-boat convoy."

"And what does this package have to do with the missing scrolls?" asked Thomas.

"The package is supposed to lead to the location of the secret Nazi Antarctic base—known as Station Two-One-One." He winked at Thomas.

"Which is where the missing scrolls are located," said Thomas, catching on.

"Exactly."

"And the Nazi treasure which, no doubt, is what you're after."

"You are astute, professor," Stone replied almost in glee. "Ten million British Pounds of gold, silver, and precious stones. Ten million pounds, professor." Stone's eyes enlarged.

Thomas could swear the man was drooling. He took a sip of

his coffee and tried to hold back a laugh. "Though this has been a very entertaining tale, I have a trusted colleague, a close friend, who'd say that it's all pure bunk."

"That wouldn't be Jeremy Nash, would it?"

This American, thought Thomas, *is full of surprises.* The professor was immediately wary. "Maybe," he said guardedly.

"We're looking for him in Germany. He's on the run, I'm afraid."

"On the run from what?"

"Murder."

Thomas actually choked on his coffee. "Ridiculous!"

"I'm afraid so."

"Why are *you* looking for him?" asked Thomas.

"Because Nash, we feel, can lead us to this package that was sent to Rudolph Hess. We believe it is somewhere in England and gives the location to Station Two-One-One."

"What do you want from me?"

"Just your help, professor. Just your help."

"What do you mean by *we,* and how do you plan to help Nash?"

Stone gave Thomas a devious smile. "I'm from New York, professor, and by *we* I mean my trusted associates. We have experience in such things."

Breaking legs for hire, thought Thomas.

"When we find Nash," Stone went on, "we'll gain his freedom and find your missing scrolls." He leaned closer to Thomas. "But first, I need to meet with the benefactor of our expedition."

THE RUNE

Nash found himself in a small apartment not too far from the crash site. The occupant of the apartment, a bent and elderly Turk named Ibrahim, was serving them tea and making sympathetic noises.

"I am sorry again to hear about your father, dear," he said, speaking surprisingly clear English. "The news came as a shock to everyone."

"Thank you, Ibrahim. I am afraid it hasn't really settled in. It has been a bit of a whirlwind day."

"Tell me about it, child."

And so, Kara did while she cared for Nash's cut forehead. She began with the horrible news of her father's murder, then meeting Nash, their escape, the BMW and its subsequent destruction.

"And you have no idea who the man that was shooting at you is?" asked Ibrahim.

"None," said Kara. "And if there was anything my father left for me in that car, we'll never know."

"And so, I am harboring a fugitive," said Ibrahim, examining Nash closely.

"I assure you, sir—"

"Relax, Mr. Nash. If Kara trusts you, then I trust you. You are welcome in my home, no matter the circumstances or the consequences."

Nash relaxed. "Thank you."

The Turk pointed at the key chain in Kara's hands. "That's a runic stone, child."

Kara blinked; no doubt surprised by the sudden shift in conversation. "Oh, yes. Father gave it to me when I was very young. I thought it was lost...." she let her voice trail. "Would you happen to know what it means, Herr Ibrahim?"

"Not off hand." He suddenly stood up. "Hang on." He briefly left the room and returned with a book. "Your father gave this to me as a Ramadan present. He knew I loved reading about ancient languages." He thumbed through the pages until he found what he was looking for. "Here it is. The runic alphabet."

Runic Alphabet

A		I		R		TH	
B		J		S		EE	
C		K		T		NG	
D		L		UV		EA	
E		M		W		ST	
F		N		X			
G		O		Y			
H		P		Z			

He turned the book so both Nash and Kara could see.

"Each rune has a corresponding English letter," noted Kara.

"Correct. And the symbol on your rune stands for the letter L. But there's more." Ibrahim turned the page. "That runic symbol also stands for *laguz* which means, roughly translated, *water in a well—bubbling up from secret depths.*"

"Sounds just like father," murmured Kara.

Nash held his tongue out of respect for the dead. Her father, he knew, was a man who was obsessed with secrets, an obsession that just might have led to his murder.

Ibrahim pointed to the key ring again. "I see there's a key attached to the rune. Do you know what it's for?"

Kara examined it. "It says Sports Club Dynamo Berlin."

"That's the old East Berlin sports club of the Ministry of Police and Public Security," said Ibrahim. "What on earth was father doing with a key to that place?"

"May I see it?" asked Nash. She handed it to him, and he examined it closely. "It's a key to a locker at the club. See here, the number fifty-seven is stamped on the back."

Ibrahim chuckled. "I've known your father for many years, and I can say without a doubt he was not into sports *or* exercise."

"Do you think your father left you something in that locker?" asked Nash.

"Only one way to find out," said Kara. She turned to the older man. "Herr Ibrahim, do you have a car?"

Ibrahim laughed. "At my age?"

"Then we'll have to call a cab," Nash replied.

"Not a good idea," Kara warned shaking her head. "We need to stay inconspicuous."

"I have just the solution," Ibrahim said. He reached over to his phone and punched in a number.

Strange Deaths

S*ome solution*, thought Nash ten minutes later. *Then again, beggars can't be choosers.*

A short, thin, young North African man wearing a blue crocheted Muslim prayer cap entered the apartment.

"This is Herr Khalid. He's from the Sudan. He runs..." Ibrahim paused, seeming to search for the appropriate words, and then continued, "an enterprising business, to say the least. Khalid does not speak much English, or German for that matter, but he has agreed to take you where you want to go...for a small price."

"Of course," agreed Kara eagerly. "Whatever he wants."

Ibrahim spoke rapidly to the Sudanese, who simply nodded. The Turk then gave Kara a hug. "Now, go find what your father has left you."

"Barak Allahu Feekum," she replied. "God bless you."

In a deserted back alley, Khalid helped them into the back of a rundown panel truck.

"I make deliveries," he said in English with a thick accent. "After that, I take you to where you need to go."

"I thought you didn't speak English," said Nash.

"I speak English when I need to," said the Sudanese bluntly, and Nash let it drop. As long as the man didn't drive them back to the police, Nash could give a damn what language he spoke.

As Khalid shut the back doors, he cautioned, "Please be careful. I have lot of sensitive equipment back here."

As the Sudanese started the truck, which rumbled violently

to life, Nash whispered to Kara, "Look at this stuff! He's got a moving Best Buy store back here."

"And all stolen, is my guess," Kara quietly replied. "Are you hungry?"

"Starving," said Nash.

"I guess we should ask Khalid to stop and get us a quick bite to eat." She knocked on the small window that opened into the cab of the truck. "Khalid. Can you stop somewhere and grab us something to eat?"

"Of course," replied the driver. "It's your dime."

As Kara sat back next to Nash, she said, "I wonder how much he's going to charge us?"

"An arm and a leg," said Nash. "But I'll take care of it. It's my fault we're in this mess."

"Pay for it with what?" asked Kara, giggling. "Last I checked your wallet and passport were downtown."

"Well, I'll pay you back—whenever."

She laughed again saying, "And explain to me why you are at fault for this mess."

"Well, I guess technically whoever murdered your father is at fault."

"I hate them, whoever they are," cursed Kara, instantly turning somber.

They were quiet, and Nash looked through the small window into the cab and out through the front windshield. Khalid had the radio tuned to some ethnic music station, and just after the last song played, a news announcer came on the air speaking in Arabic. Arabic or not, Nash heard the word "Kreuzberg" mentioned a few times.

He leaned towards the small window and asked Khalid what the news announcer was saying.

"They're speaking of yesterday and tonight. The deaths in Kreuzberg."

Nash remembered the bodies lying on the street illuminated by the burning BMW.

"What about Kreuzberg?" Kara asked.

"They say there's some kind of disease. Something killing people." He then added solemnly, "My own cousin died of it just last night."

"I'm sorry to hear that," sympathized Nash. "Does the news announcer say what the disease is?"

"No. But many have died over the last week."

What's happening? thought Nash.

"What about now?" asked Nash. "Any deaths now?"

Khalid held up a finger, listened to the newscast, and then reported. "Authorities say they think the epidemic has run its course."

Kara looked at Nash. "As the curse goes—may you live in interesting times."

"Too interesting for me," Nash asserted, shaking his head.

Kara suddenly pointed through the windshield. "Let's stop there, Khalid."

It was a schnellimbiss, the German version of a fast-food restaurant. The van pulled over to the side, and Khalid stepped into the mostly empty café. Five minutes later he came back with a handful of falafels.

Back inside the panel truck, Khalid handed one to each of them through the window. "Here. Very good. Halal."

"Halal?" asked Nash.

"Like kosher," Kara replied. "Our friend here must be Muslim."

Nash took a bite. It was heavenly. Then again, since the last time he had eaten was nearly a day ago, anything would have been heavenly.

As Khalid pulled out of the parking lot, he turned back to his passengers. "Three stops and then I take you to the sports place. Then—"

Khalid stopped abruptly. Nash looked up, wondering if everything was okay. He expected to see a police cruiser nearby. Instead, he saw there was something physically wrong with the driver.

"Khalid?" quizzed Nash.

As Nash leaned through the window into the cab, the Sudanese looked toward him with wide, terrified eyes. Half-masticated falafel fell out of his open mouth. Then he began shaking, convulsing.

Kara sat up. "What's happening? What's going on?"

"Something's wrong." Nash scrambled forward and shoved open the back door to the panel truck. Outside in the cool night air, he dashed around to the driver's side door and yanked it open. Khalid tumbled out, foaming at the mouth. Nash caught the man, and then let him slide to the pavement.

This man, Nash was certain, was quite dead.

A New Nazi Order

Johann Hoffer sat in front of Adrian Adler with a wide grin on his face. As Adler's trusted aide and, like Adler, a Knight of the Holy Lance of the Black Sun Society, Hoffer knew the importance of what had transpired this week.

It wasn't often he had the privilege of being in the inner sanctum of the leader of the Black Sun. The imposing office décor wasn't the only Nazi symbol of power. On the wall, above Adler's desk, framed in gold, was the Spear of Destiny—the Holy Lance itself—the actual spear that pierced the side of Christ at his crucifixion.

Hoffer knew that over the centuries an object claimed to be this Holy Lance had passed through the hands of some of Europe's most influential leaders—Constantine, Justinian, Charlemagne, Otto the Great, the Habsburg Emperors, and most recently Adolf Hitler. A legend had arisen that whosoever possesses this Holy Lance and understands the powers it serves, holds in his hand the destiny of the world.

Hoffer and the Society knew they held the true Holy Lance and that Himmler had Japan's greatest sword maker flown to Germany where he created an exact duplicate of it. The perfect copy then went on display in Nuremberg, from whence it was turned over to Austrian authorities at the war's end, while the real one remained in the hands of the newly reformed Black Sun Society.

As he waited anxiously for his esteemed leader to speak, Hoffer scanned the dark and windowless room decorated with Nazi paraphernalia. Two Nazi flags stood on either side of Adler's desk. One was the *Deutsch Erwache* standard, modeled after those carried by the Roman legions, while the other was a Third Reich battle flag. Adler himself was sitting behind the Fuhrer's personal cast-bronze desk, with the initials, A.H., and the Nazi Eagle insignia in raised relief on the front. On the floor, inlaid at the front of the desk, was a stylized swastika in the shape of a twelve spoke sun—the symbol of the Black Sun.

"By your smile, I gather this week's test was a success?" asked Adler, drawing a puff from his cigarette.

Hoffer nodded. "It was a complete success, Herr Adler."

Adler expected no other response. Hoffer, as a member of the Circle of Thirteen Knights of the Blood of the SS, was selected for his strength, courage, and fanatical loyalty to the Society. Along with the sign of the Black Sun on his inner arm, he wore another badge of honor—a facial scar given to him by the wild boar he had to kill, all alone in the dark woods, with only a spear and sword. It had been part of his initiation into the Black Sun Society. Hoffer had proven himself very worthy indeed.

"No incidences?" Adler queried further.

"One. Our *Einsatzgruppen* broadcast truck in Kreuzberg was destroyed in an accident. "But we were able to retrieve it."

Adler had to smile at Hoffer's personal reference to the broadcast trucks as the Einsatzgruppen—named after the *Special-operation* units of SS paramilitary death squads that took part in the systematic killing of undesirables in World War Two, including Jews, communists, intellectuals, and others.

Adler exhaled. "Good. Now on to other business. The nano-agriculture project. How does it progress?"

"Perfectly."

Again, Adler nodded, pleased.

"Shall we inform Herr Luber?" asked Hoffer hesitantly.

Adler shook his head. "Although his work creating our new nano-bioindustrial products has been very useful to our objectives, I have my doubts about the man. He's becoming...unreliable."

"But he believes in what we do."

"To a point. I'd rather keep the results of his research quiet. Though he could still be useful, he is becoming a liability."

"How?" asked Hoffer.

"Our source keeps us up to date on his meetings and conversations. Even his moods." He snuffed out his cigarette. "And his attitude is becoming a detriment to our project." Adler snapped open a silver cigarette case on his desk. He removed another cigarette and lit it. "Which brings us to our next problem." He paused. "I understand we've just about used up all the original material. We have only a small sample left."

Hoffer nodded. "In hindsight, we shouldn't have given the Italians most of the material for their biological weapon in Ethiopia—but who would have known we would lose North Africa to the British, and eventually the war. We were lucky to retrieve what we had."

Adler studied the man before him, idly twirling his SS Death's Head ring on his finger. "And we can't grow the bacteria we need from the remaining material?"

"No, Herr Adler. As Luber explained to me, the bacteria are hundreds of millions of years old and probably originate from the original primordial soup that life sprang from. So unless we find a way to recreate that soup, and win the Nobel Prize in the process," he grinned, "we have to retrieve original samples from our reserve."

"I assume, then, the research team doesn't know the real purpose of the expedition?"

"It's on a need-to-know basis, Herr Adler."

Adler smiled and nodded. "I'm expecting Herr Stone here soon. When he arrives, see him to my front office."

Hoffer stood up, clicked his heels, gave the Nazi salute, and exited the office.

The Box

With Kara driving and Khalid's dead body stowed away in the back—their roles morbidly reversed—they headed swiftly east on the autobahn.

"What do you think killed him?" asked Kara. She was still visibly shaking.

"He was eating that falafel when he died," said Nash.

"Poisoned?" she asked, glancing at him.

Nash understood her look. "I don't know. And, yes, we should be dead, too, if it was the food." He thought of the half-eaten food they had unceremoniously thrown on the pavement after seeing Khalid die.

They drove in silence as a light rain began to fall. Nash tried to put out of his mind that he was still a fugitive on the run, transporting a dead body in a truck full of undoubtedly stolen electronic equipment.

This just keeps getting better and better, he thought. *I should be in bed now, sleeping off a full meal after an evening of working on my new book.*

The book—he was behind deadline. Funny how that deadline had escaped his thoughts.

Nash thought of his sister, Alyson, in New Mexico, his only close family. And they were indeed close. He had a sudden need to hear her voice. He also thought about how he had no one else in this world who gave a damn if the police caught him or not, if he disappeared forever in a German prison, or even if he was shot running from the law.

Just his sister—and even then, she had an obligation to care about him because they were blood. Nash's few friends would soon forget him.

Suddenly feeling like crap, he looked sideways at Kara. She was sitting forward in the seat, her eyes focused intently on the road ahead. Nash knew in his heart that a woman like Kara—smart, sexy, driven, challenging—was exactly what he was looking for.

She must have sensed him looking at her. She suddenly glanced his way, held his gaze briefly, and gave him a crooked smile. Nash liked her crooked smile.

He sat back and closed his eyes, trying to ignore his growling stomach.

It was quite late when they arrived at the gym. Kara pulled into a mostly empty parking lot beside a stout, square facade. Inside, through smoky windows, Nash could see people still working out. He figured it was the German equivalent of a twenty-four hour fitness center. Whatever—he was relieved it was still open.

He somehow felt responsible for Kara. But how? Her father's murder was the reason he was in this mess. If the man had any clue who might have wanted him dead, Nash needed it for evidence. He needed it to clear his name and get out of this country.

With or without Kara?

Good question.

They entered the empty lobby and before an attendant showed up Kara took his hand and led him down a side hallway. The sign in German, he was sure, was pointing the way to the men's lockers. Indeed, she stopped before an open door. Beyond, Nash could hear showers running and occasional male laughter.

"I'd better take it from here," Nash observed.

Kara nodded and gave him the key ring with the rune. She took a seat in the lobby.

Inside the locker room, Nash maneuvered his way past several burly men in different stages of undress. He looked for the row

of lockers with the number 57, and soon found it. He paused a moment to see if anyone was watching.

No one was.

He slipped the key inside the lock and was relieved when it turned easily.

At least something's going right tonight.

He opened the locker door. Inside was a small package, wrapped in brown paper, about the size of a cigar box. He grabbed it, tucked it under his arm, relocked the locker, and quietly walked back into the lobby.

Kara fell into step casually beside him, and back inside the van, Nash handed her the box. Kara took it reverently.

"Well," asked Nash, as Kara sat there doing nothing, "are you going to open it or just hold it?"

"I'm nervous," she admitted.

"Well, I'm absolutely terrified," confided Nash.

She unwrapped the small box—carefully and agonizingly slowly, too. Nash held his tongue, though. The girl had recently lost her dad. This was, in effect, a package from the grave.

A few long moments later she held up a tattered, elongated wooden box. She frowned, looking puzzled.

"What is it?" Nash asked.

"It's my childhood pencil box."

"I'm assuming there's more than pencils inside," suggested Nash.

She nodded, taking the hint. She opened the lid of the box and peered inside. Her eyebrows immediately knitted together, causing a crease down the center of her forehead. Nash wanted to jump out of his seat, craning to get a look inside. Somehow, he controlled himself and sat where he was.

"I don't understand," sighed Kara. The disillusionment was evident on her face. "I'm so disappointed. No letter or document— just scraps of paper and old photos."

"Let me see?" Nash asked gently.

Kara handed him the pencil box and he thumbed through the contents. Scraps of paper? He was staring at a partial photocopy of an encoded message, a copy of a 1955 magazine article that spoke of secret Nazi technologies acquired by the Allies after the war, a photo of Field Marshall Erwin Rommel, a picture of someone who looked like British Royalty, another picture of a young Nazi soldier standing with his parents—and under the scraps, an old rusty hex key.

"Are these the things that my father wanted me to complete?"

Nash shook his head. "I suppose so."

"What do you make of it?" asked Kara, shrugging her shoulders.

"Well, based on the items, I'd say this has something to do with the Nazis and World War Two."

Nash tried to keep his voice even, not showing his disappointment and concern in not finding something to clear his name. And he felt angry. It looked like Tillman was tempting him—or at least his daughter—to go on some wild goose chase after one of the man's crazy Nazi theories.

Kara retrieved the box and looked through some of the items. She picked up the scrap of paper with a series of letters on it. It read:

RRHUU DZPGH IMXHZ GPILP PXLPM SAJQQ PMJQS
RJASW LSBLW GBHMJ QSWIL PXWOL WDQSN PVIJO
BRECT WLJIU JYBRK PWFPF IJQSK PWRSS WEPTM
MJRBS BJIRA BASPP IHBGP RWMWQ SOPSV PPIMJ
BISUF WIFOT KRYXB FBJRB UOHYD VOUYK XKGHB
ILLWO EPNSW FBUMQ JCJYK RCCZC JYIYQ DFANV
WDQSN PVIJO XBREC HWBIS WBIQW NKDIF SERLJ
HIBFK FKDLV NQIBR HLCJU KFTFL KSTEN YQNDQ
NTTEB TTENM QLJFS NOSUM MLQTL CTENC
QNKRE BTTBR HKLQT ELCBQ QBSFS KLTML
SSFAI NLKBR RLUKT LCJUK FTFLK FKSUC CFRFN

And on the bottom, in the corner of the copy, were the words, **Station X.**

She looked over her shoulder. "What do you make of that?"

Nash just shook his head. "No clue."

"What about the magazine article?" she asked. "It looks like it has annotations on it. It's my father's handwriting."

Nash plucked the article from the box. The article was written in German. From what Nash could tell it also had something to do with World War Two. He would ask Kara to translate it later for him. Written in one of the margins was a single word—Odinist—along with some strange symbols. Nash scratched his head. "Very odd."

She examined the picture of the young Nazi soldier standing with his parents, or what Nash assumed were his parents. As she studied it, holding it up to her face, Nash noticed some writing on the back of the photo. He pointed it out, and Kara flipped the photo over.

"They're just letters and numbers," she reported. "More code?" She set the photo down and picked up the hex key and the remaining photo of Rommel. "What is all this?"

Nash thought a moment. Outside, a man emerged from the gym with a towel over his head. Nash kept his eye on him until he stepped inside a little sports car and drove off.

God, I'm jumping at shadows.

"My best guess, as crazy as it sounds, is that these items had something to do with why your father was murdered." Nash added, "But that doesn't explain why someone would try to frame me, or why that animal was shooting at us."

"I know," said Kara. "Why just kill Father? Why frame you?" She paused a moment in reflection. "Father was crazy. I mean, at times, he was positively certifiable, especially when he would ramble ceaselessly about his conspiracy theories. And yet..."

She let her voice trail off, but Nash knew where she was going with this. "And yet," he finished, "he might just have stumbled across something very real."

"And deadly."

Kara was quiet. Rain began falling, sprinkling lightly across the windshield. She breathed deeply, then turned to Nash. "If we can figure out what these items mean, we might just find out who killed my father—and prove your innocence."

"Sounds like a long night," said Nash.

It was raining harder now. Kara took Nash's hand. "I'm sorry you got mixed up in all of this, Jeremy."

That was the first time she called him by his first name. Nash looked at her hand on his, and for the first time all night, amazingly, he didn't feel sorry at all.

Station X

Kara drove the van back towards a Berlin neighborhood near the Schonefeld Airport. Nash murmured, "That's where I wish I were now."

"Where?" Kara asked.

"In a plane. If I still had one."

"You're a pilot?"

Nash nodded.

They drove a little further, and Nash said, "We need to ditch this van."

"We will, soon," agreed Kara. "But first I want to speak with someone."

"Who?"

"His name is Karl Dieter. He's a World War Two scholar. Teaches at Humboldt University. You know. Where you held your lecture last night. In fact, he was probably at the lecture. Anyway, he's written a number of books and papers on the Holocaust and is a friend of the family."

"Does he live far from here?"

"Several kilometers. In the Prenzlauer Berg district. It's become an upscale Jewish neighborhood. A lot of Orthodox Jewish immigrants live there now. His apartment is near the Rykestrasse Synagogue."

About thirty minutes later, she stopped the truck in front of a stately brownstone walk-up. "On second thought," she said, "I think we should park further down the street. I don't want to implicate him."

She drove to the end of the block, parked the truck, and shortly they were ringing the doorbell of the Brownstone.

"Do you think it wise to leave Khalid in the van?" asked Nash.

"I don't think anyone will disturb it for a while," she responded grimly. Just then a voice came over an intercom next to the door.

"Yes. Who's this?" asked a man in German.

"Karl, this is Kara. Kara Ackerman."

"Of course! Come in. I'm in the study on the second floor."

The door clicked open, and they stepped inside. Nash nearly whistled. *College professors must make much more here than in the States.*

Kara led them up a curving, mahogany staircase and then into a massive, book-lined study. A fire crackled in a stone hearth.

"Come in, come in," implored a voice within.

They both stepped inside the warm room, and Nash was surprised to be greeted by a young man, perhaps just a few years older than himself. Dieter sported a full head of curly red hair that was quite mussed. Nash could only assume they had awakened the man.

"Kara," he greeted with a big smile, "I haven't seen you since you were a teenager. How's your family?"

And Kara, for the first time since Nash had known her, broke down in tears.

Nash watched as Alfred Tillman's young colleague held Kara while she wept and told him the entire story. Dieter, it seemed, had taken on the role of older brother to her while growing up. At least, Nash hoped that was the relationship. Despite the circumstances, he found himself jealous of the man who held Kara so warmly. When she was finished sobbing, she composed herself and pulled away from him.

"I'm sorry," she apologized, wiping tears from her flushed cheeks.

"It's quite alright," consoled Dieter. They were both speaking English for Nash's benefit.

"Karl, we need your help."

"I would say so," Dieter replied, patting her on the shoulder.

Dieter offered them both hot teas, and when they were all seated around the fire the young professor looked from Kara to Nash. "These items you have. Do you think they can really point to who murdered Alfred?" He paused, shook his head, and seemed briefly overcome with grief.

To Nash, the display of emotion almost seemed rehearsed, almost a parody of emotion.

Or just really bad acting, thought Nash.

But he shook his head, reminding himself that he had had a harrowing night and that surely his mind was playing tricks on him.

"That's why we're here," said Kara. "To see if you can make any sense out of them."

"Well, then. Let's take a look."

Kara handed the pencil box to Dieter. He set it on an ornate coffee table, opened it, and carefully withdrew the contents. He paused on the photocopy of the coded message. "Station X was the code word for Bletchley Park," Dieter noted.

"What's Bletchley Park?" asked Kara.

"Bletchley Park," Nash interrupted quickly, since he knew a little about this, "was the location of the UK's main code breaking establishment in World War Two. Codes and ciphers of several Axis countries were deciphered there, most importantly those of the German Enigma Machine."

"And the high-level intelligence produced by Bletchley Park was called Ultra," Dieter added.

"You think this is an Enigma message, then?" asked Kara.

Dieter nodded.

"But what does it say?" she asked.

"We'd need an Enigma Machine to find that out," Dieter replied.

"And what's an Enigma Machine?"

Nash jumped in again. "They were often used by Nazi Germany for the encryption and decryption of secret messages."

Geez, thought Nash, *I'm like a schoolboy showing off for the pretty girl in class.*

"Fine," said Kara. "Then where do we find an Enigma machine?"

"The only functional one in Europe is at the Deutsches Museum in Munich," Dieter said then grinned broadly. "And since they don't open until the morning, I suggest the two of you get some sleep. You both look like you've been to hell and back."

Both Nash and Kara nodded.

"If we're going to be moving around," Kara said. "I'd like to have something to put my father's materials in instead of this pencil box."

"I think we can arrange that," Dieter replied.

He walked to his desk and removed a thick leather travel pouch. "This was given to me by your father as a gift for helping him in some of his research. I know he would want you to have it."

He handed it to Kara, who took it reverently.

She emptied the pencil box and placed the contents into the leather pouch. "May I leave the pencil box here with you?" she asked, sticking the pouch in her jacket.

"Of course. Now let's get some sleep. You can stay in the spare bedroom, Kara, and Mr. Nash can have the couch."

Enigma

The next morning, after a fitful sleep on the study couch, Nash found himself with Kara in the back of Dieter's Mercedes. They were both trying to remain as inconspicuous as possible as they sped down the autobahn toward Munich.

After a while, the traffic slowed to a crawl.

"What's happening?" asked Nash. "Why are we slowing down?"

Dieter craned his neck to look towards the cars lined up in front of them. "Scheisse!" he growled. "Roadblock!"

The cars in front of them were inching slowly forward as the police check point waved some cars on and others to the side of the autobahn.

"Crap," Nash exclaimed under his breath. He started to sweat through the clothes he had been wearing for twenty-four hours. He looked at Kara to apologize for any body odor he was exhuming and saw her staring intently at the cars pulled over to the side of the road.

Nash's anxiety level rose the closer they came to the roadblock.

Finally, it was their turn. The policeman eyed Dieter, then looked directly at Nash who tried to lower himself in the passenger seat, below the gaze of the policeman. The policeman turned his head to the right to speak into his radio, all the while watching Nash.

Nash's stomach dropped.

Then, mercifully, the policeman raised his arm towards Nash— and waved them through.

"Jesus," he breathed in exasperation. "That was close."

Dieter was cataloging the vehicles pulled over to the side of the road.

Nash followed his gaze and noticed they were all expensive sports cars. Porsches, Ferraris, Lamborghinis, BMW M3s. He was about to mention that to Kara when Dieter said, "Gumball."

"What?" Nash asked.

"It's the Gumball."

"What the hell is a Gumball?" questioned Nash.

"The Gumball is a crazy alternative in the world of professional racing. Drivers undertake the challenge each year, tearing through the countryside racing each other to the finish line somewhere in Europe."

"What are the police doing?" asked Nash.

Kara smiled. "The race isn't officially on until the authorities start impounding cars. The various police forces around Europe waste little time catching up with the crazy racers."

"Let's get moving," Nash said forcefully, "before one of those police recognizes us."

Dietrich looked in the rearview mirror and said, "Something troubling you, Kara?"

The young attorney hesitated before answering. "I didn't want to bring you into this, Karl. Leaving the van on the street like that. The scare at the roadblock."

"That's my concern," he replied, glancing from the mirror to the road. Nash wished he would keep his eyes on the road. "I want to help. I respected and liked your father very much."

"You are an angel, Karl."

"Anything for the daughter of my dear friend Alfred."

Nash decided to change the subject before he got physically ill, knowing he was being unreasonably jealous, but also not caring. *I've had a shitty night,* he reasoned with himself. *I can be cranky if I want.* Nash sat forward, "So where in the museum is the Enigma Machine?"

"There are three machines, actually," Dieter replied. "One Naval Enigma with four rotors and two Army machines that employ three rotors."

"Which one should we use?" asked Kara.

"Process of elimination, I'm afraid," Dieter replied. "The Naval and one of the Army Enigmas are on display. Getting access to them would be difficult. But the second Army Enigma is kept in a storeroom at the computer department."

"How do you know that?" queried Kara, sounding slightly awed.

"I was there a month or so ago doing some research at the museum. Believe me. It's there."

"How do we get to it?" asked Nash, pushing the man.

Dieter pulled off the autobahn and headed down a boulevard towards the museum. "I know the director of the computer department. I'm pretty sure he'll give us access to it. Enigma and its history are a hobby of his, and this message should perk his interest."

They passed a sign that read, **Munich 5km**.

"We're almost there," said Dieter. "The museum is on a small island in the Isar River. Perhaps soon we'll understand the meaning behind this enigma message."

Nash tried to ignore the fact that Kara gazed at the man with what could only be described as puppy dog eyes.

Yeah, he thought. *I'm going to be sick.*

They parked fifteen minutes later and soon joined a crowd of tourists through the front gate just as the museum opened. Nash stopped in the museum gift shop and bought himself and Kara two museum logo baseball caps. Both of them had the same thought, pulling them low on their foreheads. They followed Dieter to the museum's Computer Department wing, and there, sitting proudly on display, were the two Enigma Machines.

"Wait here," Dieter said. "And try to look inconspicuous."

He left Nash and Kara and disappeared through a side door on their left that read: *Zutritt Betriebsfremden nicht gestattet*—Staff Only.

Nash hoped the man knew what he was doing.

They didn't have to wait long.

A minute or two later, the young German professor appeared in the doorway and motioned for them to follow. The two slipped away from the milling crowds, through the door, and into a short hallway. There, they followed Dieter into a tiny office and faced a small man wearing a short white sleeve shirt with two hairy arms protruding from it sitting behind a very large desk.

Dieter introduced Nash and Kara. "And this is Herr Baumrucker, head of the Computer Department here at the museum."

Baumrucker stood and shook their hands vigorously, inviting them all to take a seat in one of the chairs in front of his desk. He said eagerly, "Herr Dieter tells me you may have an Enigma message that you'd like decoded."

Kara handed the slip of paper to him. The small man sat back in his overstuffed chair and studied the message intently, stroking his chin. Absently, he lit a cigarette and studied the code further.

Nash and Kara looked at each other. Kara raised her eyes hopefully. Dieter, sitting on the other side of her, was perched on the edge of his seat, literally. Nash wondered again what the man's reasons for such concern were. Was he just a family friend, ready to help at a moment's notice? Did he have some interest in Kara herself as Nash suspected, or was there something else going on here?

You're suspicious because half of Germany is after you.

"Hmm." Baumrucker brought the paper even closer to his eyes, nearly crossing them. He smoked rapidly. "To me, this looks like only a fragment of a message." He looked up over the message suddenly, directly at Dieter. "Why do you think this is an Enigma communication?"

"The handwritten notation at the bottom of the paper," stated Dieter.

The Director lowered his eyes. "Ah, yes. Station X," he said with a big smile. He made some more noises around the unfiltered tip of his cigarette. "Yes, yes. You could be right." He fingered the piece of paper some more. "This won't be easy, you know, without any point of reference. I mean, we don't know from whom—or even to whom—or the time frame the message was made in—"

Kara, amazingly, cut him off. "We think the message has something to do with Rommel."

"Rommel?" questioned Baumrucker, perplexed. "Field Marshall Rommel?"

Kara removed the picture of Rommel from the leather pouch she withdrew from her jacket. "There has to be a connection. It was with the other materials."

The curator grinned. "Well, that's a start."

"So how do we proceed?" pressed Dieter.

Despite his reservations about the man, Nash was glad he asked the question. *After all*, he thought, *our time could be rapidly running out.* Running from the German police probably wasn't the smartest thing to do in the world—or the easiest.

"First we need to make some assumptions," Baumrucker began. "Let's start with Rommel's early campaigns in the war. The message could have been created during the invasion of France, or even during his time with the Afrika Corps." He paused, smashing out the cigarette. "If so, that means the Enigma Message was created using some of the earlier ciphers, which we have here at the department. But there is a problem."

"What problem, Herr Baumrucker?" asked Kara.

"We would need the initial settings for the Enigma machine rotors," Baumrucker replied. "Without those...well, we just can't begin."

Dieter stood and paced behind Nash and Kara. "If we began where you suggested, we could, perhaps, simply set the rotors at the Polish Positions."

Baumrucker's face lit up. "Certainly! Yes! It's worth a try."

Dieter turned to Nash and Kara, no doubt seeing their perplexion. He explained, "To decipher any code using the Enigma Machine, one needs to know the initial rotor settings. The rotors are a series of wheels inside the machine. Each wheel is numbered with Roman numerals up to twenty-six, a number corresponding with the alphabet. On the opposite side of each wheel is a corresponding number of circular electrical contacts. For example, the pin corresponding to the letter E might be wired to the contact point for the letter T on the opposite face, and so on. The Enigma's complexity, and cryptographic security, came from using several rotors in series—usually three or four."

He continued. "Anyway, to make a long story short, in nineteen thirty-nine Polish code breakers assumed that the order of letters on the rotors was the same as those on the keyboard of a German typewriter and also the Enigma keyboard. That presumption was dead wrong."

"So, they failed," Kara said.

"No," replied Dieter. "Sometimes the simplest answer is the solution. In this case it was."

"How so?" asked Nash.

"The Poles rethought the problem and guessed that perhaps the letters were not arranged around a German typewriter but in alphabetical order." He grinned. "And they were."

"And that was the breakthrough," added Baumrucker, "that helped the Allies crack the Enigma code."

"And you do know how to work this machine?" implored Nash, hopefully. Already Nash's brain hurt.

"Oh, yes," said Baumrucker, grinning. He stood. "Shall we?"

Contact

Interpol Inspector Heinrich was sitting at a Berlin café over-looking the Spree River. He was enjoying his usual sliced meat and cheese open faced sandwich for breakfast when his cell phone chirped with the sound of the refrain from Mozart's *Ninth Symphony.*

A bit annoyed at having his meal disturbed, yet knowing business came first, he answered the damn thing.

"Heinrich here."

"Herr Inspector. We have news of Nash," came the reply on the other end. "He was sighted."

"Sighted where?" asked Heinrich, his meal immediately forgotten.

"First, at the East Berlin Sports Club. A patron recognized him. Then on the autobahn by a polizei."

Plastering Jeremy Nash's face all over the news was already paying off.

"Where are you now?"

"The polizei got the tag number of the car he was riding in. We're running a trace on it now."

"Good. Find out who it belongs to. Keep me updated."

"Yes, sir."

Inspector Heinrich clicked off and returned to his sandwich. *So, Nash has made contact with his accomplices. This is working out better than I hoped.*

Nazi Treasure

Jake Stone stood in front of the impressive headquarters of *Volks-Agrarindustrie, Inc.* The offices resided in a tall modern glass skyscraper near Alexanderplatz facing the Fernsehturm TV/Radio tower—the fourth tallest freestanding structure in Europe.

He entered and took the express elevator to the top floor where he was greeted by a large security guard armed with a Glock 40 and wearing a *Volks-Agrarindustrie* patch on his shoulder. "They're expecting you," he said.

A few minutes later he was sitting in front of Adrian Adler.

"Well, Herr Stone?" he asked. "What do you have for us?"

This was Stone's first visit to Adler's large office at the *Volks-Agrarindustrie, Inc.* headquarters. He nodded to himself. The office was impressive, filled with priceless art pieces from around the world. Paintings by Renoir, 500-year-old Buddhist sculptures— even a Samurai sword on Adler's desk.

Stone knew he had made the right decision to tap Adler for the funds and resources he needed for his treasure hunting expedition.

"We've found another piece of the puzzle," Stone said excitedly. "We know that a certain package addressed to a Colonel Maximilian Hartmann, the man responsible for leading the Fuhrer Convoy, is in England. And that package, we believe, leads to the location of Station Two One One—and our treasure."

"And how will you find the package?" queried Adler.

"That's where a certain professor comes in."

"And who is this professor?"

A smile crossed Stone's face. "If I told you that, you wouldn't need me."

"I see you're an astute businessman, Herr Stone," Adler smiled back. "Good then. Tell me what you need for the expedition."

Stone pulled a manifest from his briefcase and handed it to Alder. Adler scanned the sheets and said, "Fine. But there is one condition."

"And what's that?" asked Stone, suddenly concerned.

"I'll appoint the team to go with you. Agreed?"

Stone nodded his head. "Agreed."

"Good. You have work to do. Go and find us that treasure."

As Stone left, Adler's phone rang.

"Yes?"

"Stobl, sir."

"Report."

There was a distinct hesitation on the other end of the line. Adler could only guess why. "You lost them."

"Yes, sir. After the sports club. In Kreuzberg."

This was a disappointment. Stobl had never failed before.

"Sir, I..."

"I don't want excuses. I want results," snapped Adler. He had a thought. "Why were they at the sport's club?"

"I don't know."

"Are you sure you disposed of all papers and data at Tillman's apartment?"

"Yes, sir. Everything."

I wonder if that old man...

"What about the woman? Who is she?"

"A counselor. Nash's lawyer."

Adler paused. *Why would she risk her reputation and jail to help Nash escape?* "I'll contact you when I have something," he told his henchman and promptly hung up.

Once he was gone, Adler picked up his phone and dialed an extension.

"Hoffer here," was the reply.

"We're on," Adler replied. "Be ready to leave with our team."

As he hung up, he looked out his tall office window at the Fernsehturm TV/Radio tower—and smiled—knowing that it would soon be the instrument to bring about the New Reich.

Rommel's Message

Baumrucker led the group down another hall, through a door and into a cramped storeroom.

He smiled apologetically. "We'll need to get a bit chummy in here. As you can see, there's little space for the four of us."

They squeezed into the small room, packed with dusty old electronic equipment and boxes of files. Admittedly, Nash didn't mind being more than close to Kara, although on the flip side, he did notice she was pressed up against Dieter as well.

Take the good with the bad.

Nash tried to concentrate on the present. Optimistically, he thought that as small as the room was, it was still bigger than any German jail cell he would face.

He watched as Baumrucker plugged the Enigma in and set the rotors to, apparently, the Polish Position. He stepped back and nodded. "There. She's ready."

Next, he meticulously typed the coded letters into the machine as Nash and the others waited expectantly. A moment later, he finished punching in the last of letters and announced, "Well, I'll be! We've got a hit!"

The other three squeezed towards the printed output of the machine.

"Hmm..." said Baumrucker, retrieving the message. "Like I thought. This is only a partial message."

He showed them the paper readout then read it aloud—"...*directed to transport from Tobruk National Reserves to Bremerhaven via Marseilles to Hartman. Instruct to forward to Station Two One One at 70°46 S....*"

"What's Station Two One One?" Kara asked.

Nash knew this one. "Station Two One One is an alleged secret Nazi base in Antarctica. The Hollow Earth Theory. Crypto-historians have been peddling that story for years."

"Story?" asked Kara.

"Yes. There's a popular belief—unfounded, of course—that there not only was a secret Nazi base, but that it's currently being used by what some call the Fourth Reich where, in fact, Hitler and his henchmen escaped to after the war, along with priceless booty. Artwork, precious jewels, and tons of gold and silver looted from the conquered European countries. It's also believed that secret Nazi technology far beyond what we have today was sent there after the war. Zero-point energy weapons, Nazi anti-gravity machines—flying saucers."

Nash was surprisingly pleased with himself after his mini dissertation. He swore he could sense Kara's admiration—only to be squelched by Dieter who asked, "Is it safe to say that you don't believe in the validity of Station Two One One?"

"I believe in sound reasoning and scientific fact, Mr. Dieter." Nash looked over Kara's head, staring at the young professor. He knew his look was challenging. "Don't tell me you believe in this bunk?"

"This *bunk* appears to be why Kara's father was murdered," said Dieter easily. "Do I believe in the secret base? I believe anything is possible. I also believe that where there's smoke, there's fire."

"I, too, believe anything is possible," replied Nash firmly. "I just want the proof."

"You should keep an open mind," Dieter remarked.

"Open minds are fine as long as they're not so open that one's brains fall out," Nash retorted.

"Are you boys quite done?" asked Kara.

The men zipped their lips.

She pointed to the last line of the communiqué. "Now, what are these numbers here?"

"They look like latitude coordinates," said Baumrucker, "south of the equator."

"Which are useless without a longitude," added Nash.

Kara sighed heavily. "What about these *national reserves* mentioned in the communiqué?"

Nash just frowned.

Kara saw the look on Nash's face. "What's wrong?" she asked.

"Wrong?" he replied. "Wrong? Your father has sent us on a wild goose chase after some secret Nazi base holding some supposed Nazi treasure."

"You're wrong!" she glowered. "My father was not a treasure hunter. He was a scholar."

I'm screwed, thought Nash in disgust. *I put all my hope into a man who could only be described as delusional!*

Baumrucker suddenly stood up. "Wait here," he said. He disappeared out of the room, reappearing shortly with a world atlas. He flipped through the oversized book and traced a stubby finger on the pages. He stopped and pointed. "Look for yourselves," he said.

They all did. The latitude coordinates crossed Antarctica.

"Son of a bitch," Nash exclaimed.

Baumrucker asserted, "Now we just need the longitude coordinates—"

Dieter paused a moment in thought. "Herr Baumrucker. May we use the computer in your office?"

"Of course. What are you thinking?"

"I want to scan the photo of the German soldier into your museum's network and compare it against your World War Two database."

"Do you think that would help?" questioned Kara doubtfully.

"Your father had it in the pencil box," Dieter reminded her. "It may have some significance."

He looked at Nash. "Are you game?"

Nash shrugged his shoulders and nodded. *Like I have a choice.*

Return Of The Vril

Gunter Krause, black-faced and dressed in dark green camouflaged fatigues and field boots, peered through his night-vision binoculars towards the dramatically steep cliffs of Monte Coltignone, just north of the Lake Como town of Lecco. As expected, the cave just above the shoreline was guarded by two Italian Polizia standing on a small boat dock, armed with automatic rifles.

This will be easy, he thought.

He checked the time on his watch. A little after midnight. Good. Plenty of time to find his way to the cave that contained five hundred pounds of German World War Two munitions found at the bottom of Lake Como a few months prior. The munitions were scheduled to be detonated in twelve hours, at noon. For Gunter Krause, senior member of the Vril Society, the planned detonation of the highly unstable munitions would make a perfect cover for his mission.

He'd just arrange to make it sooner.

A few weeks earlier, military divers were called in to retrieve the deadly arsenal of unexploded wartime bombs found in the deep waters of the Northern Italian Lake. The deadly arsenal included hand grenades, mortars, artillery shells, and aircraft bombs.

It included one other thing.

Something that would complete the long-sought dream of the Vril Society—access to the secret revelations of the Aryan forefathers and the location to the entrance of the Hollow Earth. And as a former member of the *Kommando Spezialkräfte*—an elite squad of Germany's Special Forces—Krause had the skills and training to complete the task assigned to him.

He tucked the night-vision goggles away. It was time to move.

Krause worked his way quietly through the small trees and scrub brush of the east shore back towards the main highway. Once there, he climbed into his four-wheel drive vehicle and drove to the far shore around the small offshoot of the inverted *Y* of Lake Como.

Under the cover of the moonless night, Krause moved through the brush of the western shore of the small lake to the high cliff above the munitions cave.

As the ex-commando slinked his way towards the cliff, he thought back over the last several months and his initiation into the Vril Society. That Krause was inducted into the Society was, to most, an anarchism—a Jew in what most believed was a Nazi Society.

But they wouldn't be entirely correct.

He was, in fact, descended from the *Ashkenazi*—medieval German-Jews who had settled along the Rhine River. Although only his mother was an *Ashkenazi*, Krause had inherited some of the genetic mutations found most frequently in Jews of Central and Eastern European descent. Such genetic mutations, he knew, could be serious and debilitating. For him, his genetic mutation had been the inability to process or respond to pain. Such a mutation had made him a perfect candidate for a pugilist life and more than capable to fulfill the current needs of the Vril.

Krause reached the edge of the cliff and focused his thoughts at the task at hand. He always had the God-given ability to clear clutter from his mind and focus.

He reached into the duffel bag at his feet and pulled out a long curl of black kernmantle rope. He attached one end to a fallen tree then walked carefully over to the sharp edge of the cliff to scan the surrounding area again. He concluded that, outside of heat-signature cameras, it was doubtful he would be spotted.

He tossed the rope over the cliff and tested it. Good enough. He next checked his sidearm but knew he probably wouldn't use it. This had to be a silent kill leaving no visible wounds.

A moment later, he rappelled into the darkness below.

As Krause descended, he heard the two young *polizias* chatting quietly on the boat dock in front of the cave entrance, their voices rising to him in a trick of acoustics. He clearly heard one of them offer another a cigarette.

Krause dropped down twenty or so yards north of them, touching quietly on the smooth rocks that littered the shoreline. He paused, listening, but there was no break in the steady banter of the two guards. Krause quietly picked his way over rocks and seaweed, keeping as close as possible to the brush that grew along the base of the cliff.

Soon, he was just a few yards from the cave entrance. The guards were laughing now. Krause crouched behind a row of heavy devil weed, watching the movement of their glowing cigarettes.

He waited.

Suddenly one of the guards stood, slinging his weapon over his shoulder, and walked in Krause's direction. The ex-commando moved his hand to his pistol and gripped the handle.

Had he been discovered? Krause doubted it. He had approached silently, and the guards hadn't missed a beat talking and smoking. More than likely—

Indeed, he heard the man unzip himself, and a moment later a strong jet of urine splashed the rocks nearby Krause. Some of the warm back spray hit Krause's neck and face. Krause didn't move or flinch. He ignored the splatter completely.

When finished, the young polizia zipped up his fly, turned... and was dead within seconds.

The trained killer leaped forward, bursting through the bushes.

The doomed polizia heard him and was about to shout when Krause's hand covered his mouth. In a practiced, violent motion, Krause turned the man's head as hard as he could to the right. The sharp *crack* of breaking vertebra briefly snapped the night air. The young man instantly went limp, and Krause dragged him deeper into the bushes, where he waited for the second guard to make his inevitable move.

He didn't have to wait long.

The second policeman, no doubt wondering why his partner's bathroom break was taking so long, was now cautiously moving toward Krause, his pistol drawn, his flashlight probing the way before him.

"Luigi?" called the man. He stepped closer towards Krause. He called out again, louder. "Luigi?"

And when the guard was within easy range of where Krause was crouching behind a gnarled tree, the young guard saw his partner's feet jutting from under the brush.

When he leaned down to investigate, Krause sprang on him and quickly dispatched the man in the same manner as his partner.

Time to get to work.

Krause dashed out into the open and over to the boat dock. Once there, he followed a pair of metal railings into the cave opening, passing a small crane.

He clicked on his flashlight and swept the powerful beam around the deep cavern. The cave was bigger than he had expected.

Stepping deeper into it, his footfalls echoing around him, his piercing flashlight soon illuminated boxes of munitions, motor shells, grenades, and bombs. He found a four-foot long, cylindrical object at the back of the cave. He recognized it immediately. A German World War Two naval Oyster mine.

His superior would be pleased.

Krause headed back to the cave opening, where he aimed his flashlight out over the small lake. He blinked the light three times, waited, then blinked it three more times.

Three seconds later, another light flashed a reply.

From somewhere on the dark lake, Krause heard the sound of a powerful motorboat. A few minutes later, a rigid inflatable

Zodiac, the kind used for amphibious assaults, pulled onto the shore. Two Vril initiates—twin brothers from Austria—stepped out of the boat and dashed over to Krause.

The ex-commando silently motioned for them to follow him, and at the back of the cave, he pointed to the cylindrical mine.

"Take this," Krause ordered.

They nodded and soon the husky initiates maneuvered a small crane in the back of the cave over to the mine, carefully hoisting it off the cave floor.

Krause watched anxiously as the two brothers loaded the volatile weapon into the boat. When done, the German breathed a sigh of relief.

There was one thing left to do.

While the twin brothers waited in the boat, Krause dragged the two dead polizia to the cave entrance, and then fetched a heavy artillery shell from inside the cavern. He removed a detonator charge and a cell phone from his fatigue jacket, expertly attaching the artillery shell to the detonator. Once done, he connected the wires of the charge to the cell phone.

He examined his handiwork once more, smiled inwardly, and then dashed off to join the Austrian brothers. Within minutes, they were speeding up Lake Como.

As they raced away, one of the twins handed Krause another cell phone.

Krause punched in a number.

He paused, then hit *send*.

Almost immediately, a massive explosion rocked the lake. A furious ball of flame blinded the south shore as a powerful shock nearly overturned the boat.

When the shockwave passed, Krause smiled.

Mission complete.

Rommel's Gold

Baumrucker led the trio back to his office and took a seat behind his desk. He took the photo and studied it for a moment. "I can't make any promises," he said. "This photograph is typical for the early part of World War Two. There are literally thousands of them out there. The young soldiers had them taken to remind them of their families and their homes."

"I understand," Kara said. "But my father left it as a clue to something, so I don't think it is just an arbitrary picture."

Baumrucker nodded, and placed the photo face down on the scanner on his desk and pushed a button. The machine lit up and a light slowly swiped across the photo. A few seconds later, the photo appeared on the computer monitor.

"Now to see if it's in our database," Baumrucker said. He typed in a few commands, and a page of search results replaced the photograph on the computer screen.

Baumrucker selected the top line and hit the enter key.

A much grainier version of the same photograph appeared with the caption, *Could a wartime photo point to looted Nazi gold?*

"Hmm… It's about Rommel's treasure myth," Baumrucker said.

"Just great!" Nash exclaimed. "I knew your father's clues would lead to something like this. Your father *was* looking for Nazi treasure."

Kara stiffened and turned to face Nash. "My father was not hunting treasure! The picture must have some other meaning."

"It does," Baumrucker said. "This article says the numbers on the back of the photo are supposed to be a secret code that leads to the whereabouts of a hoard of looted Nazi gold. The hoard was amassed by fanatical SS units operating alongside Rommel's Afrika Korps—looted from Jews in Tunisia during the North Africa campaign. It would be worth in excess of twenty million pounds today."

"Who's the German soldier in the picture?" Nash asked.

"Let me see," Baumrucker said, scrolling through the text on the screen. "His name was Walter Kirner. Near the end of the war, Kirner served at the Dachau death camp, and it was there that he learned the legend of Rommel's Treasure from one of the SS men he served with there. He wrote the coordinates of the treasure's location in code on the back of his photo."

"And we can assume," Dieter added, "that the SS thought they might be able to retrieve it if the war swung back in their favor but, of course, it didn't." He lifted the photograph off the scanner and looked at the writing on the back. "And Rommel was ordered in the enigma message to send it to Station Two One One."

"*If* you believe the enigma message to be true," Nash said. "Or any of the other umpteen-thousand treasure-hunter theories for that matter."

"Now this is very interesting." Baumrucker pointed to the computer monitor. "The set of numbers making up the code in the article doesn't match the numbers on your original. They say NHRA11hDEC+50DG. The markings in the database are very different."

Nash, Kara, and Dieter scrunched together and leaned closer to the monitor.

"I wonder which ones are correct?" Kara mussed.

Baumrucker took a large magnifying glass from the top drawer of his desk and examined the writing on the back of the photograph. "These have been altered," he said. "I can still see the indentations of the original markings under portions of this writing."

"What do you think it means, professor?" Dieter asked.

"The second coordinates for Station Two One One?" Baumrucker suggested.

"That explains why no one has ever found it," Kara said. "The

original coordinates were wrong. My father must have discovered the real ones."

"Obviously, this German soldier is connected with whatever was in North Africa and what Rommel was ordered to transport out of it." Baumrucker smiled broadly.

"Obviously?" Nash asked. "That's nothing more than wild speculation."

Dieter held up his hand. "Nash, you're not—"

"Gentlemen, and frauline," Baumrucker interrupted. "I'm sorry I couldn't be of any more help, but I have pressing matters that need to be attended to."

Dieter nodded, thanked the Director, and the three left his office.

Outside the museum, Kara turned to Nash. "I know you still think this is some kind of treasure hunt, but someone killed my father and went through a lot of trouble to frame you for it. My father thought you could help and obviously someone else wants you out of the way."

"I don't know what I can do," Nash said.

"His killer was looking for something, and I think it has to do with these clues."

"Then I would suggest we take a better look at them," Dieter suggested.

Two uniformed police officers walked past but paid them no attention.

Nash watched them until they were out of sight. "Let's find a place a little less public to do it."

"And we can grab some lunch while we're at it," Kara smiled. "All of this treasure hunting is making me famished."

Nash stared at her and then burst out laughing.

Odinist

At a local schnellimbiss, they sat at a table in the back corner and spread the clues from Kara's leather travel pouch on the table while they waited for their food to arrive.

Kara picked up the 1955 magazine article and began to read it. "This article mentions Hans Luber and the Nazi's experiments in nanotechnology as a potential weapon," she noted.

"Who was Hans Luber?" Nash asked.

"Not *was—is*." Kara corrected. "Hans Luber is my uncle."

"Maybe he can help shed some light on this puzzle," Dieter said. "Where is he now?"

"He lives in Austria. I can call him."

"Better use my phone." Dieter slid his cell phone across the table. "We can assume the police will be tracking both of yours by now."

Kara looked up the phone number in her phone and punched the numbers into Dieter's.

"Uncle Hans?" she asked. "Is that you?"

"Nein. I am Rudolf Hauser. Assistant to Herr Luber. How may I help you?"

"I'd like to speak to Herr Luber, please. This is Kara Ackerman. I'm his niece."

"The professor will be out until later this evening. Shall I take a message?"

"No," she said. "I'll try again later," and hung up.

"Can I see the article?" Dieter asked.

Kara handed it to him, and he read it from top to bottom.

"Anything?" Nash asked.

"I recognize this word from somewhere," he said, pointing to the word, *Odinist*, handwritten in the top border. "And these scribbles around the borders may be another code."

"Can you connect to the internet and look up the word?" Kara asked.

Dieter nodded, laid his cell phone on the table, and began to type. After a few seconds, he said "You're going to love this. *The Odinist* is a poem by Adolph Hitler."

"I didn't know he wrote poetry," Kara said.

"In his spare time—when not murdering half of Europe," Nash said sarcastically.

Dieter pushed another button on his phone and began to read aloud.

> *I often go on bitter nights*
> *To Wotan's oak in the quiet glade*
> *With dark powers to weave a union—*
> *The runic letters the moon makes with its magic spell*
> *And all who are full of impudence during the day*
> *Are made small by the magic formula!*
> *They draw shining steel—but instead of going into combat*
> *They solidify into stalagmites.*
> *So the false ones part from the real ones—*
> *I reach into a nest of words*
> *And then give to the good and just*
> *With my formula blessings and prosperity.*

"Well, he's no Longfellow," Nash remarked.

"It loses something in the translation," Dieter said. "I'm no fan of Adolph Hitler, but in German, it really is quite beautiful."

Kara wrinkled her nose. "Anything connected to Hitler is garbage in any language."

They stopped talking as a teenage girl brought a large tray of food and drinks to their table. She was dressed completely in black and even emphasized her love for the color by her choice of eye shadow and fingernail polish.

The girl balanced the tray on her hand as she carefully placed their drinks in front of them. "Who had the kartofflesalad?" she asked.

"I did," Kara replied, picking up the scraps of paper her father had left her and stacking them in the center of the table.

The girl bent at the waist as she extended the plate across the table. As she did, Kara gasped. The girl jumped up quickly and looked alarmed. "What's wrong?" she asked.

"It's your pendant," Kara said. "It's beautiful. I've never seen a cross quite like it before."

The girl relaxed. "It's not a cross," she said laughing. "It's the runic symbol for *N* as in Natalie, my name."

"Well then it wouldn't work for me. "I'm Kara with a *K*.

The girl set the other two plates down and went back to the front counter.

When she was gone, Kara turned to Dieter and said, "Quick! Look up the runic alphabet on the internet."

"The what?" Dieter asked, his mouth full of bratwurst.

"Her pendant. It was the same as this symbol." Kara tapped one of the handwritten scribbles along the border of the magazine article. "It's written in runic."

"As in *runic spell* from Hitler's poem? Runic spell. Spelled in runic," Dieter said. "How clever."

Dieter picked up his phone again and quickly typed in the search criteria. Kara wrote each letter down on her napkin as Dieter translated them.

When Dieter translated the last symbol, Kara said each letter individually. "I-L-O-V-E-H-I-T-L-E-R-U-N-I-T-Y. It spells *I Love Hitler Unity*."

"I love Hitler Unity! What's that? Some kind of Nazi political oath?" Nash snarled.

"This could refer to Unity Mitford," Dieter said.

"What's that?" Kara asked.

"Unity Mitford is a *who*, not a *what*," Dieter blurted out laughing. "She was English. In fact, she came from a long line of English aristocrats."

"If she was English, why do you think the *Unity* in the poem refers to her?" Kara asked.

"She was part of Hitler's inner circle, and it's rumored that she secretly gave birth to his love child in 1940."

"Another unfounded myth," Nash said, the frustration evident in his voice.

"That love child part may be myth, but her love for Hitler is well documented," Dieter told him. "My latest book is about the young woman who wrote love letters to Hitler. I have an entire chapter dedicated to her letters," Dieter said.

"You've got to be kidding," Nash commented with a raised eyebrow.

"Not at all. A German-born American military officer by the name of William Emker was sent to Berlin just after the war. During a visit to the bombed-out Chancellery he found a trove of private letters written to Hitler. The collection contains letters from hundreds of women."

"That's revolting," Kara said, her face twisted with disgust.

"And it gets even more revolting," Dieter added. "The letters were very macabre—addressed with *My Darling Sugar, Sweet Adolf,* and claptrap like that."

"What else did they say?" Kara asked.

"Oh, things like *can we meet on Christmas Eve,* or *come to my home. My parents said you can come any time so we can spend the night together in their house.* Letters like that."

"Well, that's very interesting, Dieter, but this is getting us nowhere," Nash said.

"On the contrary," Dieter replied. "It gets us to London. This clue leads us to the Mitford family."

The Promise

The tall athletic woman was escorted to a small room with no windows. There were two wooden chairs and a small table in the corner of the otherwise bare room. "Please take a seat," he said. "Dar Shamar will be with you shortly."

That's what you said four days ago, she thought, but instead said, "Thank you."

Ignoring the chair, she sat down on the floor facing the wall and maneuvered her body into the lotus position keeping her back rigid and her chin up. She wrapped her ponytail around her neck twice, closed her eyes, and began to meditate.

"I'm sorry to have kept you waiting for so long."

The woman opened her eyes, stood, and quickly, unwound her straight, blonde ponytail from her neck and allowed her hair to fall just below her knees.

The young man standing before her was tall and powerfully built. He was wearing the traditional cotton robe and brown woolen cap of his people. Despite the 100-degree heat and suffocating humidity, he didn't appear to be sweating.

The woman smiled as his eyes roamed over her body. She could tell this man was not immune to her beauty and hoped he would be as susceptible to her requests.

"I am Elsa Klein, the High Initiate of the Vril Society," she said. "You are the leader of the Tibetan Resistance Army?"

"I am Dar Shamar," he said softly. "Of the Chushi-Gangdruk."

"And you are their leader?"

He shrugged. "Let's just say that I am in a position to hear any requests made of the Chushi-Gangdruk—the Resistance Army."

"I've been waiting four days to talk to someone in the position—"

"Please sit," he offered. "Perhaps some tea while we talk?"

As if on cue, the old man who had escorted her to this room appeared in the doorway with a steaming pot of tea and two small clay cups.

After the tea was poured and the old man bowed out of the room, Shamar said, "I will listen to whatever you have to say, but—"

"The time for listening is over," the young woman said. "Now is the time for action."

"I agree with what you are saying," he said. "But you must know that we have heard all of this before. People have been coming to my family home in Tibet since the 1930s. My grandfather told stories of Germans coming to the Himalayas to search for ancient high priests—the *Masters* or *Ancients*—who they believed could conjure strange spirits and were thought to be their blood ancestors. What makes you any different?"

"For one thing," she began, "I can guarantee your people their freedom. I will take control of Tibet out of the hands of the People's Republic of China and give it back to your people."

"And what are you asking in return for our freedom?"

"All we ask," she said, "is unrestricted access to your country."

"And our secrets." Shamar smiled. He topped off her Tibetan butter tea, a concoction of tea leaves, yak butter, and salt.

"Yes," she said, sipping the sweet and salty nectar. As soon as she set her cup back on the table, he filled it back up to the brim, in accordance with Tibetan custom.

"And with our secrets, the Thule Society plans to recreate the Master Race?" the young Tibetan asked.

"We are not the Thule," she replied defensively. "The Thule focused primarily upon a materialistic and political agenda. This led to world war and eventually to the destruction of Germany.

Today, the Black Sun still follow this agenda. We are the Vril Society." She paused and tried to read his face.

"So you are not trying to recreate the Master Race?" he asked.

She drank another sip of her tea, then placed her hand over the cup so it could not be refilled. "The Vril Society places its attention on the *Other Side*. And the *Other Side* is what we seek." She leaned forward in her chair to make her point. "We want to return to Tibet and learn the secrets of the Ancients," she whispered reverently.

"I know a little about the Vril," he said contemplating his tea.

"Such as?"

"I know the original founder was also a woman, and they operated under a veil of mystery and secrecy. I know they believed in secret revelations, the coming of the New Age, and making contact with ancient peoples and inner worlds. They also believed that a superior race, the Vril-ya, lived beneath the earth, and with their help, the Vril Society planned to conquer the world with vril, a psychokinetic energy."

"You seem to know our history. But that is *history*—the past. The new Vril have no desire to conquer the world. We simply wish to become masters of the Vril. To become the master of oneself."

"I also know that the Vril was reestablished, and you were appointed their leader after the discovery of your—unique bloodline." Now the young Tibetan leaned forward and looked into her eyes.

"My agenda is quite different from my grandfather's politics," she said.

"How so?"

"Well, for one thing," she began. "My grandmother was English. From a family with ties to the House of Lords. My mother was adopted and raised by a God-fearing family in England. I was not brought up with all the Nazi rhetoric."

"Then why did the Vril choose you?"

"It is thought that my lineage will help to generate interest

in the Vril." She matched his gaze. "But surely you know all of this already."

Shamar smiled. "It is wise to know as much as possible about the people I do business with."

"I can guarantee your people their freedom," Klein said, returning to her rigid, straight-backed position on the hard wooden chair.

"But you have a problem," Shamar said.

"Two, in fact," she replied. "Tibet today is under the control of the People's Republic of China, and unrestricted access to your country by outsiders and the secrets of Ancients that dwelled there is virtually impossible." She paused a moment. "And we also need money—a lot of money."

"For?" the Tibetan asked.

"To finance our search for the Lords of Inner Earth."

"I see," he said softly as he sipped his tea.

"Agree to finance our search for the hollow earth," Klein continued, "and I promise Tibet will be free of the Chinese and back in the hands of your people in less than a month."

"And you are in a position to make this happen?"

"We have everything in place." Klein asserted. "Do we have a deal?"

"Fulfill your promise, and you will have all that you ask."

The Celestial Swastika

"Rise and shine," Dieter said, gently shaking Nash's shoulder. "We're in Paris."

Nash looked at his watch. It was late morning.

They collected their things and headed for the Eurostar ticket office to secure passage by train to London via the Chunnel.

A few hours later, the speeding train delivered them to the St. Pancras train station in London.

"How do we find this family?" asked Kara.

"One of the reporters at *The Times* is a friend of mine," Dieter said. "He interviewed the family about the myth a few years ago. He should have the address."

He pulled out his phone and punched in a number. As he spoke into the phone, Kara turned to Nash. "I could use some coffee."

"I could go for a quart or so myself," Nash said. He signaled Dieter and pointed to the Starbuck's sign across the station. Dieter nodded and mouthed the word, *Espresso,* and continued to speak into the phone.

Nash and Kara returned with the coffees, and Nash asked, "Did you get it?"

"Yes. Let's flag a cab."

The cab pulled up to a large brick and plaster multistory house.

"Looks like the family is doing well," Nash noted. "Hitler child support?"

"The family did have connections to the House of Lords," Dieter retorted. "A Lord Mitford, I believe."

"British aristocracy mingling with the Nazis. What's next?" Nash asked as they walked up the walkway.

"I don't know how well we'll be received," Dieter warned them, ringing the doorbell. "My friend told me his interviews did not go well. The family does not like to talk about this particular rumor."

"Great," Nash said. "All we need now is for—"

The door suddenly swung open, and a middle-aged woman glared at them. "What do you want?"

"We're from Berlin," Dieter told her. "We'd like to speak to someone about Unity Mitford."

"Reporters are not welcome here," the woman said sharply and started to close the door.

"Wait! Please?" Kara pleaded. "We're not reporters. Alfred Tillman was murdered, and we believe your family may have information that could help us find his killers."

"Professor Tillman? Murdered?" The woman's shoulders slumped. "You are with the police then?"

"No," Kara said. "I'm his daughter."

The woman looked at Kara for a moment, then looked quickly at the two men before returning her gaze to Kara. She opened the door and stepped backwards. "Of course. Please come inside."

She led them into the living room and motioned for them to sit on the large couch.

She took a seat opposite them. "My name is Lois Hayward. Unity Mitford was my great-aunt. I apologize for my abruptness at the door, but we have many unwanted visitors because of Unity's past associations."

"I can imagine," said Nash. "Everyone from nosey reporters to Neo-Nazis looking for a new Führer?"

Hayward nodded quickly.

Kara jumped in. "How did you know my father?"

"He came to us last year asking for our help with his research. He needed assistance with a story."

"Professor Tillman was interested in the Unity Mitford love child story?" Dieter asked.

"No. This was a story about a convoy of U-boats led by a Colonel Maximilian Hartmann."

"Let me guess. He spoke about three envelopes. Right?" Nash shook his head slowly.

"Yes," said Hayward. "You are familiar with the story?"

"I'm afraid that I am," Nash said. "It's a crypto-historian myth that has spawned a slew of urban legends."

"Ah, the story of the Holy Lance," Dieter added.

"You're the war expert," Nash told Dieter. "You can tell the story, so I don't have to stop myself from laughing halfway through it."

Dieter shrugged. "The story claims that Hartman was given three envelopes by Rudolph Hess shortly before Hess's death in Spandau prison. The first envelope contained a coded message from Professor Karl Haushofer."

"I'm not familiar with that name." Kara said.

"He was a German geo-politician," Nash interrupted, "whose ideas influenced the development of Adolf Hitler's expansionist strategies."

Dieter gave him a disapproving look.

"I'm sorry," Nash offered. "It's your lecture."

"Herr Nash is correct. Haushofer indeed molded the thinking of the Nazi inner core, and those beliefs were part of the motivation for the Nazi search for the Ark of the Covenant and Agharta, the mystical realm of enlightened beings who lived inside the hollow earth."

"What was in the second envelope?" Kara asked, intrigued.

"The second envelope," Dieter went on, "instructed Hartmann to recreate Himmler's Knights of the Grand Council. The organization was also to be called by a new name, Knights of the Holy Lance. The third envelope was supposed to either contain a large amount of cash to recreate the Knights of the Holy Lance—or some kind of artifact."

"It wasn't cash," Lois Hayward informed them.

"What makes you say that?" Dieter asked.

"Professor Tillman called me several times about the story," Hayward said. "During the last call, he told me that he had discovered something that told him what exactly the artifact was. When I told him that our family had what he was looking for, he came to see me."

Dieter jumped to his feet. "You have the artifact?" He looked at his companions, who were staring back at him, and exclaimed, "This is really fantastic."

"We *did*. I gave it to Professor Tillman when he was here. We had the key to what he was looking for—literally."

"The key?" Kara asked. "A key?" She reached into the leather travel pouch in her jacket and pulled out the old rusty hex key. "Are you talking about this key?"

"Yes," Hayward replied. "I gave that to your father thinking he could use it in the research he was doing. Did he tell you what it was for?"

"No. He didn't. Do you know?"

Hayward shook her head.

"Ms. Hayward, how did you come by the key?" Nash asked.

"We found it inside a locked box in a cousin's safe deposit box after his death many years ago. Whatever it was, my cousin must have thought it valuable. The family kept it as a curiosity."

"May I ask the name of your cousin?" Dieter asked.

"Sir Nigel Humphrey."

"*Sir*?" Kara asked.

"Yes. He was a member of the House of Lords in the nineteen thirties. Another dark chapter, unfortunately, in our family history."

"How so?" Kara leaned forward.

"He was a Nazi sympathizer like several members of the Royals back then. It was rumored he worked with the Nazis on ancient disease cures. Our family believed he worked with Nazi biologists as part of a secret Nazi technology project with esoteric undertones."

"What did you mean by *esoteric* undertones?" Kara asked.

"The occult," Hayward said, lowering her eyes.

"The crypto-history version goes something like this," Nash said. "The Nazis, in their desperation to avoid their looming disaster and win the war, experimented with a science—an occult science— that had never remotely been considered."

"Occult science?" asked Kara.

"Occult science is defined as containing artifacts, ancient mysteries, various esoteric or occult traditions, and actual physical material or other types of physical paraphernalia," Dieter explained.

"And somewhere in these wild ideas a new technology was to be born," Nash added. "So far advanced for its time that it had to be suppressed by the powers that be to the present day."

"Who?" asked Kara. "Who suppressed it?"

"You know," Nash said. "The proverbial, *They*. The *They* that always suppresses the truth. The truth of Nazi UFOs and atom bombs, Zero Point Energy devices, ice bombs, V-3s, 4s, and 5s, super bombs and vortex guns...then top it off with the belief of the Nazi Occult Bureau, that super beings lived inside the hollow earth, and it gets even nuttier from there."

"Herr Nash," Dieter commented. "I know you don't believe in—"

"Enter the Thule and Vril Societies," Nash ignored the interruption and continued to speak. "They believed that a quarter of a million years ago an alien race from outer space mated with mankind and assimilated. The Nazis believed these beings and their offspring had superpowers and that by purifying the human race of undesirables these Supermen will emerge, taking their rightful place as rulers of the world. The Ahnenebe SS searched the world for anything that could be spun into their quest for racial superiority."

"Nazism was not just a political movement but an occult religion with Hitler as the Messiah," he continued. "His beliefs were based on a twisted version of ancient law borrowing any belief of any kind from any religion to adapt to the Aryan cause of world domination."

Nash paused for effect. "And there's the whole sick Nazi occult nightmare in a nutshell."

"But what does this have to do with my father's research?" Kara asked, puzzled.

"Maybe I can answer that," Dieter said. "Kara, can I see the items—the clues that your father left you?"

She handed him the leather pouch, and he took out the picture of the Englishman. "Would this be your cousin?"

"Yes," the English woman replied. "That's Sir Humphrey."

"Ms. Hayward, did Sir Humphrey talk much about the Nazi occult with your family?"

"Yes. Quite often. He was obsessed with it. I was young at that time, but I do remember him speaking often about something called the Celestial Swastika and Station Two One One. He thought that somehow, they were connected." She shook her head. "He was old and dying and his mental capacity was fading fast. We thought they were just the rantings of an old man. Could they have been true?"

"I wonder..." Dieter said aloud.

"What are you thinking?" Kara asked.

Dieter withdrew the picture of the German soldier from the pouch. He turned it over and looked at the code on the back. "Let's assume something. As I said before, suppose the second set of coordinates to Station Two One One are these letters and numbers on the back of this photograph. Your father included all these different scraps of paper for a reason."

"We agreed they must be connected somehow," Kara said. She turned to Nash. "Agreed?"

Nash nodded.

"Good." Dieter continued, "Now the Unity Mitford clue, the picture of Sir Humphrey, his interest in the Nazi occult and the hollow earth, and the story of the German soldier, the Rommel message—I believe they all add up."

"Add up to what?" asked Nash in frustration. "What the devil are you getting at?"

"To where Station Two One One is located. The celestial swastika. That's the connection. Sir Humphrey might have been right."

"And how is that?" questioned Nash, impatiently.

"The celestial swastika is created by the rotation of Ursa Minor around the Polaris, the brightest star in Ursa Minor, at the end of the handle of the Little Dipper. The northern axis of the earth points toward it."

He pulled out his pen and drew an image of the Little Dipper rotating around a point on the back of the soldier's picture.

"And?" Nash said.

"And according to Nazi beliefs, the celestial swastika points to the Ultima Thule—the ancient country at the top of the world where the entrance to inner earth would be found."

"I'm sorry, but I don't understand any of this," Kara sighed.

Nash pointed to the letters and numbers on the back of the German soldier's photo. "Are you saying these are the coordinates of Ursa Minor?"

"What do you think? Kara tells me you're a pilot."

"May I have your pen?" he said.

Dieter handed it to him, and Nash started to manipulate the

figures on the back of the photo. "If these are celestial coordinates and we separate them to make sense of that we have…"

NH RA11h

DEC+50 Degrees

"Whadaya know," Nash pondered. "Ursa Minor."

Dieter had a self-righteous smirk on his face. "Here's where it gets interesting. Polaris also points to the Prime Meridian that goes around the globe to Antarctica and runs through the region known as Queen Maude Land.

"*Neuschwabenland*," Nash said almost under his breath.

"Yes. Nazi Antarctica," Dieter said. "Its location must be where the Prime Meridian intersects with the latitude in Rommel's message."

Nash nodded slowly. At least this much made sense.

"Let's say that my father found this secret Nazi base," Kara said. "Is that grounds to have him murdered, Jeremy framed, and the two of us nearly killed by some madman?"

"Not that he found it," Dieter replied. "But what may be *in* it."

"What do mean?" Nash asked.

"Perhaps an artifact. Your last diatribe about Nazi secret weapons, Nash. Remember?"

"You're saying Kara's father found a Nazi UFO?" Nash asked sarcastically.

"What I'm saying is that Tillman's clues point to *something* that he might have discovered."

"What about the article that mentions my uncle and the secret Nazi research? Could he know what my father discovered?"

"Only one way to find out," Nash said. "Can we go see him?"

"I'll call him again," Kara said.

They thanked Hayward for her hospitality and stood to leave.

"Ms. Hayward," Dieter said. "Would it be possible to use your water closet?"

"Of course." Hayward pointed the way to her bathroom.

"And could I ask you to call us a taxi?"

Dieter locked the bathroom door, leaned back against it, and closed his eyes for a few seconds. He pulled out his phone, punched a number on the speed dial and waited.

"Stone."

"It's Dieter. I—"

Stone cut him off. "Dieter, I paid you good money to locate the Hartman information. I found what I needed myself. And I found someone who could help me locate Nash."

"I've earned your money," Dieter said. "I have the Hartman information, and I have Nash. I'm with him now. We're in England."

"What does he know?" Stone asked.

"Enough. We're taking the Chunnel back to the Continent tonight."

"Tell me what—"

"I can't talk now. I'll contact you as soon as I can." Dieter hung up, flushed the toilet, and exited the bathroom.

While they waited for the cab at the curb, Kara used Dieter's phone to call her uncle.

"Uncle Hans? It's Kara."

"Kara! How are you? It's been too long. How's your father?"

Kara was silent a moment then said, "He's dead. Murdered."

"My God!" Luber replied. "When? How?"

She cut him off. "Listen. I don't have much time. Someone framed an American for Father's murder. I have him here with me. He's going to help find who did it."

"You're at the jail now?" Luber asked.

"No. We're in England. I broke him out of the police station."

"*Kara!*" Hans nearly shouted. "What are doing? Turn him over immediately to the authorities!"

"I can't. Father wanted the American to help me." Tears started to tear up in her eyes. "I think he knew he was going to be killed."

"Kara, I—"

"Please, you're the only family I have left," Kara pleaded.

There was a long pause. "Of course, child. When will you be here?"

"Thank you, Uncle Hans." She wiped the tears from her eyes. "We'll be there tomorrow."

Lois Hayward watched through the crack in the curtains until the cab pulled away from the curb. She picked up the phone and dialed a number from memory.

"Ya?"

"This is Lois Hayward," she said.

"I know who you are," the man said. "Why are you calling?"

"You told me to let you know if anyone was asking about Professor Tillman."

"Who was it?"

"What about the money?" Hayward asked. "You promised us the money."

"You'll be paid," the man said. "The Black Sun honors its promises. Now, tell me who was there."

"Jeremy Nash. He was with another man and Professor Tillman's daughter. I believe they are going to see her uncle."

The Tap

Klaus Heinrich sat at his desk at the Berlin Interpol Office reading through Nash's file. "Where are you?" he muttered.

The phone on his desk began to ring. Heinrich looked at the Caller-ID and scooped up the phone. "Tell me you've got something for me."

"The car Nash was seen in on the autobahn belongs to a Karl Dieter."

"Good work," Heinrich said. "Track down Dieter and get a tap on his phone."

"Right away, Herr Inspector."

Heinrich hung up the phone and added Karl Dieter's name under Kara Ackerman's on the sheet of paper in Nash's file marked *Persons of Interest*. He underlined the name twice.

"With some luck, Interpol will have you back in custody very soon, Herr Nash," he said aloud as he closed the file.

The Chunnel

The trio boarded the Eurostar and made their way to the rear of the train. They sat as far away from the two other men in the carriage as possible.

"How about something to eat or drink?" Dieter asked.

"I could use another cup of coffee," Kara said.

"Me, too," Nash added.

"Karl, would you mind getting us some coffee from the café car?" Kara asked. "Jeremy and I need to stay as far under the radar as possible."

"No problem," Dieter said. "I'll be back in a few minutes."

As Dieter closed the sealed doors between the cars, Kara said, "I really don't know if my uncle can be of help or if he knew why my father was murdered, so don't get your hopes up, Jeremy."

"He must know some reason why your father was killed, or your father wouldn't have included that magazine article in your pencil box. I'm hoping he knows something about the artifact your father was hunting."

Kara smiled. "So, you're saying that my father may not have been the kook you thought he was? The great skeptic is having a change of heart?"

"I'm saying that he might have been murdered for something tangible he stumbled upon. He may not have even been aware of what it was. I'm still not warming to the idea of some half-baked theory about the hollow earth or Nazi treasure."

"Discover what that artifact is and we find who murdered him?"

"Or get one step closer. And I believe—" Nash froze and stared over Kara's shoulder.

Kara turned around and saw a tall muscular blond-headed man standing in the doorway of the next car looking through the door window of the café car. He was smiling.

"Shit!" Nash shouted. "It's that madman. Let's go!" He stood up, pulled Kara to her feet, and ran towards the doors leading to the next passenger compartment.

Just as they reached the doors, the glass window exploded in front of them. Several large holes appeared along the door frame.

"Shit!" Nash shouted, pulling Kara down into a crouched position.

One of the other two men in the compartment jumped up and grabbed the gun with the long silencer that Stobl was pointing at Nash. The other man tried to climb over in front of the seat. Stobl punched the man trying to wrestle the gun away. The man's nose crunched, and blood splattered across his face.

The other man managed to get over the seat and into the aisle. Stobl shot him right between the eyes. He crumped into the aisle. Stobl turned and shot the man with the broken nose in the chest.

Nash yanked the door to the next carriage open and grabbed Kara's arm. As he pulled her backwards, Stobl scrambled over the body of the dead man blocking the aisle. He grabbed Kara by the throat and pushed her body at Nash. The impact made them both crumble to the ground. He grabbed Kara's throat again and easily lifted her off the ground.

Stobl smiled and once again pointed his pistol at Nash.

An unknown passenger entered their car from the café car with a tray of food and three drinks. He dropped the tray when he saw his two dead companions. "Help! Somebody help me," he shouted.

"Maybe God will help you," Stobl said and shot him twice.

Stobl, now distracted, gave Nash an opportunity. He grabbed the small fire extinguisher attached by a cable beside the door and swung it at Stobl as he was turning back around.

Stobl raised his pistol arm and took the brunt of the blow

to his forearm. The pistol dropped to the floor with a clatter. He released his grip on Kara's throat and squatted to retrieve the gun.

Nash swung the fire extinguisher again and hit him in the center of his large forehead. Stobl fell forward and lay still.

"Get his gun." Kara's voice was no louder than a whisper as she rubbed her throat and gasped for breath.

"What?" Nash asked. "Are you alright?"

"His gun," she squawked. "Get his gun!"

Nash knelt and frantically searched for his weapon. "I don't see it," he said. "He must have fallen on it." He tried to turn the large man over but couldn't budge him.

"Then we need to get out of here," Kara said.

"Agreed." Nash opened the door to the next carriage and guided Kara through it.

Almost as soon as the door closed, Stobl's frame filled the window.

"Jesus!" Kara shouted. "Who is this guy?"

Kara and Nash ran to the other end of the carriage and went through the door and passed from the passenger carriage to the vehicle carriage and started weaving through the cars and trucks.

"Now where do we go?" Kara asked.

"Upstairs," Nash said. "To the upper level."

"We need to find help," Kara said, climbing the stairs behind him. "They have security on the train. Maybe we can double back to one of the passenger cars and sneak by him."

"We're wide open here," Nash replied. "Not much cover to—"

He stopped when a bullet pinged against the steel ramp just below his feet. He looked down and saw Stobl maneuvering under them to get a clear shot.

"Keep moving," Nash shouted.

When they arrived at the top, Nash pushed Kara in front of him. "You take the lead while I watch for him."

Kara moved quickly through the vehicles, and Nash followed her while keeping a look out for Stobl to breach the top of the stairs.

As they reached the middle of the carriage, Kara suddenly stopped. Nash nearly plowed into her.

"What's wrong?" Nash whispered.

"Look." Kara pointed just beyond the car in front of her.

There was nothing between them and their passenger carriage. The rest of the ramp was devoid of vehicles.

"We'll be sitting ducks!" she cried.

A bullet ricocheted off from the car in front of them.

"Get back!" Nash yelled.

A second bullet caught Kara in the side and spun her around, throwing her to the ground.

Kara! Oh, God!

Nash grabbed her arms and pulled her towards him behind a small truck and hopefully out of the line of fire.

"Kara! Are you OK? Where did you get hit?"

"I ... I don't know." She looked down and felt around her side. Her fingers found a hole in her jacket that contained the thick leather pouch holding her father's clues. She pulled out the pouch and saw a spent bullet lodged in it.

They stared at each other in astonishment until more bullets peppered the metal ramp and vehicles around them.

They crawled deeper into the maze of vehicles.

"I smell smoke," Nash said.

"So, do I. Do you think he's trying to burn us out?"

"No," Nash said. "He'd be trapped in here, too. Wait here."

Nash crawled past several more cars, then crouched beside a large panel truck and slid along its length. He carefully peeked over the hood and then fell back to the ground and scurried back to her.

"It looks like one of his bullets hit an old diesel Mercedes. There's a lot of smoke coming from the rear end."

"What do we do?" she asked.

"We try to get across that ramp as fast as possible and pray for more luck."

They moved back to the last level of vehicles. Nash got down on his stomach and looked under the car in front of him. "When I tell you that it's clear, run. Don't stop. Don't look back. I'll be right behind you."

Nash returned to his feet and inched toward the back of the car. "Now!"

Kara took two steps when a loud explosion rocked the entire carriage. She hit the ground and rolled to the edge of the ramp. Nash grabbed her arm and tried to pull her back up.

"Pull yourself up," he shouted.

Before she could react, a second explosion ripped through the carriage, pulling her out of Nash's grip. She fell to the floor below them. Nash jumped down and landed by her side. He quickly looked around for Stobl but couldn't see anything because of the thick black smoke.

Two more explosions erupted above them almost in unison, throwing the train beneath their feet severely to the left then to the right.

"More vehicles are igniting," he screamed. "We've got to get out of here."

The carriage started to tilt on its side. There were a series of loud scraping sounds, all the lights went out, a chain of explosions, wild movements—then all went still.

Kara awoke and found herself on top of Nash. He moaned softly.

"What...What happened?"

The flickering flames burning in the carriage around them showed a bizarre scene. Though none of the vehicles in the carriage had been dislodged from their ramps, several were hanging from them in precarious positions.

The smell of gasoline and burning metal was thick in the air.

"We've got to get out of here," he yelled again. "Can you walk?"

Kara slowly got to her feet. "Yes, I think I'm okay."

Nash looked back toward the passenger car they came from,

but the way was blocked by dangling vehicles. He looked behind him and saw that the vehicle carriage loading doors were slightly ajar, one hanging off its track a little.

Nash guided Kara along. "Faster," he ordered, pushing Kara ahead and almost shoving her off her feet. "Faster. Faster," he implored.

"What happened to the fire suppressant system these carriages have?" Kara wondered out loud.

"Probably knocked out by the explosions. Please keep moving."

They reached the loading doors, and Nash climbed up first. The doors were not only ajar but crumpled and torn with shards of sharp metal protruding on all sides. When he was on top of the carriage, he looked back down the Chunnel. The rest of the train had detached from the vehicle carriage. The rear locomotive was perched at a dangerous angle on its side.

"Give me your hands," he said.

Kara threw her hands above her head and Nash pulled her to the top of the carriage.

"I heard something down there," she said. "Dieter?"

"We're not waiting to find out who it is," Nash replied. He stood up and looked down the Chunnel. "There's supposed to be an emergency crossover link to the central service tunnel here somewhere."

He helped Kara down off the carriage and over the rear locomotive. They looked into the cab as they climbed over the engine and saw the motorman was dead.

Kara stared at the lifeless man.

"Nothing we can do for him. We gotta go. We should follow these lights," Nash said, pointing down the tunnel towards the amber emergency lights in the distance.

"What about the fire?" Kara asked.

"The service tunnel will seal behind us."

"Wait," Kara said. "Hear that? I hear something. Maybe it's help."

"And maybe it's the crazy man with the gun. Keep moving."

They were about fifty yards from the emergency lights when there was another enormous explosion. They looked behind them and saw a fireball enveloping the tunnel.

Stobl pulled the debris off his beaten body and crawled out of the remains of the vehicle carriage. Clothes torn and bloodied, he climbed over the deformed metal and the battered cars.

The rear portion of the vehicle carriage was lodged in the sides of the tunnel, and the rear locomotive was on its side blocking his view. He heard voices behind him. Far down the tunnel. French voices.

Scheisse! Fireman.

He ran towards an emergency crossover link behind him just as a hot fireball roared towards him—sucking the air from the tunnel as it went. He entered the emergency link just in time and sealed the door behind him.

With the fireball rolling towards them, Nash unceremoniously pushed Kara through the emergency exit door, followed, and sealed it behind them as the roar of the conflagration passed by. A few moments later they reached the service tunnel.
Nash could see the silhouette of a man coming down the dimly lit tunnel towards them. He instinctively pulled Kara behind him.

A tall stocky figure approached thorough the dim light, reached out for Nash, and said, "Êtes-vous deux d'accord?"

French!

It was a maintenance worker. Nash sighed in relief.

"Oui. Très bien," Kara replied.

"Thank God!" Nash said.

"Ah! Englishman." He reached for Kara as two more maintenance men carrying oxygen masks came up behind. "Come. This way."

Setback

Gunter Krause hit the alarm clock hard and rolled out of the massive bed in the Vril mansion. It was 5 a.m. and he was exhausted, but he had much to do before the High Initiate of the Vril Society returned later in the morning.

He and the Bauer twins had driven down every dirt road and goat path between there and Lake Como last night with the instrument that would free Tibet and open the way to Inner Earth and the Ancients. She had instructed them to stay off the main roads, and the trip had taken an extra four hours.

He walked to the kitchen and started a pot of coffee. Yawning, he added an extra scoop to the coffee maker. "Today, strong is good," he said and then headed back to the shower.

After his shower and a quick shave, he poured himself a large cup of coffee, grabbed the morning newspaper from the front lawn, and went out on the back deck to make sure there was no mention of last night's activities in this morning's news.

He sat down at the table and unfolded the paper.

The headline immediately grabbed his attention.

Local Professor Murdered In His Home

No! No! It can't be!

He read the entire article. It was indeed Tillman that was murdered.

They had a suspect. Someone named Nash. But Nash escaped.

Who the hell is Nash? And why did he murder Professor Tillman?

Now wide awake, Krause kicked over the table and threw his cup at a large oak tree bordering the lake.

Their only lead to hollow earth was gone.

A Deadly Secret

"Dieter!" Kara cried. "We've got to find Dieter."

Nash felt a sudden twinge of jealousy. "If he survived, he'll meet us at your uncle's house. He knows where we are going, and we can't draw attention to ourselves."

Kara looked back over her shoulder, but Nash pulled her into the line of frightened passengers and emergency personnel that were moving away from the Chunnel.

Nash washed his face and combed his fingers through his hair. "Passable," he said aloud. "Not great, but passable."

He exited the restroom at the train station and waited for Kara to do the same. She came out a few minutes later wearing a different blouse, and her hair looked perfect. She was even wearing mascara.

"How—?" Nash looked confused.

"We women stick together," she said, laughing. "I met a woman in the bathroom who took pity on my torn shirt and disheveled appearance. She gave me this blouse from her luggage, and she had almost a full beauty salon in her purse."

"I was happy just to wash my face," Nash said laughing. "Maybe next time I'll go into the ladies room."

Kara smiled broadly and waved her arm towards the restroom. "Be my guest."

They were both laughing as they walked through the train station.

"How far is it to your uncle's place?"

"He lives just outside of Kleinau," Kara said. "We'll need to make three transfers between Calais and Kleinau, so it will take the better part of the day."

"Kleinau? Isn't that—"

"Yes," Kara replied. "Hitler's birthplace."

"Irony at its best."

They boarded the train and settled into their seats. Within minutes, Kara rested her head on Nash's shoulder and fell asleep. He dozed off a few minutes later with a smile on his face.

The sun was about to set when they exited the train station.

"Let's get a cab," Nash said.

"Do you mind walking?" Kara asked. "It's less than a mile from here, and I've been sitting for too long. My legs and backside are numb."

"I could use the exercise myself," Nash agreed.

They walked through the center of the city full of narrow streets and Baroque merchant's houses with pastel-color facades. On their way to Luber's house, they passed a medieval main tower, or Torturm, with a little carillon on top.

"This is the street," Kara said, pointing ahead of them.

As they walked, Nash pointed to a massive slab of granite that was coarsely carved and decorated with intricate lines. "What's that?" he asked.

"It's from the concentration camp at Mauthausen. It reads, *Für Frieden, Freiheit und Demokratie—Nie wieder Faschismus—Millionen Tote mahnen.* For peace, freedom and democracy—Never again fascism—millions of dead remind."

"Fitting," Nash noted.

"There's my uncle's house," Kara said pointing to their right.

They climbed the small set of steps to the front door and rang the doorbell.

A dour looking man opened the door. "What is your business here?"

"We're here to see my uncle. I'm Kara Ackerman."

"Herr Luber is expecting you. Follow me."

Hauser led them into a sitting room off the entrance and pointed to a couch by the wall. "Wait there," he said gruffly.

"How are you going to approach this?" Nash asked as he sat down next to her.

"Remember what I said at the police station? A direct approach is sometimes the best approach. I'm going to—"

"Kara!" Luber walked into the room and took both of her hands in his as she stood. He glanced over at Nash. "And this must be your American."

Nash stood and extended his hand. "Jeremy Nash. Nice to meet you Herr Professor."

Luber ignored Nash's outstretched hand. "So, what's this all about, Kara? Why do you think I can help?"

"One of the things Father left me was an old science magazine article that quoted you several times concerning secret Nazi technologies acquired by the Allies after the war."

Nash jumped in. "We think it has something to do with why Kara's father was murdered—a murder I was framed for, but I can assure you that I am innocent."

"That should be for the courts to decide," Luber mumbled without looking at Nash.

"Uncle Hans, the article was mainly about research in nanotechnology during World War Two. We're thinking that father may have discovered something about that and was killed for it. Would you know what my father found?"

Luber was silent for a moment, then he took Kara's hands again and held them tightly. "I'll tell you what I told your father when he came to see me. Let it go. Do not pursue it if you value your lives."

"I'm being framed for murder," Nash said. "My life is ruined if we can't figure this thing out."

Luber glanced at Nash and then back at Kara. "Please turn yourselves in to the police. You will be safe there."

"I can't do that, Uncle."

Luber sighed. "It's late. Stay the night, and we'll discuss it again in the morning. I hope by then you will have changed your mind."

Kara started to protest but Nash interrupted. "Thank you, Herr Professor. That would be fine."

"Good. Rudolf, my assistant, will show you to your rooms."

Luber rang for Hauser, and moments later they were led to their bedrooms.

After Kara and Nash were escorted up the stairs, Luber picked up the phone and dialed a number.

A man answered. "Kleinau Polizei."

Kara listened at the door to her bedroom until she heard the door to the next room close and Hauser's footsteps go back down the stairs. She slipped out of her room and knocked softly on the Nash's door.

He opened the door before her third knock. "I was just coming to talk to you," he said, opening the door wide enough for her to slip inside.

"Why didn't you let me press him?" she asked, sitting down on the edge of the bed. "I'm good at that sort of thing. It's my job, remember?"

"Didn't you think his assistant appeared a little too quickly when he rang for him?" Nash asked. "Almost as if he was just around the corner in the entry hall?"

"Eavesdropping?" she asked.

"Maybe. Probably. This whole thing just doesn't smell right," Nash said. "Your uncle didn't even ask any questions about your father."

"What are you suggesting?"

"That maybe someone else has already answered all of his questions."

"Who?" Kara stood up quickly.

"I don't know. The police, maybe."

"So, what do you want to do?"

"Leave. Now."

The Tip Off

Adrian Adler sat at the head of an ornately carved dining table that could comfortably hold twenty people. The dining room also boasted a fireplace that made up the entire north wall. It was one of twenty-seven rooms in his palatial home in Prenzlauer Berg, one of the wealthier neighborhoods in Berlin.

As usual, Adler was alone. He preferred it that way, enjoying his own company—and that of his dog—to that of most people.

He picked up the bottle of twenty-eight-year-old Riesling and poured a small amount into his glass. He swirled the wine in the glass for several seconds, then lifted it to his nose and let the petrol note envelop him. He took a small sip and allowed the wine to attack his taste buds before swallowing.

"Perfection," he remarked.

Next, he lifted the domed stainless steel cloche from the plate in front of him and breathed deeply as the smell of roasted grouse wafted through the air.

One of the two massive oak doors that led to the kitchen opened, and the butler stepped through holding a cell phone. "Phone call, Herr Adler."

"Take a message," he growled. "I'm eating."

"It's Herr Hauser," the butler said nervously. "I told him you were indisposed, but he insisted. He says it's very important."

Adler pushed his plate away and pulled his napkin from his collar and dropped it on the table. He looked at the butler and said, "What are you waiting for? Hand me the phone."

He snatched the phone from the butler's nervous grip and brought it to his ear. "What is it Hauser? What do you have for me?"

"There's someone named Nash here. He's with a woman. Herr Luber's niece."

"What do they want?"

"They spoke with Herr Luber. I couldn't hear what they were saying, but I'm afraid he may have told them something."

"I'll take it from here," Adler said, and hung up the phone without waiting for a reply.

He tossed the phone down on the table and pulled his cell phone out of his jacket pocket. He pushed a single speed dial number.

"Yes, sir?"

"Stobl, Nash is at Luber's," Adler said. "Kill them both—and the woman who is with him, too."

"I'll take care of it."

"Just don't disappoint me again." Adler hung up. He poured a full glass of Riesling and then rang the small bell on the table.

The waiter immediately came through the kitchen door.

"I'm finished," Adler said, motioning to the uneaten Grouse on the table. "Feed this to my dog. De-bone it first."

A Strange Arrest

Nash took Kara's hand and slowly descended the stairway.

"I'm not sure—"

Nash turned toward her, pushed his index finger to his mouth and signaled her to be quiet. He pointed to the light shining from under the closed kitchen door. As if on cue, muffled voices suddenly erupted from the kitchen.

Nash froze and held his breath. The voices continued, and the kitchen door remained closed, so he quickly pulled Kara down the stairs, across the room, and out the front door.

They were half a block away when they saw two late-model, dark-colored sedans pull in front of Luber's house.

"I knew it," Nash said. "Your uncle turned us in."

"You don't know that," Kara told him. "We may have been followed or maybe—maybe it was Hauser. You saw how he looked at us."

"We're too out in the open to argue about this here." Nash motioned to an alleyway between two large houses ahead of them. "Let's get off the main street and try to figure things out."

Once in the alley, they walked quickly to the end. It opened into a small park.

"Behind those benches," Nash whispered. "We can hide in those trees."

They squatted in the small grove of trees and peered out into the darkness.

"How well do you know the area?" Nash asked. "We need to go—"

A branch cracked loudly behind them. They spun around but were blinded by a spotlight.

"You go where I tell you." A tall, burly man wearing a tailored black suit took several steps toward them. The suit did little to hide the size of the man's massive chest and arms.

Nash stood up, and the large man lowered the spotlight and raised the pistol he was holding in his other hand. "You two will come with me, now." He directed them back the way they had come.

As they entered the alley, the man fell back a few steps and pulled out his cell phone. "I've got them. We're on our way back."

When they were in front of Luber's house, two men, dressed in the same suits and obviously working out in the same gym as the man who apprehended them, pushed Nash and Kara up against one of the dark sedans and frisked them. Once they were satisfied the two prisoners weren't hiding any weapons, they handcuffed them and pushed them into the back of the car.

Another man with the same tailor and physical build walked up the path to the house and knocked on the front door. Luber opened it a crack and peered out. The man said something to him and Luber nodded, looked at Kara through the car window, and quickly closed the door.

The man turned around and said something to the others. The two who had frisked and handcuffed Nash and Kara rushed to the empty car and got in. The other man got into the passenger side of the front seat of Nash and Kara's car.

The man Nash now assumed was the supervisor stood in front of the car with his phone to his ear. He listened for a minute, spoke a few words, and pocketed the phone. He turned back and looked at the front door of the house for a few seconds, then climbed into the driver's seat of the car.

They drove slowly down the street. Once they turned the corner, the driver said, "We're clear. Take off their cuffs."

Loose Ends

Stobl approached Luber's house as the two dark colored sedans pulled away from the curb. He pulled over about a hundred yards away and watched the darkened house for almost a half hour. When he was sure that the vehicles weren't coming back, he slipped out of his car and made his way silently to Luber's house.

He rapped twice on the front door and then moved into the shadows. Hauser opened the door and looked around. Stobl stepped out of the darkness and Hauser quickly ushered him into the house.

"Why were the police here?" Stobl asked.

"They came for Nash...and the woman," Hauser said weakly. "But they weren't here. They left the house before the men arrived."

"They've escaped again?" Stobl's voice was irate.

"No. They caught them," Hauser said. He looked down at the ground and added, "But they weren't the police. At least not the local police."

Stobl contemplated that for a moment. "Where's Luber?"

"Upstairs. He said he wasn't feeling well and retired just after the police—the men—left."

"I need to speak to him," Stobl snarled. "Stay here and watch the street. Let me know if we have any more visitors."

Hauser nodded and watched Stobl climb the stairs. He went to the front window and peered through the gap in the curtains. A moment later, he heard a muffled sound, and something hit the floor hard above him.

Hauser closed his eyes and said a silent prayer. He finished the prayer and turned slowly around. Stobl was standing at the foot of the stairs.

"I'm ready," Hauser said.

"No loose ends," Stobl said, smiling.

He lifted his pistol and pulled the trigger twice. Two muffled shots tore into Hauser's chest. The first shot went clean through and shattered a photograph on the wall of Hans Luber and Alfred Tillman as young men. They had their arms around each other, and they were both smiling.

Bait

Nash and Kara were escorted to a room on the third floor furnished with a large table surrounded by twelve elegant chairs. There were ornately framed landscape paintings on the wall and a fully stocked bar in the corner sporting crystal glasses and goblets.

"This looks more like a corporate conference room than an interrogation room," Nash observed.

Kara looked out of one of the large windows and remarked, "And this isn't the Kleinau police station. I'm not sure where we are."

The door opened, and the man with close cropped hair stepped inside. "Please sit down." He motioned to the table.

"My name is Captain Dietrich." He looked directly at Nash. "I'm with the GSG-9, and we need your help."

"Who or what the devil is the GSG-9, and why do they need my help?"

"They're an ultra-secretive, paramilitary arm of the German Federal Police," Kara interjected.

"We're an anti-terrorism squad nowadays," the man corrected.

The man who caught them in the park came into the room carrying a large file.

"This is Lieutenant Lenz," Dietrich told them.

"What do you want of us?" asked Kara.

"Not you, frauline. Herr Nash," Dietrich said. He turned back to Nash. "We need your help to stop a terrorist attack planned here in Germany."

Nash was set aback. "And if I don't cooperate?" Nash finally asked.

"We'll turn you over to Interpol," Lenz replied.

"What about the Kleinau police?"

"They will cooperate." Lenz said. "They have to."

"So, why me? I'm not sure what kind of help I can be?" Nash brooded, almost to himself.

"We have information that a terrorist cell is planning an attack here in Germany. They're members of the Vril Society, a throwback to the Nazis. Have you heard of them?"

Nash nodded. "They're a cult that believed in the so called 'Ancients who had spiritual powers—*supermen*—who lived inside the earth. Real nut jobs."

"Correct," Dietrich replied. "The hollow earth. We have intel that they've raised a large sum of money to finance an attack on their own soil."

"I don't understand. What does this have to do with me?"

"We've announced to the media," Lenz began, "that you and the frauline were arrested and are being held here in Kleinau."

Dietrich broke in. "And we'll add that your motivation for killing Tillman was to keep him from disclosing the location of the hollow earth so you can take all the credit."

"That's absurd!" cried Nash. "First, I didn't kill Tillman. Second, who would believe such a cock-eyed story?"

Dietrich gave Nash a knowing look.

"You're probably right," Nash said. "The Vril are just crazy enough to believe it." Nash slumped in his chair. "You're setting a trap. And I'm the bait?"

Dietrich and Lenz both nodded.

"What about Interpol?" Nash asked. "When they know you have me, won't they want me back?"

Dietrich smiled. "We take precedence. Terrorism trumps a simple murder."

"And it doesn't matter that he's innocent or that my father's murderer is still free?" Kara asked, very agitated at this point.

"Everything will be made right after we stop this attack," Lenz told her.

"What about Kara?" Nash asked. "If I do this, is she free to go?"

"No." Dietrich replied. "It's been in the news. It's known that she is on the run with you. If she's not with you, they may get suspicious."

Nash looked at Kara. "I'm sorry."

"You'll both be safe." Dietrich assured them.

Complications

The two men sat huddled in the corner of a small gasthaus in Berlin.

"He's gone," Dieter said. "And things have gotten more complicated."

"How so?" asked Stone.

"After being separated from Nash and Kara on the Chunnel, I made my way to Kara's uncle's house to meet them. When I arrived, I found that Luber and his assistant had been murdered." He took another sip of his espresso. "And Nash is the prime suspect."

"How'd they figure that?"

"Kara Ackerman's uncle called the Kleinau police and told them Nash was there. He and Kara were gone when they arrived, and they found the two dead bodies. They assumed Nash killed them. He is already wanted for the one murder, so it wasn't a stretch for them."

"You're right. That does complicate things." Stone stared into his coffee. "We'll have to wait and see what my network turns up."

"Well, I hope you find him before the police do.

"But you *do* know the coordinates of Station Two One One?" Stone asked.

"Yes, but Nash has the hex key."

Stone nodded. "Ah, yet another complication."

Reprieve

Elsa Klein stood in front of the rain-streaked window with her back to Gunter Krause. She had been excited when she first arrived from India, but now her mood was as dark as the storm clouds building over the Black Forest mansion.

"Leave it to a filthy Jew to ruin our plans," she hissed.

The large German Jew flinched and said, "His murderer has been arrested. We could still salvage things."

"How?" She spun around and glared at him.

"He knows where the location is." Krause smiled. "We'll make him tell us what Tillman couldn't."

"Where are they holding him?"

"He's at the Kleinau police station. An easy target."

"Perhaps." She furrowed her brow. "But we should take precautions."

"I've already started," he said, holding out his arm and showing her the fresh stitches on his wrist.

She leaned over and took his hand. Krause felt a shiver run through his body. "We can't fail on this. We are so close. We have our means and have our material." She then squeezed his hand tightly—too tightly—and bored into his eyes. "I want you to take personal charge of this. No mistakes. Understood?"

He nodded. His training and acceptance in the Vril would allow nothing else.

"Now. Here's the plan," she said.

The Plan

Nash and Kara were escorted to a tiny windowless room. Two small cots sat in the center.

"I trust this will be suitable," Lenz said.

"What are we doing here?" Nash asked. "I thought we were staying in the police station."

"We felt you and frauline Ackerman would be safer here during the operation."

"And how long do we stay here?" Nash queried.

"If the Vril take the bait, they should make their move tonight. We've told the press that we're transferring you two to our headquarters in Bonn tomorrow morning."

"And if they don't bite?" asked Kara.

"Then it won't turn out very well for both of you."

"Interpol?" Nash asked.

"Just relax," Lenz said, "and let us do our job."

Krause scanned the outside of the Kleinau police station with his night vision binoculars from the roof of a two-story building across the street. It was quiet. There had been no movement in or out of the police station for the last hour.

He took the penlight out of his pocket and pointed it at the car parked down the street. He flashed it twice and watched as two men, armed with Glock 40s, got out of the car, and made their way to the side entrance of the police station. Once there, one of the men flashed his own small light twice. Krause scanned the area one last time and then hurried to join his team.

They jimmied the lock on the door, put on night goggles, drew their pistols, and slipped into the building. Through the green haze of the night goggles they systematically searched and cleared each room, ending with an empty cellblock.

The two men turned to Krause. He took a step toward them and took off his goggles.

"They must be—"

One of the men dropped to his knees and then fell over sideways. The other started choking and went down in a similar fashion.

Krause put his goggles back over his eyes and looked around the hallway. When he looked up, he saw a thick mist coming from the air ducts.

He coughed twice and then blacked out.

Dietrich watched the security monitors and smiled when the three men collapsed.

"That was too easy," he said. He picked up his walkie-talkie and pressed the button. "They're down. Flush the air and retrieve them. We'll take them to Bonn for interrogation."

"I'll make the necessary preparations for the trip," Lenz assured him. "What do you want to do with Nash and the frauline?"

"We'll bring them with us," Dietrich said.

"Damn it!" insisted Nash. "You said you'd release us after you caught the Vril crazies."

"Change of plans." Dietrich exclaimed. "Interpol wants you. We had no choice." He flashed a crooked smile. "It seems you've been very busy since your arrival in Germany, Mr. Nash."

"What do you mean?"

"You're now wanted for the murders of Hans Luber and Rudolf Hauser."

"What?" cried Kara. "My uncle is dead?"

"Yes. And you and Nash are the prime suspects."

"That's ridiculous," Nash cried. "He was alive when we left him. We had nothing to do with it."

"I'm just a humble public servant," Dietrich replied. "Take it up with Interpol." He picked up his briefcase. "It's time to go." He motioned to Lenz. "Take them to the car."

A Bridge Too Far

Horst Bauer was ground hugging, flying the Huey helicopter within a few feet of the treetops. A daunting task in daylight, but at 2 a.m. on a cloudy night, this flight would have killed most pilots.

Horst expertly guided the craft toward the blip displayed on the GPS mounted to the console in front of him. The signal that was coming from the biometric tracking device implanted in Krause's wrist was getting stronger. And when it moved within the second concentric circle on the screen, he glanced over his shoulder and shouted, "Ten kilometers."

His twin brother, Marco, jumped to his feet and slid the side door open. "How far are they from the autobahn?" he shouted.

"We'll intercept them about four or five kilometers before they reach it."

"Good," Marco said, his words lost in the whooshing sounds of the spinning blades overhead. He moved quickly to the metal case in the rear and started popping open its latches.

A small convoy consisting of a white van sandwiched between two black Mercedes—blacked out—sped down the nearly abandoned highway toward the border of Austria and Germany. Dietrich decided that a post-midnight transport would be safer, as they would encounter far less vehicles this late at night.

The lead car contained four heavily armed guards. The van had two armed guards in the cab section and the three shackled Vril prisoners and Lenz in its separate, fully armored cab.

Nash, Kara, and Dietrich were in the car at the rear.

"I don't understand any of this." Kara looked across the back seat at Nash. "First my father and now my uncle. Who's doing this and why?"

"And the crazy man who tried to kill us," Nash added. "There's no way these things aren't related."

"Stop talking," Dietrich ordered. "You'll have plenty of time to confess once we get to Bonn."

"You know we didn't kill anyone, Dietrich," Nash blurted out. "They were both alive when we left in *your* custody."

"I only know what I'm told." Dietrich pushed the button on the small walkie-talkie on his shoulder. "Status check."

The walkie-talkie on Lenz shoulder came to life. "Status check."

"Car number one check."

Lenz looked at the three prisoners who were shackled to the floor in the rear of the van. Krause met his gaze and smiled.

"Transport check." Lenz spoke into the walkie-talkie but didn't take his eyes off Krause. He released the button on the walkie-talkie and snarled, "What in the hell do you have to smile about?"

"Just your stupidity," Krause said.

"My stupidity? You're the ones shackled to the floor."

"All part of the plan." Krause straightened his back as far as the shackles would allow and waved a mock *bye-bye* with his right hand.

Lenz rapped three times on the sliding door that separated the cab from the transport cabin. The door slid open.

"How much further to the autobahn?" Lenz asked, still staring at Krause.

"A kilometer or so beyond this bridge," the driver replied. "We will..."

A loud explosion rocked the van, fire engulfed the cab and a blazing stream of hot flame shot through the small door Lenz was looking through.

Marco snapped the safety harness onto his belt, pulled his night-vision goggles on and leaned out the door of the Huey. He scanned the area in front of him and pulled himself back into the helicopter. "The bridge," he shouted. "Take us to the far end of that bridge."

Horst nodded and maneuvered the craft into place.

As the helicopter hovered over the bridge, Marco extended the firing tube of the shoulder-held light anti-tank weapon, leaned out the door again and squinted through the sight of the weapon. He exhaled as the first set of headlights passed and pulled the trigger when the second set of lights came into view.

An orange ball of flame engulfed the center of the bridge as the cab of the armored van exploded. The passenger section jackknifed, flipped onto its side and skidded through the fiery remains of the cab.

Marco smiled and swung back into the Huey to retrieve another anti-tank weapon.

"Jesus Christ!" Nash cried as a huge explosion in front of them rocked their vehicle. He leaned forward and looked out the windshield as the van ahead of them skidded sideways and flipped on its side.

Dietrich expertly maneuvered the Mercedes around the van and what remained of its cab.

As Dietrich accelerated, a sharp piercing flame of light came from the sky at the far end of the bridge. The lead Mercedes was instantly consumed by a conflagration of twisted metal and flames.

"They've got a rocket launcher!" Dietrich cried, pulling the wheel hard to the left. He just missed the flaming wreck but skimmed an abutment and tore through the guard rail.

Dietrich's head slammed against the window as both driver side tires of the Mercedes went off the bridge. The vehicle started

to slide forward but got hung on the metal guard rail. It bucked and rocked several times.

Kara was crumpled against the door, unmoving. Nash unfastened his seatbelt and gently shook her. "Kara, are you okay?"

"She's dead," Dietrich said. "And we'll be dead, too, if we don't get out of here." He leaned over and started to pull himself to the passenger side door. As he did, the Mercedes groaned and slipped forward several feet.

"Don't move, Dietrich," Nash cautioned. "Shifting your weight will make us fall."

Dietrich ignored him and pulled himself across the front seat, pushed open his door and jumped out. Miraculously, the car didn't fall.

Nash tried to open his door, but it wouldn't budge. "Dietrich, the door is safety locked. You'll have to open it from the outside."

There was no reply.

"Damn it, Dietrich!" yelled Nash. "Help us out of here. You—"

The Mercedes lurched and slid several more feet.

Horst landed about fifty yards behind the rear section of the armored van. He and Marco grabbed their automatic weapons and ran toward the back of the van.

"Inside the van," Marco shouted. "Move as far forward as you can." He waited several seconds before pointing his weapon at the locked door handle and then pulled the trigger.

The door swung open and one of the Vril members fell out onto the tarmac, dead.

"Krause," Marco shouted. "Are you all right?"

"I am now. What took you so long?" Krause moved forward and pulled himself out the door.

Horst and Marco reached into the van and pulled out the other Vril. He was bleeding badly from a large laceration across his chest. Marco picked him up and carried him to the chopper.

Horst dragged Lenz out by his feet. He landed on the concrete facedown. Horst rolled him over. Lenz was dead, most of his face melted away from the blast. Horst stared at him for a moment and then turned to Krause and said, "The only good polizei are dead polizei."

Krause nodded. "Get Nash and the frauline."

Dietrich backed into Nash's line of sight.

"Dietrich, you bastard," Nash screamed. "Open the door."

Dietrich did a weird half-turn and flung himself back into the vehicle. He lay across the front seat with his feet hanging out the door. Nash leaned over the seat and grabbed Dietrich's shirt. He pulled him up by the collar. There was a bullet hole where his left eye had been. Nash dropped him, causing his body to roll against the dashboard and shift the weight inside the vehicle.

The Mercedes groaned and began to move slowly over the bridge.

The rear window exploded, and tiny fragments of glass peppered Nash. Before he could react, two large arms reached in, grabbed Kara by the shoulders, and pulled her out.

The Mercedes lunged again.

Nash closed his eyes as he felt it ever so slowly teeter and slip from under him towards the river below. Suddenly, arms grabbed him by the scruff of his jacket and jerked him up and out of the Mercedes just as it broke loose from its restraints and plunged into the darkness below.

Nash looked up at his saviors. Two men, twins, were standing over Kara's body and pointing automatic weapons at him.

"Herr Nash," one of them said. "There's someone waiting to meet you." He roughly pulled Nash to his feet and covered his mouth and nose with a strange-smelling cloth.

"Whazza do dat?" Nash slurred through the cloth and collapsed into the large man's arm.

An Apocalypse Revealed

Nash blinked several times and tried to focus his eyes. He pushed himself to a sitting position and looked around the room.

There was a rustic sitting area with an antique work desk in the corner and a wall of stocked bookshelves beside it. A large flat-screen television was hanging from the wall across from him. The wall opposite the door was completely covered with full-length curtains, but the light peeking through suggested there was a window behind them. He was sitting on a four-poster bed that was covered with a variety of throw pillows.

He rubbed his eyes again and tried to remember where he was.

"Shit!" he hissed and jumped down off the bed. He tried the door first, but it was locked. He pressed his ear against it and listened for several seconds. Hearing nothing, he grabbed the door handle and pulled as hard as he could. The door was solid oak and didn't even flex.

Nash moved quickly across the room and searched through the curtains until he found a seam. He pulled them slightly apart and looked out. The house overlooked a large lake. He pulled the curtains all the way apart to find a wall of glass, floor-to-ceiling windows from one end to the other. Nash followed the seams of the glass but found no openings.

An enormous air conditioning unit blocked most of his view to the left, but he could clearly see the blades of a helicopter protruding above it. He went to the desk and pulled the chair to the window and stood on it.

The helicopter was about fifty yards in front of a boat dock. There was a speedboat on one side of the dock and a World War

Two-era single-engine airplane on the other. The plane was made of corrugated metal and had been converted to a float plane by the addition of pontoons.

"A World War Two Junkers F-13," Nash marveled out loud.

Several men were scurrying around the boat dock. One man was placing Taiwanese flags on the rear of the speedboat while another was loading signs hand painted with Chinese symbols into the cargo hold.

Someone was painting Medical Evac markings on the side of the helicopter.

A tall, athletic, middle-aged woman with blonde hair that hung below her knees—and two men armed with automatic weapons—walked into view. They watched the progress for several minutes. Suddenly, the woman turned around, looked directly at Nash, and smiled.

He jumped and almost fell off the chair.

She said something to the two armed guards, and they all moved quickly back the way they came.

A minute later, Nash heard a key in the door behind him. He jumped down from the chair just as Krause opened the door. "Herr Nash," he snarled. "Kommen sie mitt."

Nash was escorted down a long hallway into a huge room. It had a rustic elegance with large hewn post-and-beam logs towering twenty feet above them, carved from the trees of the nearby forest. In the rear of the room was a massive stone fireplace that emanated whiffs of acrid burnt wood. The fireplace was cradled between two floor-to-ceiling grand windows providing breathtaking vistas of the lake and the forest beyond.

"Admiring our humble haus?" a female voice emanated from behind.

Nash turned toward the woman he had seen near the boat dock as she drifted up beside him.

"House?" Nash asked. "It looks more like a luxury hotel. I guess terrorism really pays."

"Would a terrorist rescue you and your companion from your captors?"

"Rescue?" Nash's voice elevated to such a level that the armed guard raised his weapon. "You killed my companion and kidnapped me."

"Bring her," the woman ordered.

Krause sneered at Nash for a second longer, then turned and left. A minute later, he returned pushing Kara in front of him.

"Kara!" Nash cried with delight and hugged her. "I thought you were dead."

"I don't know what happened," she sighed, hugging him tightly. "I woke up a little while ago in some fancy bedroom."

"How touching," the woman sniffed. There was a certain coldness about her. Her steely blue eyes were cruel looking. And the way she was looking at Kara. There was a burning contempt in her eyes. "If you and your Jewish friend are finished, we have much to discuss, Herr Nash."

"You seem to know who we are," Nash replied. "Who are you?"

"My name is Elsa Klein. I am High Initiate of the Vril Society." She pointed to a pair of couches on either side of a large heavy glass and wood coffee table. "Please sit."

Nash and Kara took their seats beside each other while Klein sat on the opposite sofa.

"Are you familiar with the Vril Society, Herr Nash?"

"Some," he replied. "At the turn of the century, many secret societies developed in Germany. One of these groups was the Vril Society. In 1917, four members of the original Vril Society met in a cafe in Vienna. There was a woman and three men. The woman saw herself as a spiritual medium." Nash gave Klein a knowing look. "I suppose you've assumed that mantle."

Klein nodded and gave a thin-lipped smile, leaned over and pulled a long, slim cigarette from a silver box on the coffee table. She offered one to Nash—ignoring Kara.

He declined.

She lit it and inhaled a puff, blowing smoke out her nostrils.

"What does all this have to with us?" asked Kara impatiently.

Klein blew another puff of smoke from her thin lips. Still ignoring Kara, she stood and walked over to Nash. Standing above him, her voice became animated as if she was revealing a sacred truth. "We believe a superior race, a subterranean matriarchy, called the Vril-ya, lives beneath the earth, and with their help, our reconstituted Society plans to conquer the world with psychokinetic energy called the Vril Force."

Nash looked up at the towering woman. "And you want us to tell you the location of the entry to this inner earth."

"Precisely," she said. She pointed an accusing finger at Kara. "*Her* father," she almost spat the word, *her*, "found the entrance to the inner earth. We had planned to meet with Tillman, but you killed him before we could reach him."

Nash became incensed. "I did no such thing. I didn't kill Kara's father. I was framed. And now we're—"

"Irrelevant!" Krause yelled. "You *do* know the location. Tillman told you. Right?"

"He didn't tell me anything," Nash protested. "To be honest, I thought he was a conspiracy kook." He looked sympathetically at Kara.

"We know nothing," Kara said. "My father was murdered before he could tell us anything."

Klein nodded, and Krause pushed the muzzle of his gun into Kara's back.

"Perhaps you should reconsider," Klein told Kara. "I'd hate to have Jew blood ruin my carpet, but the thought excites me a little, too."

Kara grimaced and gave Klein an evil look. "My father left a series of clues that pointed to the location of something called Station Two One One. We know little of what it is supposed to be or what's in it."

"It's the code word to the entrance to the inner earth," Klein said solemnly. "The home of the Ancients, the Masters of the Vril." Her voice dropped to a reverent whisper. "Shambhala."

Despite their predicament, Nash had to snicker. "Yeah. I know the song."

"You will not be joking later, Herr Nash," she snarled, "because *you* will be taking us there tonight. We leave for Colonia Dignidad and then Antarctica after we complete a small mission."

"Colonia Dignidad?" Kara asked. "What's that?"

"A supposed Nazi community in southern Chile, south of Santiago," Nash said.

"Your knowledge of the war surprises me, Herr Nash," Klein said, gliding back to her seat. "I see we made the right decision choosing you to help us."

"Do I have a choice?"

"Not one that ends well for either of you," Klein answered. "We need to take steps to free Tibet from China's control, and then we leave."

"Free Tibet? Just like that?" Nash said snapping his fingers. "How do you do that?"

"Simple," she answered nonchalantly. "We start World War Three."

"World War Three?" Nash jumped up, but Krause pushed him back onto the couch.

"And then we'll finish what my grandfather started," Klein said. "The purification of the human race."

"Your grandfather?" Kara asked. "What do you mean?"

"Hitler," Nash said. "I'm guessing she's Unity Mitford's granddaughter."

"*Oh my God!*" Kara shrieked. "This is insane."

"Shut up, Jew!" Klein screamed. "You and your kind have no place in our world."

"But Klein is a Jewish name," Nash said calmly.

"The Vril made sure my father was adopted by a Jewish family for his own protection," Klein said. "But he was educated by members of our society that taught him everything he needed to know. The dirty Jews that adopted him were killed when he was of age. I am the purebred result."

"Purebred? But your mother—"

"My mother was handpicked from the others. She was superior in every way."

"The others?" Nash asked.

"Hitler's other children." Klein smirked. "His legacy must live on."

"Your mother and father were both Hitler's children?" Kara gasped. "No wonder you're crazy. You're inbred from pure insanity."

Klein backhanded Kara across the face and spit on her.

Nash pulled Kara's quivering body close to his and looked at Klein. "You'll never get away with this."

"I have already channeled the Vril force, and the voices of the Ancients have acknowledged our success."

"I won't—"

"Take them away." Klein dismissed them with a wave of her hand. "We have work to do, and I grow tired of this game."

She summoned the twins, Marco and Horst, and they escorted Kara and Nash back to their rooms.

A Gilded Cage

The twins stopped at the door to the bedroom where Nash had awakened earlier. Marco opened the door and moved aside, allowing Nash to walk by.

Kara stood beside Horst. Defiant tears streaked her face.

"Let Kara stay in here with me," Nash said.

"So, you can plan your escape?" Marco sneered. "The windows are shatterproof, and these doors are two inches thick."

"Then you don't have anything to worry about," Nash said. "She's been through a lot lately, and I don't want her to be alone."

The twins looked at each other, and one of them winked. "We understand, Herr Nash." They started to laugh but allowed Kara to step inside the room. Once the heavy door was closed, they heard the key turn in the lock.

"Are you okay?" Nash asked softly, pulling her into his arms.

"I'm fine," she said, but her body was still shaking. "I just hate being *her* prisoner."

"Well, I've been in worse prisons," Nash commented, nodding and looking around the room.

Kara wiped the tears from her eyes, sighed, and sat down on the bed. "We need to do something. I for one don't want to be a guest at this Colonia whatever."

"Colonia Dignidad," Nash replied.

"What is that place, anyway?"

"It's almost a state-within-a-state in Chile. The community is ringed by barbed wire fencing. Originally, it was home to about three hundred refugees from Nazi Germany and their descendants—and it has a nasty reputation," he added.

"How so?"

"There's a story about a writer named Peter Lavenda who went to the secret Nazi colony and barely managed to escape with his life. He was investigating rumors of mysterious deaths, torture, sexual abuse of children, and the practice of the black arts combining traditional Voodoo ritual with Nazi occultism."

"Whatever this colony is," Kara said, "it certainly sounds like a place neither of us wants to visit." She paused for a second, collecting her thoughts. "And who the hell are these Vril people?"

"Don't you know your own history?" Nash asked. "I thought they taught the German youth about the Nazi-era in school now."

"History, yes. Weird occult shit, no."

"Well, as the story goes, the Vril were a secret society who discussed the coming of the New Age and making contact with ancient peoples and inner worlds. The Vril Society's pedigree, so to speak, dates back to Karl Haushofer—the founder of the *Bruder des Lichts*—the Brothers of the Light—sometimes known as the Luminous Lodge." He looked around the room. The irony of the name and the building they found themselves in did not escape him.

He continued. "Haushofer sent annual expeditions to Tibet from 1926 to 1943. Their mission was to make contact with the Aryan forefathers in Shambhala and Agharti, hidden subterranean cities beneath the Himalayas. The people there were the guardians of secret occult powers, especially the Vril, and the missions sought their aid in harnessing those powers for creating the Aryan master race."

Nash noticed Kara bristle at those last three words, but he continued. "The Nazis believed the ancient high priests were their blood ancestors. As they tell it, after the great flood, certain high priests went by boat from Atlantis to the Himalayas of Tibet—the original race of Aryan Godmen and ancestors of all Indian and European peoples."

"Explain this then," Kara said. "How can white Aryan people evolve from dark skinned Tibetans? And how do you explain that

none of the Nazi high leadership had blond hair and blue eyes. So much for the perfect Aryan human."

"Simple, really," Nash replied. "If you look at the highest human cultures and civilizations, they were fair skinned. Even with many dark peoples, the ruling caste or race is fairer in color than the rest and has, therefore, evidently immigrated from somewhere else. It's understood that those people slowly emigrated to the north and gradually became white. In response to their more challenging environments, the Nordic peoples had to develop their intellectual powers to survive the more brutal climates."

"But that doesn't make them a Master Race," she commented.

"No, but people like Klein and her followers think so. They believe that Aryans are determined by their superior intellect and culture, not the color of their skin."

"What's with her uber-long hair?" Kara asked.

"The Vril woman grew their hair as long as they could. They believed it was an antenna to communicate with the spirits."

Kara rolled her eyes.

"Now you're getting a taste of what I've had to deal with for most of my career. The nut jobs don't just stop at the conspiracy theories. They're crazy enough to believe anything."

"Even starting World War Three?"

"Yes," Nash said. "She said they were doing it to free Tibet from China." He looked at the television on the wall. "We need to see the news."

He found the remote control on the stand next to the bed, turned the TV on and started flipping through the channels until he found a news channel.

There was a picture of a group of Chinese officials exiting a government-looking building. A split screen showed a file video of a large paddle wheel all lit up and sailing down a wide river.

"What is the news anchor saying?" he asked. "My German is only fair."

Kara listened for a moment, then started to translate. "He's reporting on the EU-Asia Economic Conference held in Frankfurt. That's the Chinese contingent led by the Premier, his second in command, and most of the top Chinese Administration officials." She paused to listen more. "They just finished a week-long meeting... it made strides towards import/export agreements... blah, blah, blah."

"What's he saying about that boat on the river?"

"That's the Rhine-River-Lights boat cruise, the *Rhine in Flames* festival. It takes place this time of year. Lots of music, dancing and fireworks happening on any number of boat cruises down the Rhine. The Premier and his entourage will be sailing on one of the yachts to watch the fireworks."

"Fireworks?" Nash asked. "Lots of noise?"

"What are you saying?" Kara asked.

"A lot of distraction and potential confusion," Nash said. "Good time to mount an attack on the Premier."

"I don't see it," Kara disagreed shaking her head. "Security will be as tight as a drum. They'll have patrol boats all around the Premier's yacht and other boats in front sweeping for mines."

"And I bet you won't be able to get within a hundred meters of the river front when the yacht passes," Nash added.

The picture on the television now showed many small boats flying Taiwanese flags and signs written in Chinese.

Nash jumped up from the bed and pointed at the television. "What's he saying?"

"He says there's going to be a flotilla protest by the Taiwanese. They're going to try and sail around the yacht holding the Premier and his Administration."

"I know how they're going to do it," Nash told her. "I saw them putting those same flags and protest signs on a speedboat docked out back."

"I don't understand how that will start a World War," Kara said.

"Fuzzy logic," Nash said. "If China responds militarily against Taiwan over the assassination of their Premier and important officials of their Administration, the United States will respond according to treaty and protect Taiwan against invasion."

"And once China is defeated, Tibet would be free." Kara shook her head. "That's insane. They're betting everything on the assumption that China would be defeated."

"That, and the vision of success that their spiritual leader channeled from the Vril," Nash added.

A Strange Request

Just before dusk, Krause and one of the twins burst into Nash and Kara's room, escorted them down to the boat dock, and onto the Junkers float plane. Klein and the second twin were waiting for them in the plane. Several minutes later the group took off over the lake and into the setting sun.

An hour or so later, in the dimming light of the day, Nash could see a wide river below the opening clouds. The Junkers flew on several more minutes then began to circle, rapidly losing altitude.

Nash could see the river coming up fast. He and Kara gripped the armrest of their seats as the Junkers banked and turned, positioning itself over the river.

Nash held his breath as the plane lined itself up with the river below and then seemed to hover for a moment. A few seconds later he felt the pontoons of the Junkers make contact with the water.

The pilot pulled back on the throttle, slowed the plane down, and steered it towards the bank of the river.

Floodlights flashed on in front of them, and Nash could see a figure standing on a boat dock as the floatplane maneuvered alongside.

The figure on the dock, a thin man in his early thirties with a five o'clock shadow, secured the plane to the boat dock.

Klein and Krause stepped out first and motioned to the twins to take Nash and Kara to the large steel hangar at the far end of the boat dock.

The thin, young man watched Nash and Kara as they left for the hanger.

When they were gone, he removed his phone from his pocket and opened a recent email. Attached to the email was a picture—a picture of Nash.

"Son-of-a-bitch," he whispered under his breath.

"Where do you think we are?" wondered Nash.

It was a bit damp in the sparse back room of the hanger, and except for a few boxes, there was little to sit on.

Kara unconsciously pulled her jacket up over her shoulders. "From what I could see from the plane, I think we're in the narrow Rhine valley gorge near Boppard."

"I'm betting that's one of the towns on the *Rhine in Flames* cruise," Nash said.

"Yes, it is."

She stood up and walked toward the locked door, turned the door handle once, then shrugged. "Worth a try, right?"

Nash smiled. The woman never gave up. He liked that in her.

"Did you notice the chopper and speed boat there in the hangar?" she asked.

"Yes," he replied. "The helicopter they probably used to fly us into the lodge now has the markings of a medical EVAC chopper, and the Zodiac speed boat is the one I saw them loading the protest signs and Taiwanese flags on."

"They've thought this through," Kara observed. "In the commotion and confusion, they'll just fly out of the area in the medical EVAC chopper and take us to Nazi South America."

"And whatever they plan to use to blow up the yacht," Nash added, "can be maneuvered through the Taiwanese protest boats without suspicion."

"And the other private boats that will sail down the river," Kara added. "But how do they plan to blow up the yacht? Security isn't going to let any boat get within a hundred yards of that boat."

"I've had a few close encounters with nut jobs. What they lack in sanity they make up in depraved intelligence." Nash looked at his watch. "It's getting late. I assume the *Rhine in Flames* cruise has already begun upriver."

Kara nodded.

They heard the door to their jail unlock. Nash looked quickly around the room. A few feet away, an empty schnapps bottle lay on the floor. Nash scurried over and scooped it up.

The door opened a crack and the man they saw securing the Junkers to the boat dock slipped inside and quickly closed it.

Nash held the empty bottle behind his back.

"You're Jeremy Nash," he stated, almost as a question.

Nash looked at him suspiciously. "Yes, I am." He raised his voice. "What the hell do you want?"

The young man's voice dropped to a whisper. "Keep your voice down. We don't want them to hear."

"Who are you?" Kara asked.

"My name is Albert Marsh. I'm a stringer for the Associated Press."

"Don't tell me," Nash said caustically. "You're doing a human-interest story on hostages."

"I'm serious, Mr. Nash. We have to stop Klein. I'm here to help you."

"Why should we believe you?" Kara suspiciously asked.

"I'm working undercover. I'm an investigative reporter. I worked my way into the Vril Society over the past two years. Me and a few others who, if you don't stop Klein, you will meet tonight. They are part of the crew of a Vril ship anchored in Bremerhaven that's leaving for South America tonight."

"So, what are you doing here?" Kara asked.

"They needed an extra hand down here. I volunteered so I could get close to Klein and find out what she has planned."

"You mean you don't know?" Kara asked.

"Not until now."

"How are they going to blow up the Premier's yacht?" Nash asked.

"They have a naval mine, and Klein is going to use it to blow up the yacht."

"They can't," Kara said. "Security would be sweeping ahead of the ship. It's standard procedure."

"They can't sweep for this." Marsh said. "They have an old World War Two Oyster mine. It doesn't work magnetically. It's a pressure sensitive mine that needs no signal to arm. It's detonated by the pressure wave a ship makes going over it. No mine sweeper could duplicate the wave because each pressure wave is unique to the size and speed of the ship."

"And they've calibrated the mine for the Premier's yacht," Nash noted.

"He and his entourage will be on the Goethe, a reconditioned paddle wheel. They plan to drop the mine off downstream in front of it with that speed boat out there, and when the Goethe goes over it," he paused. "You get the picture."

"Why us?" Nash asked. "And how do you even know who I am?"

"I can't do it alone," Marsh replied. "I need help. As for knowing you, your photograph was sent out to a network of people."

"Sent out by whom?"

"It's not important, and I don't have time to go into it right now," Marsh replied.

"So how do we stop Klein?" asked Kara.

"That's up to you. Now go. I'll run interference and try to divert Klein's muscle. You've got to stop that speed boat. Krause and Marco already left with the mine."

"Do you have any weapons?" Nash asked, holding the empty liquor bottle in front of him. "I doubt this will help much against automatic weapons."

Marsh shook his head. "They keep close control over them."

Kara and Nash started for the door when Marsh said, "By the way, Nash. You owe me."

"What are you talking about? Owe you what?"

"I want you to meet me after this—if you get out alive. We have a lot to talk about."

"Like what?"

"There's no time now. Let's say, you've made a very powerful enemy."

"Tell me something I don't know."

"You don't know this."

"Marsh, I—"

They heard a noise outside the room. "We're running out of time."

"Wait," Nash said grabbing Marsh's arm. "What do we do with Kara?"

"I'm going with you," she said. "You can't do it alone."

"I don't think—" Nash began to say.

"I have martial arts training. Do you?"

Nash shrugged. He was sure she could handle herself in any combat situation, and he couldn't do this alone.

"I'm glad you two have that settled," Marsh said. "Wait a few minutes and let me distract whoever is out there. It's imperative that you stop that speed boat."

"Have the authorities been notified about any of this?" Kara asked.

"No, there's not enough time and too much to explain." Marsh replied. "It's up to you."

A Gruesome End

After Marsh left the room, Nash and Kara waited a few moments, then made their way quietly through the hangar.

"How are we going to stop them?" Kara whispered.

Nash motioned towards the floatplane at the rear of the large hangar. It had its wheels extended under the pontoons, resting on the concrete floor. It was backed up into the hangar facing the open hangar doors. "I fly. Remember?"

"We're going to fly to the speed boat?" she asked.

"That's the plan."

"Then what?"

"Haven't thought that far ahead yet. Come on."

Marsh was at the front of the hanger talking to Elsa Klein and Horst, occupying their attention. The Vril goddess had her long hair tied up in a top knot and twirled an errant stand of hair with her finger. She looked almost innocently benign.

Nash and Kara crept along the back wall until they were behind the plane. They knelt and peeked under the fuselage between the pontoons and watched the trio, now less than fifty yards directly in front of them.

Klein handed Marsh a small device. He nodded curtly, clicked his heels together, spun around, and walked out of sight.

"I'm glad he's on our side," Nash whispered when they were out of sight.

"Yeah, that was creepy. All that was missing was the *Heil Hitler* salute."

"It's now or never," Nash said, standing up and moving quickly around the plane.

They opened the doors and climbed into the pilot and co-pilot seats of the Junkers. Nash did a brief survey of the cockpit, initiated the ignition sequence, and started up the single engine.

It roared to life, the engine spitting out smoke.

Startled, Klein and Horst swung around when they heard the engine turn over then ran towards the float plane. Klein was unarmed but Horst drew his Glock. He was about to fire at the plane when Klein stopped him.

"No!" she ordered, pushing the gun toward the ceiling. "Don't damage the plane." She pointed at the hangar doors. Horst nodded and sprinted to the door controls while she ran towards the plane.

Nash stood on the brakes and kicked the engine into full gear. The entire metal hangar rattled above them as the sound of the engine reverberated throughout the structure. "Hold on," he yelled over the engine roar.

Kara grabbed hold of the steering wheel in front of her for support, and as the RPMs of the engine reached a feverish pitch, the Junkers literally rose on its hind quarters and lurched down the hanger towards the doors.

Nash momentarily lost control of the powerful plane when Kara accidentally stood on the rudder controls. The plane skidded to the left, smashing into a pile of 50-gallon barrels of aviation fuel. Kara screamed as they came cascading down over the side of the Junkers and fuel emptied through the open side windows behind them.

Nash fought with the controls and began to accelerate again, but the plane began to slide on the aviation fuel covering the floor.

The massive hanger doors slowly slid sideways. It was now a race between the closing hangar doors and the barreling floatplane. Nash struggled with the plane, trying to keep it moving forward, but it continued to skid from one side to the other on the slippery hangar floor. He let up on the throttle to help regain control of the plane but the Junkers slid out from under his grip.

"Nash!" Kara screamed, pointed, and pushed back into her seat as far as she could go, putting as much distance possible between her and the end of a pistol pointed at her through the windshield.

It was Horst. He had somehow managed to climb onto the engine cowling and was pointing his pistol at Kara through the windshield.

Nash instinctively hit the brakes trying to throw him from the cowling.

Horst dropped his pistol but managed to hold tight as his feet and lower torso slid back and forth.

"Look out," Kara screamed.

Nash looked up and saw the parked helicopter looming up before them. He pulled the controls to the left and pumped up the plane's acceleration.

Nash and Kara were thrown sideways as the Junkers glanced off the chopper. When they righted themselves, they saw a large smear of blood on the passenger side of the windshield. Kara leaned forward and looked out just as Horst's headless torso slid off the plane.

"*Oh my God!*" Kara cried.

Horst's head was hanging from the chopper blade.

Kara gagged as Nash hit the throttle hard, spun the Junkers around and pointed it toward the closing doors.

"Hold on," Nash yelled. "This is going to be close."

"We're not going to make it," Kara whimpered.

"Won't have to." Nash pulled the engine accelerator controls back hard, trying to get the last bit of acceleration out of the engine.

The float plane lurched forward.

Nash held his breath and braced himself for the inevitable impact.

Kara said a silent prayer.

The plane's wings hit the closing doors hard, shearing them off with the sound of screeching metal. The doors collapsed around the Junkers, but the now-wingless floatplane lurched twice and managed to clear the hangar and roll onto the river on its underbelly pontoons.

"My God!" Kara cried. "We're through."

"Let's get to the flotilla," Nash said, pointing the plane downstream.

After a prolonged silence, Kara said, "I wonder if they're giving out a prize for the most peculiar looking boat this year."

Nash laughed and shook his head.

Attack On The Goethe

"We're here." Kara pointed to a group of boats ahead of them. Several of the boats were flying Chinese banners.

"Look for the speedboat," Nash said, slowing the wingless floatplane and maneuvering through the line of boats.

The firework spectacle was just starting. The star blast, lightning bombs, and other exploding firework displays drew bright pictures in the moonless sky with each explosion. The hills bordering the river made the noise echo even louder.

"There!" Kara pointed to a Zodiac speedboat leisurely moving downstream toward the flotilla.

Nash guided the floatplane toward the boat. As they neared, the fireworks lit up the area surrounding the boat. Nash saw Marco driving the speed boat while Krause worked on a cylindrical object hanging from the rear.

"That's got to be the Oyster mine." Nash pointed to the plane's steering wheel and said, "I need you to take over."

"But I can't fly," Kara said in surprise.

"We're not flying this thing. It's just a clumsy boat now. Use the rudder controls at your feet and get me as close to the speed boat as you can."

"What are you going to do?"

"Just get me near that boat."

He opened his door and slid out onto the pontoon as she moved into his seat and took the wheel.

The water rushed by under his feet, and the spray of the river stung his face. He closed the door and started to inch forward across the long narrow pontoon.

When he was about three feet in front of the door, someone grabbed him around the waist and pulled him backwards.

He turned to see Klein squatting on the pontoon, both legs wrapped around the landing gear.

What the hell…!

She pushed her upper body backwards, pulling him off balance.

He fell forward and immediately grabbed her neck. She twisted her body and swung her legs out from under the plane. She quickly stood up and pushed down on his shoulders, forcing him on his back. Her strength was incredible, but she was off balance. Nash twisted and swept his right leg under her body. He connected with both of her legs, forcing her to topple on top of him.

When she regained her balance, she was sitting on his chest. He tried to push her off, but she was too strong. She grabbed his head and forced his body over the pontoon and near the rushing river. Spray stung his face as he strained to keep her from pushing his head into the river.

Klein suddenly released him, stood up and stumbled backwards. Nash leaned forward and saw Kara hanging out of the pilot-side door. She was pulling Klein backwards by her topknot.

Nash tried to stand up to help Kara, but the floatplane bounced around wildly as Kara accidentally pushed the rudder controls during her struggle with Klein.

Out of control, the plane collided with the Zodiac, throwing Nash off the pontoon and onto a surprised Krause.

The floatplane peeled off to the left leaving Nash and Krause struggling in the speedboat. Marco looked back over his shoulder, corrected his predetermined course, and entered the flotilla of Taiwanese boats.

Krause scowled and punched Nash is the face sending him sprawling towards the front of the boat. He drew his Glock and pointed it at Nash. "You're making it increasingly difficult to follow orders and keep you alive, Herr Nash."

Nash started to stand up, but Krause ordered, "Keep still! She needs you alive, but she didn't say anything about not shooting you in the kneecap."

Krause backed up to the mine that was hanging from the rear of the speedboat. "This is our destiny," he said, reaching for the bomb's release mechanism.

Kara struggled to regain control of the floatplane. Once she did, she started scanning the area below for Klein, who had disappeared after Nash leapt into the Zodiac.

As Kara leaned over and looked as far back on the pilot-side pontoon as she could, the co-pilot side door opened. Klein jumped through it, grabbed Kara by the hair, and smashed her face into the control panel several times. Kara put her hands on the panel and pushed backwards, throwing a wild elbow toward her attacker. It caught Klein squarely on the jaw, knocking her backwards.

As the two women fought, the plane jerked back and forth, roaring down the river toward the flotilla of Taiwanese protest boats. The out-of-control Junkers scattered the small boats as it careened wildly from side to side.

Klein pushed Kara backwards into the co-pilot's seat, pressing her knee into Kara's chest. She wrapped both hands around Kara's throat and began to strangle her.

Kara thrashed back and forth and pushed her attacker into the steering wheel again. The plane lurched violently to its right and crashed into something, throwing Klein into the windshield.

Krause stopped and looked up over Nash's shoulder—surprise etched his face. Nash turned to see the floatplane heading directly for them. He dove to the floor as Krause fired two shots at him, grazing his shoulder with one of the rounds.

The impact threw Krause backwards.

Nash, holding his injured shoulder, struggled to regain his

balance as the speedboat veered to the right nearly colliding with the floatplane again.

Nash grabbed the back of one of the seats to maintain his balance. He turned to see Marco driving the speedboat slumped over the steering wheel, a large stain growing across the back of his shirt courtesy of the other of Krause's bullets.

Krause struggled to his hands and knees and reached for the gun in front of him.

Nash looked around frantically and grabbed the boat anchor from behind the seat. As Krause leveled the gun, Nash stepped forward and swung the small anchor, hitting him in the chest and knocking him backwards. Nash jabbed the anchor forward, catching Krause in the stomach.

Krause doubled over and Nash, ignoring the pain in his burning shoulder, raised the anchor over his head and hit Krause in the face. Krause dropped the pistol and stumbled backwards, his nose broken and bloodied.

The back of his legs hit the side of the boat and Krause tumbled backwards into the river.

Nash dropped the anchor and sank to his knees, gripping his wounded shoulder.

The mine!

Nash jumped up and made his way the back of the speed boat.

The cylinder was gone.

Flashpoint

When the Junkers crashed into the speedboat, Klein was momentarily thrown back off Kara and slammed against the pilot's seat. Scratched and bloodied, the Vril leader tried to get up but fell between the seats, screeching at Kara like a banshee.

"You filthy Jew!" Klein screamed. "I'll kill you!" She jumped up and lunged at Kara but lost her footing as the out of control floatplane bounced wildly, hurtling towards the riverbank.

Kara grabbed Klein in a headlock and pushed her into the rear of the plane.

Klein spun around with a vicious smile on her face. She had a flare gun in her hand, and she pointed it at Kara.

"Go ahead, you fucking Nazi. Shoot and we'll both die!" Kara spat.

Klein paused but did not lower the flare gun.

"There's aviation fuel all over back there," Kara screamed. "It splashed in when we hit the barrels in the hanger. Smell it?"

Klein sniffed the air and then raised her free hand to her nose. She scowled and threw the flare gun at Kara, just missing her head.

Kara spun around, scooped up the flare gun and fired it at Klein, then pushed open the door and dove out into the water.

When her head broke the surface of the water, the plane was completely engulfed in flames. She could hear Klein's screams and see her hapless shape thrashing around inside of the plane.

Die, you Nazi Bitch.

Kara started to swim toward the shore.

Nash looked downstream to see the Goethe, with only a single security boat, approaching him. The other security boats were speeding towards the out-of-control Junkers that was headed toward the riverbank.

The lone security boat, with its red and blue lights flashing, was headed towards Nash and the flotilla.

Nash rushed to the front of the speed boat and pushed the dead Marco out of the driver's seat. He grabbed the wheel and spun it around, pointing the boat directly at the paddlewheel. He pulled back on the throttle and sped downriver.

The security boat bore down on Nash shouting orders in German over its loudspeaker.

As Nash was getting closer to the paddlewheel, the Junkers burst into flames. The figure of a lone person completely engulfed in flames could be seen through the plane's windows.

"Kara!" Nash cried but did not alter his heading.

The plane exploded in a fiery orange ball raining debris on the pursuing security and flotilla boats.

Nash tried to use the flotilla of Taiwanese protest boats as a shield by maneuvering through them, but the police on the security boat started firing their automatic weapons anyway. One of the boats to Nash's left exploded as it was riddled with bullets.

Nash hunkered down as low as he could in the Zodiac, keeping the now turbulent river—and the Goethe—in view.

Bullets peppered the Zodiac, spitting up pieces of plastic, rubber, and wood all around him, but he pressed on. He worked his way left and right, back and forth, dodging bullets, racing through the flotilla, knowing the mine was less than a hundred yards behind him.

Many of the boats scrambled out of the way and headed towards the riverbank.

Through the chaos of scattering boats and shouting protesters, Nash tried shake his pursuers by cutting hard to the left, but to no avail.

As he approached the Goethe, several bullets hit the back of the Zodiac causing it to belch flame and smoke.

The black smoke seemed to be blinding the security boat because the gunfire stopped.

The paddlewheel was now directly in front of him. He could see people running in panic on the decks as he hurtled toward them.

"Turn, you fool!" Nash screamed.

It was almost as if the captain heard his shouts because the paddlewheel started to turn toward the shore.

As soon as the Goethe started to turn away from the submerged mine, Nash spun the wheel of the Zodiac and veered off to the right. An immense rumbling thud shook the speedboat. It was followed by a gusher of water that swamped the Zodiac, throwing Nash into the river. He went underwater but fought hard against the strong waves that rippled out from the mine's detonation.

When he surfaced, he saw the Goethe, miraculously unscathed, steaming up the river.

Ignoring the pain in his shoulder, Nash turned and swam in the dark water towards the east bank.

When he reached the shore, he collapsed on the rocky bank and lay there a moment gathering his strength.

"Jeremy, are you okay?"

Nash looked up to see Kara making her way down the bank.

"How do you... what did you..." he slurred.

"Marsh pulled me out of the river," she said, coughing up the remainder of water in her lungs. "Klein had sent him on ahead to film the attack."

"Klein... the plane?" Nash coughed several times.

"She's dead," Kara said. "The plane exploded."

Nash nodded.

"Where's Marsh?"

Kara looked around. "I don't know. I saw what happened, and I ran to the closest place to where you went into the water. That was pretty gutsy, Jeremy. You could have been killed."

He only nodded.

"We better get out of here," she said. "The river will be crawling with security any moment now. We should try and find—"

Nash looked up at Kara. Her eyeballs were wide with fright.

Nash craned his head around and saw Krause on the river walk. He was bloodied, one arm dangling uselessly at his side. The other arm had his automatic pistol pointing at them.

Nash pulled Kara to him and shielded her with his body.

The Vril killer snarled down at them and cocked his pistol. He suddenly stiffened, swayed and then fell over the river walk guard rail down. He hit the riverbank hard at their feet, groaned and rolled over on his back.

"That's twice I saved your ass, Nash." Marsh was standing on the river walk holding the remains of the large video camera that he had just used to put away Krause. "We need to go, now."

They walked quickly to a small sedan parked just off the river walk.

"There's someone who wants to meet you," Marsh told Nash. "It's okay. No authorities. And we need to have that shoulder looked at, too."

They nodded and climbed into the small VW sedan and drove off.

"Who wants to meet me?" Nash asked.

"Let's say, a friend."

They turned a corner and pulled to a stop under a streetlight in front of a closed coffee shop.

Karl Dieter stepped out of the shadows.

"Karl!" Kara pushed open her door and ran to him. She threw her arms around him, nearly knocking him over.

Nash silently watched them through the car window. It was easy to see that he wasn't as happy to see Dieter as Kara did.

"Is this who wants to meet me?" Nash asked.

"No," Marsh said, watching the interaction between Kara and Dieter. "But he'll take you to him."

Nash reached for the door handle, and Marsh said, "Remember, I need you to meet me when this is over."

"How? When?"

"You have enough to concern you now. I'll contact you when the time is right."

Nash looked at him, nodded, and got out of the car.

"We thought you were killed in the Chunnel explosion," Nash told Dieter, trying to be as accommodating as possible.

Dieter shook his head. "I was lucky. I got out with some of the other passengers." He paused for a second. "Did they ever find out what happened?"

Nash and Kara explained their ordeal with the madman that caused the catastrophe.

"My God," Dieter exclaimed. "You're lucky to be alive."

"You don't know the half of it," Nash said. "Now, who are we supposed to be meeting?"

"I'll tell you all I know at my place." He pointed to his car parked just down the street. "Get in. We have a lot to discuss."

Doubling Down

It was nearly midnight. The lights in Adler's private office were the only signs of life in the otherwise abandoned Volks-Agrarindustrie building.

"They're worried." Johann Hoffer uncrossed his legs and shifted his hands nervously in his lap as the one-eyed, jet-black Doberman Pincher watched his every move. "They're even speculating to our benefit."

"It's the same story in *Die Welt*," Adler said. He dropped the folded newspaper on the top of the cast-bronze desk that had once belonged to Adolph Hitler. "They're raising the speculation of an ethnic disease. They're being very sensitive about it, but you don't have to read too far between the lines to see it."

"All is as you said it would be," Hoffer said.

Adler flipped open his silver cigarette case and stuffed a long, filterless cigarette into his mouth. "Turkish tobacco," he said. "At least those Muslims are good for something." He extended the ornate case across the desk. "Care for one?"

As Hoffer leaned forward, the Doberman perked his ears up and bared his teeth. Hoffer slowly relaxed back into his chair and shook his head.

Adler laughed and scratched the dog on his long snout. "Don't mind Adolph. He doesn't like anyone but me, but you're safe as long as I like you."

Adler lit his cigarette and leaned back in his chair. He blew a smoke ring into the air and said, "Our test this week has raised concerns with the papers and television networks, but it's not enough. Perhaps it's time we make them all a little more insensitive."

"Are you suggesting we stage another incident?" Hoffer asked.

"Precisely."

"Another test will exhaust the material we have," Hoffer advised. "We'll have nothing left."

"Stone has found the location of Station Two One One," Adler said. "Soon, we will have all the material we need."

Hoffer nodded. "Who do we go after?"

"I think it's the Jews' turn." His upper lip rippled into a sneer. The dog growled. "Send out your," he gave Hoffer a quick smile, "your Einsatzgruppen."

"Do you have a specific location in mind?"

"Hit the Prenzlauer Berg district," Adler hissed. "And do it tonight."

Escape Into Horror

The chirping of the phone made Interpol Inspector Klaus Heinrich jump out of bed. He snatched up the cordless phone.

"Ya?"

"We've got them, sir."

"Are they in custody?" Heinrich asked.

"Not yet. They're in the Prenzlauer Berg district. We got lucky with the tap on Dieter's phone."

"Have the local police pick them up."

"Yes, sir. Right away."

Heinrich ended the call and reached for a pack of cigarettes sitting on his nightstand. He lit one, took a long drag and then dialed a Berlin phone number.

When Nash and Kara arrived at Dieter's apartment, Nash was surprised to find a familiar face sitting in the living room next to a stranger, dressed in a tan safari jacket.

"Raymond!" Nash exclaimed. "What the devil are you doing in Berlin?"

"Hoping to save your ass," Professor Raymond Thomas replied.

"Don't tell me you're involved in this, too."

"He's with me," the other man said. He held out his hand. "Let me introduce myself. My name's Jake Stone."

"You're American," Nash noted.

"Afraid so," Stone said. "And that's not the only thing we have in common. We're both after the same thing."

"And that is..." Nash said warily.

"Station Two One One," Stone replied. "And the Nazi treasure hidden within its walls."

"Treasure hunters? You've got to be kidding me."

"On the contrary, Mr. Nash," Stone disagreed. "We're quite serious."

Nash looked at Professor Thomas. "Raymond, I never thought you would believe in this tripe."

"Look Jeremy, if what he says about the scrolls I've been searching for is even half true, it's worth the gamble."

"So, it's the scrolls again?" Nash smiled. "You and your dusty old scrolls."

"You know those scrolls are the Holy Grail of my linguistic research. I've been searching for them ever since—"

"And that search is what brought us together," Stone said.

"I know you don't believe in the Nazi treasure myths, my old friend, but this is different. We have plenty of documentation concerning the Nazi's removal of the scrolls from Egypt." Professor Thomas put his hand on Nash's shoulder. Nash recoiled and howled in pain.

"Are you alright, old man?"

"No, I'm not alright! I was shot," Nash said. "It's just a flesh wound, the bullet just grazed me, but it still hurts like hell."

"Are you well enough to make this journey?"

"What journey?" Nash asked.

"We have a cargo jet sitting on the runway at Tempelhof," Stone cut in. "It'll take us to a base owned by our financiers in Antarctica. We'll be picked up soon."

Nash looked around the room. All eyes were on him.

"This path was always leading us to Station Two One One," Nash said. "Who am I to argue?"

"Good," said Stone, clapping his hands. "Then we're off. I have an SUV downstairs."

A few minutes later, the four men and Kara climbed into Stone's SUV. It was a brute of a machine sitting on huge tires and stood four feet off the ground. Nash marveled how Stone could maneuver such a beast through Germany's tight roads.

They drove through the haze of Prenzlauer Berg district just before sunrise as drops of dew clung to the windshield.

"How far to Tempelhof?" Nash asked.

"We're not going there yet," Stone answered. "First we..."

Stone pause as he looked past Nash and saw a blue and white Mercedes bearing down on them. On top of it was a flashing blue light. "Crap! Police!" he cried.

Nash turned around and saw another patrol car pull in behind the first from a side street.

His stomach dropped.

He turned to Kara to speak but stopped when he saw her fixated on something in front of them. She had raised her hand and was pointing at something—then gasped.

Nash looked to where Kara pointed, and the color flushed from his face. Directly to his right in the street in front of them, three people stumbled off the curb and into the SUV's path.

"Christ! Stone! In front of us!"

Stone turned his attention from the police cars, now wailing their sirens behind them, to the new threat. He reacted immediately turning the wheel of the SUV and, as he did, he narrowly missed the three men falling—really collapsing—into the street.

"What the hell!" Stone cried.

Stone screeched the SUV to a halt just as a small sedan careened around the corner, out of control, and ran over the three men.

"Jesus Christ!" yelled Thomas.

The others stared in disbelief.

On the tail of Thomas's last syllable, the careening sedan was followed by an old VW bus. It plowed into the sedan, pushing it into a lamp post—knocking it over in a sea of sparks—and through a plate glass window of a kosher foods store.

"Mein Gott!" yelled Kara. Then she screamed.

Nash looked over at Kara just as a crazed man slammed against his passenger window, screaming in German. He tried to pull open his door. Stone saw the attempt and hit the accelerator, pulling away from the madman just as a woman threw herself across his hood and vomited onto the windshield. Stone automatically recoiled away from the windshield and slammed the car in reverse. He then took a quick glance in his rearview mirror, expecting to see the police bearing down on them.

Not so.

The police cars following them were not as lucky as Stone.

Amid dying and dead residents lying in the street were the two police cars. One was on its side in flames, under the remains of the destroyed streetlight. The other was amid the remains of an Israeli food café, its entire front end smashed, leaking fluid and covered with dying patrons, tables and chairs.

Nash hit Stone on his back. "Let's go!" he yelled. "What... Why..." stammered Stone, pointing at the carnage before his eyes.

"Not now!" yelled Dieter. "Go! *Schnell!*"

Stone dropped the SUV into drive and sped down a side street spewing smoke and burnt rubber into the air as he went. At the end of the block, his eyes, locked on his rear-view mirror, beheld a frightening sight.

Three, four... no, several men and women—even a young child—were either dead still on the pavement or were in convulsions. Others, seemingly unaffected by whatever was killing their neighbors, were leaning down trying to help them. Even more residents were stumbling into his path from his left.

"What the hell is happening?" screamed Thomas.

The sound of more police sirens echoed down the street. Dieter turned to Stone and yelled, "We'll never reach the airport. Police cars will be all over us."

Stone made a sharp right onto a main drag and said, "No, they won't." He pointed to what looked like a small park up ahead.

"Unless they can fly."

A few moments later Stone pulled the SUV into a gated driveway, through a small grove of trees, and pulled up to a large warehouse looking building.

"Everyone out!" Stone yelled. "Follow me."

The American fortune hunter led the group up a set of steel stairs that ran three stories up along the side of the building to the roof.

"What are we doing here?" Nash asked, catching his breath when they reached the top.

"We're waiting for our pickup," Stone replied.

As if on cue, they heard the unmistakable sound of a helicopter chopping through the early morning air. A dark colored, unmarked commercial helicopter approached the roof and landed, blowing dust and dirt into the group's faces.

Stone nodded smugly. "Next stop—Tempelhof."

They quickly climbed in, and as it took off, skimming the roof tops, Dieter and the others looked down through the early light of the morning at the havoc on the streets below.

"Holocaust," Dieter hissed in anger. "Holocaust."

Tempelhof Airport

The chopper landed at the extreme north end of the Tempelhof terminal. When it was on the helipad, a man approached, his head low, protecting his face from the swirling ground debris.

The doors opened on the chopper, Stone stepped out, and walked over to the man. He had blond hair and a facial scar on a heartless, chiseled face. Something about him—his stance, maybe, or his demeanor—reminded Nash of the madman who pursued them through the streets of Berlin and the Chunnel.

"This is our team," Stone said excitedly. "This is Professor Thomas, Kara Ackerman, Karl Dieter, and this is Jeremy Nash. He found the location of Station Two One One. Jeremy, this is Herr Hoffer. He's the right-hand man of our benefactor."

Nash held out his hand and thought he caught a glimpse of recognition in Hoffer's face.

"Herr Nash," he said, shaking Nash's hand amiably. "Happy to meet the man responsible for making us all rich."

"To be honest, Mr. Hoffer, I'm not a treasure hunter," Nash explained.

"Regardless," Hoffer said. "The location of Station Two One One puts us all that much closer to the treasure. Now we have a plane to catch."

He led the group into the terminal.

"This is breathtaking." Professor Thomas stopped in the middle of the crescent-shaped terminal and looked around.

"It was built in the nineteen thirties," Hoffer said. "The tall expanse of floor to ceiling windows was designed to impress foreign guests to the new Reich. The unusual design of the terminal also had a specific purpose. It was meant to be an air stadium for 100,000 spectators that Hitler would talk to at an annual air show."

"And the terminal had a more apocalyptic use," Dieter added. "Deep under the airport is a maze of tunnels that still exist today, forty kilometers in length on six levels used as a wartime aircraft factory producing Focke-Wulf 190 fighter planes. The tunnels were also connected to the Nazi nerve center of Ministries in old East Berlin."

"Well, the Nazi thing puts a damper on it," Professor Thomas said, "but it's still architecturally amazing."

"We've got to get moving now," Hoffer advised. "The plane is almost loaded."

"Loaded with what?" Nash asked.

"We have a C-5 Galaxy cargo plane loaded with more than two tons of supplies and equipment, a pair of snow cats and a chopper."

"Antarctica, here we come." Stone clapped his hands together.

"We'll have to make a refueling stop in South Africa before we get to our base camp on the Antarctic shelf." Hoffer pointed to a coffee machine sitting on a table off to the right. "Warm up. We'll be loading very soon."

Hoffer left the group and walked to a place out of ear shot. He pulled out his phone and punched in a number.

"This is Adler."

"We have the team."

"Good."

"And something else. Nash is here. He's the one who knows where the Station is. The woman… Tillman's daughter is with him."

There was a long silence at the end of the line.

"Sir?"

"You are not to harm Nash until we have the material in hand."

"Yes, sir." Hoffer said.

"Then kill them all."

Nazi Antarctica

With a grueling thirty-six hours of travel behind them, the C-5 Galaxy descended into a bleak landscape of ice and snow that extended as far as the eye could see.

Nash looked out his window and saw a blue icy runway covered with a thin layer of compacted snow. Next to it was a sprawling network of large, poundcake-shaped, red and white metal buildings perched on stilts.

"Queen Maud Land?" Professor Thomas asked, leaning over the back of Nash's seat.

"Ya. Neuschwabenland," Dieter replied.

The wheels of the Galaxy touched down, and the lumbering cargo jet steered towards the metal buildings.

The turbofan jets powered down as the C-5 Galaxy came to halt.

"Put on your artic coats and bundle up," Hoffer ordered. "Don't let the sunny air fool you. It's biting cold out there—and windy."

The occupants bundled up in parkas and waited at the exit doors. When they opened, a blast of freezing air whipped their faces.

"Not the dusty tombs and museums you usually haunt," Nash remarked to Professor Thomas. "Still feel your scrolls are worth this?"

"Those scrolls are priceless."

They were led off the cargo jet to the stairs of the nearest entrance to the building complex—and blessed warmth. Once inside, Hoffer motioned for them to follow him.

They passed what looked like a well-equipped science lab with a clean room as they were ushered down a semi-dark hallway. At the end of the hallway was a modern-looking, wood paneled conference room, lit by fluorescent recessed lights.

They removed their parkas and found seats around an ebony conference table.

"Herr Nash," Hoffer said. "Please show us the location of Station Two One One and tell us how you determined its locality."

Nash asked Kara for the leather document holder, and as he showed Hoffer the contents, he explained how they pieced together the clues.

"Amazing," Hoffer exclaimed. "This location you found is in the Mühlig-Hoffmann Mountain range. Quite a bit of detective work you two did here."

"Dieter helped," Kara said.

"I can see that." He looked at Dieter who looked down at the table and fidgeted with his hands.

"Well," Hoffer said, striking his hands on the table. "We need our rest. We leave for our objective in ten hours." He stood up as an act of finality. "We'll eat supper and then you will be shown to your quarters."

"A hot meal would be great," Professor Thomas remarked.

"Let's hope it's not our last," Nash said as he looked out the small, double-paned window coated with ice. "It looks like a storm is brewing."

Into The Abyss

Nash awoke to the sound of someone giving commands in the hallway. He pulled himself off the small cot he was sleeping on, nudged his bunkmate, Professor Thomas, and made his way to the door. He opened it to see Hoffer talking to two burley men.

Hoffer saw him and said, "Good, you're up. Wake the others in your group and meet us in the conference room." He turned and led his two compatriots down the hallway.

"What's up?" Professor Thomas asked when Nash closed the door.

"I guess it's time to go treasure hunting."

"A few things before we leave," Hoffer said, standing at the head of the conference table. "We're using two snow cats. Nash, the frauline, and the professor will ride with me, along with a driver and one of my men. Dieter and Stone will ride in the other with a driver and my other compatriot."

He pointed to the two hard-looking men in the room. "These men are well-seasoned. They've had years of experience in the Antarctic environment and know their way around Queen Maud Land. They will be our guides. Listen to what they tell you, and you'll have a good chance of surviving the journey." He paused a moment. "Does anyone have any questions?"

No one responded.

"Good, then we go."

The two teams made their way to the vehicle hanger connected to the building and loaded onto the two red, enclosed-cab, truck sized, fully tracked vehicles. The two guides loaded an impressive amount of mountain climbing gear in the back of each snow cat while the group donned Artic clothing and heavy insulated boots.

The engines started up, and the large hanger doors opened to an orange glow on the horizon. A few moments later, they drove into a lightly falling snow and over the Antarctic ice sheet.

"This is eerie," Professor Thomas remarked looking over the bleak flat landscape. "Almost otherworldly."

"You've seen nothing yet," replied Hoffer. "The region is filled with peaks and mountains. Little was known of this area until the Germans made aerial photos of it in 1939."

"Stone said something about that," Professor Thomas remarked.

"And I bet," Nash said, "he told you that a Captain Wilhelm Bernhard, commanding a U-boat, set off to the Antarctic in April of nineteen forty-five."

Hoffer glanced back at Nash and smiled. "Very good, Herr Nash. Der Fuhrer Convoy. Supposedly, sixteen crew members of the U-boat landed on the Antarctic shore and deposited numerous boxes that contained documents and relics from the Third Reich in a network of tunnels, somewhere in this chain of mountains."

Nash couldn't contain himself. "And I suppose we'll find the remains of Hitler and Eva Braun there too?" he said. "Or maybe the Holy Grail and the Spear of Destiny!"

"You don't believe that such a secret base is possible, Herr Nash?" asked Hoffer. "Even though you hold in your hand the exact coordinates of such a base, don't you think that all myths have some basis in fact?"

"There are other explanations. It could just be an old World War Two weather station or something."

"Tales of ancient tunnels," Hoffer replied, "leading through the Mühlig-Hoffmann Mountains appear at first, far-fetched. But wouldn't a cavern network, glacially eroded enough, appear unnatural and thus be explained as a tunnel?"

"I don't believe—"

"The British had secret wartime bases, so why not the Nazis? Some Japanese soldiers fought on for over twenty years on forgotten Pacific islands, so why not pockets of Germans? In fact, the Nazi Werewolves were active in occupied Germany after the surrender of the Reich and isolated attacks occurred years after the Nazis were defeated. Perhaps you should keep a more open mind."

"I've heard more than my share of conspiracy theories and treasure myths," Nash commented. "None of them have ever been proven."

Hoffer just shrugged his shoulders. "Well, we'll find out soon enough."

They continued for hours through a stunning landscape of bright blue ice caves and glaciers, endless white snow fields, and craggy mountains towering above the plain white surface of the ice sheet, one evoking a row of flesh-tearing teeth.

"Look at that," Professor Thomas exclaimed pointing to a string of fang-like imposing mountains to their right.

"Those are of the Jaws of Fenris," Hoffer told him. "They get their name from a fierce wolf in Norse myth."

"This place would be a paradise for mountaineers," Kara remarked.

"Don't tell me," Nash said. "You mountain climb?"

"On occasion," she replied. "We have a mountain in southern Germany on the border with Austria. It's called the Zugspitze." She held up both arms and flexed them in a weightlifters position. "I've done a lot of climbing there. Keeps me in shape."

Hoffer tapped the driver on the shoulder. "Slow down and tell the other cat to watch for crevasses. They'll be easy to miss under all this ice and snow." The driver nodded and radioed the second snow cat.

Hoffer checked the GPS reading, then pulled out a pair of binoculars and scanned the horizon. "There!" he said excitedly, pointing to a series of rocky outcroppings. "If your deciphering of the clues is correct, that would be our destination."

The two cats lumbered towards the rocky outcroppings, and five minutes later they reached the coordinates given by Nash.

"Grab your climbing helmets and follow me," Hoffer ordered.

The guides unloaded heavy back packs and hefted them over their shoulders. A few minutes later, they led the team to several outcroppings of rock.

"You all wait here." The lead guide turned to his partner and said, "Let's see what we can find."

A strong, cold wind came up blowing snow around the group as the two guides disappeared into the swirling white cloud.

The others pulled their hoods over their heads and fitted their face masks and goggles against the biting wind.

Dieter moved from one foot to the other, hugging his arms in front of him trying to stay warm.

Nash nudged Professor Thomas and said with a straight face, "Keep an eye out for polar bears."

"Polar bears?" He looked around quickly.

Kara and Stone both laughed.

"What's so funny?"

"They're pulling your leg," Hoffer said. "There are no polar bears in Antarctica."

"Very funny, Jeremy. Maybe you should—"

One of the guides suddenly appeared. "We've found something."

The group followed the guide through the dramatically reduced visibility of blowing snow.

"Careful where you step," Hoffer said. "Keep your head about you."

They approached a small crevasse inside a grouping of ice and rock. The guide standing by the crevasse had unpacked the mountain climbing gear from the backpacks and was attaching ropes to pitons on the rocky wall.

"We go down," the guide leading them said, pointing to the icy chute at his feet. He pulled a heavy flashlight from his belt and shined it down the chute.

"Turn on your helmet lights," Hoffer said.

"Has any of you climbed before?" one of the guides asked.

"I have," Kara answered.

"You follow me."

Kara was fitted into a rope sling that wrapped around her legs and rear. The guide attached a d-ring to the rope harness and then attached the ring to the heavy twisted nylon rope that was threaded through the piton attached to the rock wall. He dropped the rope down the icy chute.

"Now watch me, then the frauline," the guide commanded. "Do as we do." He switched off his flashlight and attached it to his utility belt. He turned around, leaned back in his rope harness, put one hand behind his back and the other on the nylon rope—then kicked off.

The group watched as he rappelled down the craggy ice cave into the chute, lit only by the small beam of his helmet light.

Kara was next. Repeating the same procedure, and looking like she had done this sort of thing all her life, she disappeared into the crevasse.

"I'll go next," Nash said, still looking down into the crevasse where Kara had disappeared just seconds before. The guide fitted him up then led Nash to where the crevasse began its steep descent. Nash took a deep breath and then lowered himself down into the icy shaft.

"Take it slow," the guide ordered. "Try and keep your feet on the rock and not the ice.

Nash looked ahead at the splash of light from his helmet lamp before him as the surrounding darkness masked the chasm below, and all he could imagine was ice.

He slipped twice, but he was able, after much concentration and much trepidation, to find the proper footholds. After repelling into the darkness for what felt like an eternity, illuminated only by his helmet light, he landed at the bottom of the shaft.

"Pretty good for a bookworm," Kara said.

Nash turned, and his helmet light shined on her face. She was smiling.

Nash thought back over his chilling experiences of the last two weeks and weakly replied, "If you only knew."

Several minutes later, the entire group, their helmet light beams bouncing off the craggy walls, was making its way into a dark cave, assisted by the powerful flashlight of the lead guide.

Hoffer walked up beside Nash. "Tell me, Herr Nash. Is this a cave or a tunnel?" He pointed his flashlight towards an area up front of them. It seemed to be made of a different material, smooth as ice but much darker.

"It could be nothing more than a freak of nature," Nash replied. "I think the scientific term is *glacial erosion.*"

"You're talking to a dyed-in-the-wool, pure skeptic," Professor Thomas told Hoffer. "Believe me. Don't try arguing with him. It gets you—" His foot caught something, and he stumbled forward and fell to his knees.

"Are you alright?" Nash asked.

Professor Thomas looked down at his ankle. "I'm tangled up in some sort of wire."

"Don't move!" Stone ordered.

Professor Thomas reached for the wire imprisoning his foot.

"I said, *don't move!*" he ordered again, loudly, and jammed his foot on the professor's ankle.

"Ow!" Thomas cried. "What the hell are you doing!?"

Stone reached down and inspected the rusty wire around Thomas's ankle. "Jesus," he whispered under his breath. He looked up at the others and yelled, "No one move."

As the others watched in puzzlement, Stone motioned for one of the guides. "See this?"

He nodded and said, "Let me handle this."

They all watched as he carefully unwrapped the wire from Thomas's foot.

When he had freed Thomas's foot from the wire, he followed it back towards the wall of the tunnel where it was snagged in a jagged crack in the floor. He unhooked the wire from its restraint and followed it back into a crevice in the tunnel wall. He reached inside and pulled out what looked like a grimy, rusted World War Two Wehrmacht stick grenade. "That was a trip wire! We were very lucky it didn't pull the detonator cord on the grenade." He detached the stick grenade from the trip wire and placed it gently on the floor behind him.

Stone touched Nash on the shoulder. "Still think this is a weather station? I don't know many that welcome visitors with a booby trap."

"Let's just keep going," Nash commented, grimly.

Station Two One One

The guides took the lead and moved slowly through the tunnel, scanning the area for more trip wires or booby traps. The tunnel soon opened into a series of made-made rooms that had been cut into the rock.

"Wait here," the lead guide ordered as he and his partner entered the first room. The beams from their flashlights bounced around the room for a moment before one of them called, "All clear."

The group cautiously went into the room single file. Both guides were standing in front of the only object in the room, a small obelisk about a meter tall.

"What is it?" Professor Thomas asked.

"I'm not sure," Hoffer answered, moving closer to it. The others followed him, surrounding the obelisk.

"There's an inscription on it," Stone noted as he kneeled in front of it. "I think it's in German. Hard to read. What does it say?"

Hoffer took a flashlight from one of the guides, knelt and focused on the weathered words etched on the obelisk. "It reads: *There are truly more things in heaven and 'in' earth than man has dreamt. Beyond this point is AGHARTA.* It's Signed, *Haushofer, 1943.*"

"*Haushofer?*" Kara turned to Nash. "Isn't that the name of the man with the coded message in that first envelope the Unity family in London told us about?"

"And the man," Stone informed them, "who actively molded the thinking of the Nazi inner core, and those beliefs were part of the motivation for the Nazi search for the Ark of the Covenant and Agharta." He looked at Professor Thomas. "And the man who sent annual expeditions to Tibet to find, and then to maintain, contact with the Aryan forefathers in Shambhala and Agharti—*the inner earth*."

"What do you believe now, Herr Nash?" Hoffer asked, his tone suggesting it was more of a statement than a question.

Everyone looked at Nash.

"I'll be damned," Nash said and shrugged his shoulders in surrender.

"The box!" Professor Thomas said in a demanding tone. "Let's find the box!"

Kara looked at Nash. They both had the same thought.

What box?

"What box?" Nash asked. "What are you talking about?"

"The scrolls!"

"And the gold and jewels." Stone added.

"According to what we know," Hoffer told Nash, "there's a box here containing the treasures of the Nazi regime. And it's somewhere in this Station." He signaled to the two guides. "You know what we're looking for."

They nodded, walked down the narrow hallway and went into the next set of rooms.

"Let's do some searching ourselves," Hoffer said. "Nash, take the frauline and the professor and search the rooms on the right. Dieter, Stone and I will search the rooms on the left. Everyone watch out for more booby traps."

Professor Thomas led Nash and Kara through the inky darkness with only a stream of light from his bobbing helmet marking the path.

He stepped into the first room and stopped dead in his tracks. Nash bumped into him making him take a step forward. The professor immediately recoiled, pushing Nash back into Kara.

"What's wrong?" Nash asked, moving around to the side of the professor.

"Oh my God!" Kara put her hand over her mouth as her words echoed through the room.

All three of their helmet lights focused on the same target, the frozen body of a man. He was dressed in a World War Two Kriegsmarine uniform. His eyes were black luminous pools, with ice encrusted across his face in a horrid mask—icicles dripping from his nose and mouth. He was hunched over a radio on a large table, his forearm extended awkwardly away from his body, towards the receiver, frozen in place.

"*I … Dear God! … I …*" Professor Thomas stuttered and pushed back a step farther.

Nash placed his hand on Thomas's shoulders. "Raymond, are you alright?" he asked. "I thought this would be par for the course in your line of work. Mummies and such."

"I deal with dusty old scrolls, as you say, and engraved hieroglyphics—not dead bodies."

"Nash! Get over here!" Hoffer shouted from another room.

The three made their way into the next room and saw Hoffer, Dieter, Stone, and the two guides standing over a large, metal footlocker encrusted with dirt and ice.

"I think we've found it," Stone said, clapping his hands together.

"This is the Reich's lost treasure?" Kara asked. "I thought it would be bigger."

"Whatever it is," Nash said to Kara, "we need to open it. Hopefully it will get us closer to finding the people who framed me and murdered your father."

"Yes," said Professor Thomas said excitedly, as he stepped closer to the chest. "By all means, let's open it."

The guides dropped several light sticks around the box, lighting the center of the room.

"Herr Nash," Hoffer said. "Please give me the key."

"What key?" Nash tried to look puzzled.

"The hex key, Herr Nash," Hoffer pushed. "The artifact in Hartman's third envelope that was given to you in London."

"How do you know about that?"

"That's irrelevant," Hoffer snapped back. "Now give me the key."

Both guides stepped forward, flanking Hoffer, and drew their pistols.

"What the devil is going on here?" Professor Thomas asked.

"Shut up!" ordered Hoffer. "The key, Herr Nash." He held out an ungloved hand.

"Kara, give me the pouch," Nash asked.

She unzipped her parka, pulled out the leather pouch, and handed it to him.

Hoffer snatched it out of Nash's hand.

"Why are you threatening us?" Stone asked. "I had a deal with your boss. Are you trying to cut me out of my share?"

"Dummkopf," Hoffer whispered and just shook head. He motioned to the two henchmen who moved forward and made the group back up against the wall. Hoffer knelt by the metal box and wiped the crusty snow off the top of it. He emptied the contents of Kara's leather pouch on the ground beside him and plucked out the hex key.

"The box is attached to a detonator inside. Its contents were never to be accessed by non-authorized personnel." Hoffer inserted the key into the hexagonal lock and slowly turned the key twice to the left, once to the right, then once more to the left. With each turn, tumblers sounded from within the box. "Two, one, one," he whispered.

Hoffer opened the lid of the metal footlocker and peered inside. He reached in and pulled out a box the size of a small cooler.

"Can't be much treasure in there," Stone said aloud.

"More valuable than any treasure you know." Hoffer closed the footlocker and carefully placed the small box on top. Using the hex key once again, he opened it. A strange greenish glow emanated from inside, lighting Hoffer's face. He was smiling. "*Wunderbar!*"

Hoffer stood up and looked at the guides. "We have it. You know what to do."

"Wait!" Stone shouted. "Where's the gold? The jewels?"

"And the scrolls?" Professor Thomas's voice was weak, defeated. "Where are the scrolls?"

"There's nothing of the sort," Dieter shouted from the rear of the room.

One of the guides shone his flashlights over at where Dieter was standing and all eyes turned to him. He was holding the stick grenade from the booby trap.

The detonator cord was dangling ominously from it.

"Jesus Christ, Karl!" Kara cried. "What are you doing?"

"Preventing another holocaust," was his curt reply. He pushed the grenade out in front of him. "Move away from the box, Hoffer—and your goons, too."

Hoffer and his men reluctantly complied, backing slowly away from the box.

This was getting too confusing for Nash. *Nazi treasure? Scrolls? Now a holocaust?* "Dieter. What the devil is going on?" Nash asked.

"There's no lost Nazi treasure or ancient scrolls in that box," Dieter said. "Just the seeds of a second holocaust perpetuated by them." He pointed the grenade at Hoffer. "Tell them!" he ordered.

Hoffer just stood there. He refused to speak.

"Then I will," Dieter growled. He walked to the open metal box at his feet, waving the armed grenade from side to side, and pulled out a vial of greenish glowing liquid. He stood up and showed it to the group. "This is what they're after, and they used you, Stone, with the help of Nash there, to find it."

"What is it?" Kara asked.

"An ancient bacteria. A bacteria no human being has a defense against. And they plan to use it to create civil war in Europe."

"Are you out of your mind, Dieter?" Stone shouted.

"How do you know this?" Nash asked.

Dieter looked over at Kara. "Several weeks ago, your father came to me for help. He told me that he found something strange in his research on the hollow earth theory."

187

"Why come to you?" Kara asked.

"Because I am a World War Two scholar and a good friend."

"So, what did my father say?" Kara's voice was shaky.

"He asked me for help in researching some of his findings," Dieter continued. "I realized he found this Station, an old Nazi base that held a terrible secret. And he had inadvertently uncovered a neo-Nazi organization called the Black Sun, financed and controlled by Hoffer's boss, Adrian Adler. Adler had been searching for this base for many years."

"Go on," Nash prodded. "Who is this Adler?"

"Adler is the CEO and Chairman of the Board of Volks-Agrarindustrie," Dieter informed them. "It's actually a conglomerate of companies that rule over an immense agri-business empire. This empire not only grew, packaged and distributed food to countries throughout Europe, but had a lucrative research and development arm creating genetically modified foods."

"And my father was murdered for that?"

"I'm sorry, Kara. Somehow, they found out about your father's research and the fact that he had accidentally stumbled upon their conspiracy. Before he died, he told me to find Nash and uncover the plot. You did that for me."

"Then why frame Jeremy for his murder?" Kara had tears in her eyes.

"Your father said Nash was the only person who could untangle the web of clues that he pieced together." Dieter looked down into the metal box. "Now, this poison must be destroyed, and disaster averted."

Dieter raised his arm and was about to pull the detonator cord when Stone shouted, "You madman. You'll kill us all!" He leapt at Dieter, throwing him over a desk and onto the floor.

The two struggled behind the upturned desk as Stone grabbed Dieter's hand to stop him from pulling the detonator cord.

As the two men struggled, one of Hoffer's henchmen fired shots at the two struggling men, and the others scrambled for cover.

Hoffer reached out and stopped him from firing another round. He motioned for them to grab the metal box and exit the room.

Stone held Dieter's arm with a grip like a vise. He slammed the arm onto the ground several times trying to make Dieter drop the grenade. When that failed, Stone rolled onto him and punched him in the face several times. Dieter's head rolled to the side, and he lay still. Stone reached down and pulled the grenade out of Dieter's hand, but the detonator cord was wrapped around his finger. Stone's tug pulled it out of the grenade.

"Take cover!" Stone shouted. He hefted Dieter over his shoulder and jumped through the door into the next room.

Nash, Kara and Thomas sprawled out on the ground behind some of the old equipment in the room.

Just before the explosion, Nash rolled on top of Kara to shield her body. After a deafening roar, Nash felt a searing heat on his back and heard the sound of the ceiling collapsing in a rain of rock and ice.

A Runic Clue

Hoffer and his two henchmen ran towards the crevasse. When they got to the ropes, an explosion shook the ground below them. Smoke and mist filled the caverns.

Satisfied that the others were dead, he slipped into his harness. He clutched the small box in one hand and the rope in the other. The two men tightened the slack in the rope and pulled him to the top, then followed suit.

They hiked back through the swirling snow to the rock out-croppings near the two snow cats. The guides started down the hill, but Hoffer said, "Wait a minute."

He set the box on the ground and removed his backpack. He took the satellite phone out and punched several buttons and spoke quickly into the phone. When he was finished, he pointed to a flat area of ice about a mile to their south. "We'll take one of the snow cats there, and the chopper will pick us up. Let's get moving."

"Are you alright?" Nash asked Kara as he rolled off from her.

"I-I think so." She sat up and looked around.

"And I'm fine, too," Professor Thomas said. "Thanks for asking."

The three got to their feet and surveyed the wreckage that was once a room. Pieces of rock ceiling had collapsed from the blast, covering most of the room, and the air was filled with grey silt and flakes of ice. Both exit doors were completely blocked by debris.

"We were lucky," Nash commented, looking around the room. "I'm guessing that old grenade lost much of its muster. It could have been worse."

"Lucky?" Professor Thomas laughed nervously. "Well, I suppose we could be dead." He paused a moment to take in all that he had experienced. "Tell me, Nash," he huffed. "Is this what you call scholarly research?"

"Where are Karl and that fortune hunter?" Kara asked.

"Stone pulled Dieter through that door." Nash pointed to the large pile of ice and rock hiding the door completely.

"Did you hear that?" Professor Thomas asked.

"Quiet," Kara said. "Listen."

Voices were coming from behind the rubble leading to the next room.

"It sounds like Karl!" Kara cried. She ran over to what once was an entrance to the adjacent room. "Karl! Is that you? Are you alright?"

A muffled voice behind the debris replied, "Yes. We're both okay. We're digging from this side. You do the same on yours."

Several minutes later, Stone and Dieter appeared from the debris, but only a few seconds passed when Stone jumped at Dieter and pinned him against a wall. "You stupid son-of-bitch," he screamed. "You were willing to kill us all!"

Dieter offered no resistance and waited for Stone to do his worst, but Nash pulled him off. "That's enough!" yelled Nash. "We have bigger problems now."

But Stone would not be sated. He ranted on. "I don't believe this," he shouted at no one in particular. "That son-of-bitch, Adler, tricked me!" He repeated over and over that he had a deal. That Dieter tricked him into helping him get into this predicament.

"I wouldn't talk, Stone," Kara angrily cried. "You and Dieter used Jeremy for your own ends."

"Adler tricked me. And this son-of-a-bitch convinced me to go along with the whole thing and then tried to kill us all."

"Alright," Nash shouted. "Let's take it down a notch, folks." Nash needed them calm. "Whoever did what to whom is of little consequence now." He gave Stone a long, hard look. "Just who or what in the devil are you, anyway?"

Stone calmed down and sat on a piece of wooden table. "As you might suspect, I'm a treasure hunter and soldier of fortune."

"How did you get involved with this guy, Adler?" Nash queried.

Stone looked around at the others. "Treasure hunting is not cheap. It takes a lot of money to mount an expedition like this."

"So Adler financed this?"

"In a way. I was in Berlin looking for clues to the lost Reichsbank gold reserves—"

"Lost Reichsbank gold?" Kara interrupted.

"Yes. Just days before Berlin fell, the Nazis spirited away the gold in the Reichsbank vaults to potash mines in southern Germany. After the war, the gold was discovered, and an accounting was done and compared to the Reichsbank records. There were gold bars that were unaccounted for. A lot of them, actually. As the story goes, the missing gold is still somewhere below the Reichsbank in a maze of tunnels and bunkers under Berlin.

"We have documented accounts that the gold was taken out of the bank through the tunnels that make up the subway system running throughout Berlin. We also know that the *ghost station*, the main subway station in East Berlin that was under the Reichstag building complex, was used by the Nazis to move the gold through the metro network and out of the city. This *ghost station* was buried after the war.

"I knew if I could find it, I would find the remaining gold."

"How did Adler fit into the picture?" Nash asked. "Did he finance this wild gold hunt of yours?"

"No. Adler told me he was close to finding this Station Two One One and the lost Nazi treasure in it. He said he would finance my Reichsbank expedition if I would help him with this one."

"And you would get a share of the Nazi treasure from this station?" Nash asked.

"Well, yes. He offered me ten percent of anything we found."

"And what about the scrolls? Were they real?" asked the professor.

"You got me," Stone shrugged. "I thought you could get me to Nash so..."

"Yeah," Thomas sneered. *So.*

"No." Stone looked around at the group again. "Listen. I'm sorry, professor. Adler said Nash was necessary for this operation to succeed, but he wasn't cooperating. I did my research and found the connection between the two of you. I thought you could get me to Nash so—"

"What about my father?" Kara said turning to Dieter. "Tell us what he uncovered that cost him his life, and why was Jeremy framed for it?"

"I can't imagine why they framed Nash," Dieter replied. "But I do know that you've made a very powerful enemy."

"I've heard that before," Nash said. "Who is it?"

"I don't know that either."

"You're not just some scholarly researcher, are you?"

Dieter stared down at his feet then a determined look crossed his face. "I'm a member of *Operation Last Chance*," he said.

"Christ," Stone explained. "You're a Nazi hunter!"

"For the uninitiated and just out of curiosity," Professor Thomas said, "What is Operation Last Chance."

"It's a group that still seeks justice after the war." Dieter stepped into the center of the group. "Operation Last Chance's objective is to track down ex-Nazis still hiding and bring them to justice. The Black Sun never really went away. Although illegal, it was kept alive and fully restored by neo-Nazis, some of them very rich and very powerful."

"Like Volks-Agrarindustrie?" Nash questioned.

"Correct. But they are not alone. They are part of a very large international grouping of companies whose mission is something we have not been able to decipher."

"If what you are saying is correct, what about this bacteria and a new holocaust?"

"We at Operation Last Chance believe the Volks-Agrarindustrie has a secret lab somewhere under Berlin—somewhere in the thousands of unmapped tunnels and bunkers."

"Why down there?" asked Kara. "Why not in their regular labs at their research facilities?"

"Because they must be doing something illegal," Nash told her.

"Correct," Dieter said.

"Then why not just expose them?" Professor Thomas asked.

"Right, professor," Stone replied. "Just march into a multi-billion euro company and accuse them of being a front for neo-Nazis?"

"And since we don't know where this secret lab is, we can't shut it down. The only option left was to stop them at the source." He pointed to the floor at his feet. "We couldn't let them get their hands on more bacteria."

"More?" Nash stepped forward. "They had it before this expedition?"

"Yes. You all saw their latest test on our way to the cargo jet."

"All of the dead bodies in the Jewish neighborhood?" Kara said softly. "My God!"

"That was a small sampling," Dieter said. "I knew I had to stop them, no matter the cost."

"What about this bacteria?" Nash pressed. "Where did it come from?"

"Just before the war," Dieter began, "the Germans did extensive exploration of Antarctica. Specifically, this region we're in."

"Yes," replied Nash. "We're quite familiar with that fact."

"Right. Anyway," Dieter continued, "they discovered vast regions that were surprisingly free of ice, as well as warm water lakes and cave inlets. They even found a large hot-water geothermal lake deep below the surface. These lakes haven't seen the light of day for millions of years."

"And these lakes contained a bacteria that also hadn't been seen before." Professor Thomas noted.

"Yes," Dieter replied. "The Germans discovered a primordial bacteria strain that neither animals nor humans were immune to. They speculated it was a pre-historic life form that had been preserved in the Antarctic ice. Somehow, their scientists turned it into a biological weapon."

"But if they plan to use this weapon to create a second holocaust," Kara said, "what's to stop everyone in the population from contracting the disease and not just a specific ethnic group?"

"And how did they get it into the population in the first place?" Nash asked.

"Through the food," Dieter replied. "Through genetically enhanced ethnic foods that are kosher and halal and other ethnic type foods."

"But non-ethnic people eat those foods," Professor Thomas interjected. "How come they didn't contract the disease?"

"And why did the epidemic only last a short time while the foods were always available?" Kara asked.

Dieter shook his head. "I'm afraid I don't have the answers to either of those questions. That's why we knew we'd never be able to convince the authorities to believe us." He paused a moment. "But I do know this. In less than a week, Muslims throughout Europe will be celebrating Eid, the end of Ramadan and their fasting."

"And if they launch the bioweapon," Nash noted, "when Muslims are breaking their fast and eating the halal foods supplied by the biggest ethic food distributor in Europe and start mysteriously dying—"

"It will scare the hell out of the indigent Europeans," Dieter continued, "who are already spinning theories about ethnic diseases contaminating the natural German population."

"That would be the spark that ignites a simmering hatred over Muslin integration." Professor Thomas noted.

"And that same spark would start a civil war," Stone added. "Tailor made by the Black Sun.

"Exactly," Dieter replied. "We have to get back to Berlin and find a way to stop them."

"And how are we going to do that?" Stone asked. "We're trapped down here."

"If there's one thing that a decade of crawling around in caves and underground bunkers looking for treasure has taught me," Stone said, "is that there is almost always a second tunnel or escape somewhere."

"That's true," Professor Thomas added. "Even the pyramids in Egypt had escape tunnels."

"Look around," Nash said, "there may be an exit somewhere." The small group searched around the rubble, running the beam of their helmet lights over every nook and cranny in the dilapidated room.

"There's nothing," Stone said. "I would have bet that we'd find another way out of here."

"We need a treasure map with a big X on it," Kara said.

Stone laughed. "I've seen more than my share of treasure maps—both real and manufactured—but I've never seen one where X marks the spot."

"Except for maybe in an Indiana Jones movie," Professor Thomas said, hoping to lighten the mood.

"What about the other room?" Dieter asked. "It only had one way in and out."

"It's worth a try," Stone said. "I'll crawl back through the hole and check it out."

"I'll go with you." Nash followed Stone through the small hole in the debris.

Once inside, Stone and Nash began to search the smaller room.

After several minutes, Stone said, "There's a weird looking symbol on the wall over here, but there's no door or anything."

Nash moved over next to him and shined his helmet light on the marking. The symbol was carved into the stone. It stood about three feet high and looked like a reversed number seven.

"I'll be damned," Nash said, excitedly.

"What is it?"

"Get the others," Nash said. "I think we found our way out."

Stone scrambled back to the small tunnel joining the two rooms and called the others.

Once everyone was standing in front of the symbol, Nash turned to Kara. "Let me see your father's key ring?"

She reached into her pocket and pulled it out.

Nash held it up in front of his helmet light so that everyone could see that the symbol on the keychain matched the symbol carved into the wall.

"They're the same," Professor Thomas admitted. "But how does that get us out of here?"

"An old Muslin friend of Kara's father told us that this is a figure from the runic alphabet."

"The letter *L*," Kara said.

"He also said that it stood for *laguz* which roughly translates to *water in a well, bubbling up from secret depths*." Nash put his hands on the wall on both sides of the symbol. "The wall is cooler around the symbol."

"I don't understand," Kara said.

"It's not the same material as the rest of the wall," Nash explained. "I'm betting it's concrete. Someone give me one of those rocks. One about the size of a football."

Dieter brought him a rock from the debris pile. Nash gripped it with both hands, lifted it above his head and smashed it into the center of the large rune. A large crack appeared in the wall. Nash hit it again, and the rock smashed completely through the wall.

As everyone moved in for a closer look, a rush of frigid air blew out into their faces.

Nash reached into the hole, grabbed the back of the wall, and pulled. He danced backwards as a large chunk of concrete fell to the floor in front of him. He moved back to the wall and leaned as far inside of the hole as he could, shining his helmet light all around. He pulled himself out of the hole and said with relief and delight, "There's a circular stairwell attached to the wall. It goes down as far as my light will see."

"I'll be damned," Professor Thomas said, laughing. "It looks like X really does mark the spot."

The Lake

Nash peered down into the ever-widening passage as his helmet light followed an iron handrail attached to the metal stairs, circling into the shaft below.

"There's a handrail of sorts attached to the wall."

"Is it safe?" Professor Thomas asked.

"I don't know," Nash replied. "The stairway is made out of metal, but who knows how old it is, and it feels pretty damp in there."

"It seems to be our only hope of getting out of here," Professor Thomas observed. "I just don't want to die doing it."

Nash turned to Dieter. "There's still a backpack in the other room. The guard carrying the box of bacteria left it. It had climbing gear attached to it."

"I'll get it." Dieter went back to the small tunnel in the debris blocking the door between the two rooms.

Dieter returned a minute later with the backpack. Kara opened it and started rummaging through it. She pulled out a coiled nylon rope and started to unwind it.

"We need to loop this around something stable," she said. "We can use it to help support our weight on the staircase."

"And to save our necks if we fall," Professor Thomas added.

"I was purposely leaving that part out," Kara said, laughing.

Nash and Dieter pushed a heavy desk up to the wall just below the entrance to the tunnel and looped the rope around it while Kara rigged another climbing harness for all of the group.

"This is going to be different than when we came down here," she warned them. "You won't be repelling. We'll just use the rope as a safety harness."

"Oh, thank God," Professor Thomas exclaimed breathlessly. "I don't know if I could have done that again."

"That surprises me, professor," Dieter said. "You look like you're in better shape than I am."

"Physically, I'm fit," Professor Thomas replied. "But I have a bad case of acrophobia, you know."

"I never knew you were afraid of heights," Nash told him.

"Well, I don't do much climbing at the university," he said, laughing nervously.

"I'll go first." Kara said. "You can follow me when I give you the all clear."

"Maybe I should go first," Nash offered.

"I'm the only experienced climber here," she said. "Plus, I weigh less than any of you. Let me test the stairs first."

She climbed up on the desk and tied the nylon rope around her midsection. "Keep a little bit of tension on this line."

Nash grabbed the rope and wrapped it around his waist while Kara climbed through the hole in the wall and lowered herself to the first step. The stairway groaned from her weight but held fast. She pulled on the handrail with both hands. Satisfied it would hold, she slowly started her descent. When she reached the fifth step, the rope tied around her waist tightened and pulled her back a little.

"Hey," she yelled up the tunnel. "What's happening."

"Oh, sorry," Nash replied. "Was that too tight?"

"For a noose, no, but for a safety rope, yeah, a little."

"Okay," Nash said. "I think I've got it now."

Kara felt the tension around her midsection slack. She smiled to herself and continued to descend the circular stairway. Her helmet light finally shined on the floor below. She looked up and gauged that she was about halfway down.

"Looks like it's about forty feet down," she yelled. "I'll be on the ground—"

The step she was standing on buckled in the middle making the stairway sway a little. Kara grabbed the handrail and pulled herself back up a step. "There's a broken step about halfway down. You'll have to watch for it."

It took several more minutes, but she finally reached the bottom.

"I'm untying the rope," she called up. "Pull it back up and tie it around the next person while I look around."

"Don't go too far away," Nash called down. "It may not be safe."

Kara, ignoring the concern in his voice, stooped down and walked through the indented arches of the narrow long tunnel.

The ice gave off a soft but chilling light—sort of a glowing blue-green color, as light from somewhere was filtered through the overhanging snow and ice. The glow completely outlined the ice cave from the frozen floor to the ceiling. Shards of bluish stalactite spikes of ice hung from the ceiling of the corridor leading to the inner cave chambers.

Kara switched off her helmet light and the glow seemed to get brighter.

She was about to turn back to the stairway when she heard something behind her.

She turned and said, "I told you to wait until—"

Standing in front of her, and as surprised as she was at the uncomfortable situation, was a large elephant seal. Kara stood perfectly still. Overcoming its initial surprise, the lumbering behemoth grunted once, turned, and slipped back into the hole in the floor of the ice it came from. A few beats later, Kara heard the sound of splashing water.

Kara let out a long breath and sighed. She returned to the stairway. Once there, she called up to Nash. "It's alright to come down. Just take it slow and be careful."

"Who's next?" Dieter asked.

Nash started to reply, but Professor Thomas stepped forward and said, "I'd better go next. I'm afraid I'll lose my nerve if I wait any longer."

"It'll be fine, Raymond. We'll have you tethered to the safety line the whole way down." Nash put his hand on the professor's shoulder.

They tied the line around his waist and fastened it to his climbing harness. Dieter and Stone took up the slack as Nash helped the professor climb onto the desk.

"I'm just not sure I can do this." Professor Thomas looked through the hole in the wall into the darkness below.

"Kara's at the bottom, and we've got you from this side," Nash reassured him. "If we have to, we can just lower you all the way down."

Professor Thomas took a deep breath and climbed through the hole and onto the top step of the winding stairway. He stood there for a long moment before starting his descent.

Each step made the stairway creak and groan under his weight. When he was about halfway down, the stairway began to shutter. He froze and said a silent prayer until it settled.

Professor Thomas leaned forward and looked at Kara's helmet light below him. He guessed it to be less than twenty feet away.

All at once, the step he was standing on broke through and he fell forward. The safety rope tightened around his waist and crotch. He screamed as he hung suspended in midair.

Stone and Dieter were dragged forward to the large desk. They braced their feet against the bottom of it and pulled back on the safety rope with all of their might. Nash jumped onto the desk and leaned his body through the hole in the wall.
"We've got you, Raymond. You're not gonna fall."

Professor Thomas had stopped screaming, but he was breathing so quickly that he started to hyperventilate.

Nash watched as he started to curl his body into the fetal position. When he lifted his legs, his center of gravity changed, turning him upside down. He let out one last scream and then fell silent. His body relaxed and slumped forward, his arms and legs dangling.

"My God!" Nash shouted. "Kara, I think he passed out. "I'm coming down after him."

"Wait!" she cried out. "Your weight may be too much for the stairs. Several of them have already broken through. Let me climb up from here and when I do, you guys can lower him with the rope."

Nash hesitated for a moment as he watched his friend swinging helplessly. He finally called, "Okay, let us know when you are in position."

He pulled his head out of the hole and climbed down from the desk. He went behind Stone and Dieter and wrapped a length of the rope around his waist three times, then he sat down on the floor.

"I've got a hold," he called. "Stone, relax your grip and allow his weight to come back to me."

Stone did as asked and the rope tightened on Nash. Dieter did the same thing and Nash was pulled a few inches closer to the desk.

"Come behind me and help me stand up when Kara gets into position."

"I'm right below him," Kara shouted. "I can't hold his weight on my own, but I can guide him down."

"On my count of three," Nash called and nodded to the other men. "One … Two … Three!"

On three, he allowed his body to be pulled into a standing position while Stone and Dieter held his shoulders. About three feet of rope slid through the hole in the wall.

"Okay," Kara shouted. "I have him."

Nash slowly wrapped the rope around his body several more times. "Don't let me move forward," he cautioned. He slowly started to turn clockwise, allowing more of the rope to slide through the hole in the wall. Dieter held his upper body while Stone wrapped another section of the back of the rope around his waist each time he turned.

It seemed to take forever, but Kara finally shouted up. "He's on the ground. He's okay. He's awake and talking now." She paused for a few seconds. "I've got the rope untied from his harness. You can pull it back up."

Dieter retrieved the rope while Nash sat down on the floor and took several deep breaths.

"We'll have to repel down," Dieter observed. "We don't need to go through that again."

"Agreed." Nash laughed nervously.

When they were all at the base of the stairway, Dieter grabbed the rope and yanked it hard. The loose end shot back up through the tunnel, around the desk and landed at his feet.

"Karl!" Kara cried. "No!"

"What? I—"

"We have no way of getting back up there now," she told them. "If this turns out to be a dead end, we're stuck down here."

"I didn't think about that," Dieter admitted apologetically.

"What's done is done," Nash said. "Let's just move forward."

Kara led them through the arches and into the narrow passageway. Each of them switched off their helmet lights as they stepped into the cavern. They walked in single file, moving deeper into the ice chamber.

"See the walls?" Professor Thomas ran his hand along the ice. "They were smooth before. Now look. This scalloping indicates erosion by air currents."

"Maybe Nash was right," Dieter said hopefully, "and we'll find an exit to the surface."

A blast of cold air chilled their faces.

"That's wind," Stone cried out. *"Wind!"*

The group walked further, and as they walked, a crystal palace more than fifty feet high started to take shape. The ethereal blue light got brighter as they walked further into the cavern.

There was a large chamber to the rear of the grotto. Something big moved quickly across the opening to the chamber, and there was a large splash.

"Did you see that?" Dieter whispered.

"What was it?" Stone took a step backwards.

"I don't know." Nash's voice sounded nervous. "It was moving too fast, but it was big."

Kara burst out laughing. "It was a seal. I saw one when I first came down the ladder."

"Nice of you to warn us," Professor Thomas said.

"Sorry, I forgot about it." Kara said, still laughing. "I had a lot on my mind, what with saving you and all."

"Yeah, thanks." Professor Thomas looked at the ground.

"I heard it go into the water," Nash told them. "Let's check it out."

As they moved into the rear chamber, a twisting ice bridge came into view. It spanned over a vast lake of greenish-blue water.

"This must be the lake where they found the primordial bacteria," Stone said.

"How do we get across?" Dieter asked. "There's no other way out of here."

"Over that ice bridge to there." Nash pointed to a ray of daylight coming from above the almost sheer ice cliffs surrounding the lake. "That's our way out."

"You call that a bridge?" Professor Thomas said. "It looks more like a giant icicle."

"We don't have many options, Raymond."

"This just keeps getting better and better," Thomas whined.

"It'll be easier this time," Kara told him. "We'll form a daisy chain. You can be in the middle." She took off her backpack and pulled out the nylon rope and the d-ring harnesses. "Put the harnesses back on."

When they were finished, she said, "We'll move across in six-foot intervals. Clip your d-rings to the rope."

"I'll go first," Nash said.

Kara stepped close to him. "Maybe you should go after Professor Thomas."

Nash looked at his old friend. He had his eyes closed and was shifting his weight from foot to foot nervously.

"Stay near him," Kara said. "Your voice may help him get through this."

Nash nodded and walked behind Professor Thomas. He hooked his d-ring onto the rope and then leaned forward and similarly fastened the professor to the rope ahead of him.

Kara led the group onto the ice bridge. She was about thirty feet out with the professor six feet behind her followed by Nash, Stone, and Dieter when the ice started to crack.

The section directly behind Kara sheered away with a frightening sound and fell into the water making a huge splash. Professor Thomas tried to catch his balance, but he toppled over the edge. Nash pulled back hard on the guide rope, while Kara leaped across the abyss and slid back down the bridge.

"Help me," the professor screamed. "My God, help me." With nothing but air below his dangling feet, he swung there back and forth, in the icy space above the lake.

Nash and Kara pulled back on their ends of the rope, pulling the professor to the edge of the broken bridge.

"Almost lost you there, old man." Nash smiled as they pulled Professor Thomas back up onto the ice bridge.

The professor crawled onto the remainder of the bridge and rolled onto his back. He took several deep breaths.

Nash looked back on what was left of the ice bridge and sighed, "Well, that's that."

"Now what?" Dieter asked.

"There's only one avenue left," Kara said, pointing straight up to an ice ledge winding around a sheer cliff, smooth as blue glass, to the sunlight above. "It's not an ideal way out, but it's all we have, and I think we can do it. We *have* to do it!"

She emptied the backpack at her feet. "There's ice screws here."

"And what do we do with those?" Dieter asked.

"We do a running belay," Kara replied.

"I'm afraid to ask, but how do we do that?" Nash replied.

She gathered up the ice screws, placed them in the pocket of her parka, then leaned down again and wrapped the coil of nylon rope over her shoulder. "Follow me."

She led them to the start of the narrow ledge at the base of the ice cliff. She walked several feet up onto the edge and rotated the first screw into the ice, attached a d-ring from her pocket and fed the rope through it. She walked up further along the frozen path, screwed in another ice screw anchor, attached a d-ring, and fed her rope through that.

"The rope and these anchors will hold us if any of us should slip off the path," she informed them, looking back over her shoulder. "Just attach and feed your rope through the d-rings as you go. When you get to an ice screw, detach your d-ring, and reattach it onto the rope on the other side. Got it?"

Everyone but Professor Thomas nodded. He just kept staring back at the demolished ice bridge. Nash hooked his d-ring onto the rope and then reached behind him and did the same thing with the professor's. He turned and gave Kara a thumbs up sign.

"Follow me, and don't look down," Kara ordered and began to inch her way forward.

Step by careful step, the group made its way up the frozen narrow ledge. Short moments of terror came and passed when pieces of the ice ledge crumbled off as they walked.

Nash opened and closed his fists several times. His hands were getting numb, and it was becoming increasingly difficult to reattach his and the professor's d-rings onto the rope as they passed each ice screw. He looked back and saw Dieter working his hands in the same manner.

After about an hour of climbing, Kara neared the top of the ice cliff. She could see the path leading into the streaming sunlight. "We're almost there," she called back to them.

"Thank God!" Professor Thomas said, rushing forward.

The ice ledge crumbled beneath his feet, making him stop in his tracks. He flattened his body against the wall and wouldn't move.

Dieter started to move forward, but the ledge in front of him broke away in several large chunks, leaving a lip about three feet wide for the professor to stand on.

Kara moved quickly back to Nash and said, "Jeremy, tie this around you and hold it tight while I work my way back along the ledge."

He did as she instructed, and she pushed her body against his as she moved along him and started inching down the narrow ledge.

Nash watched and held his breath as she worked her way toward the broken section of the ledge. Small shards of the ledge started to fall away after every few steps she took.

Kara knelt down and looked across the gap at Professor Thomas. He was holding onto one of the ice screws.

"Are you okay?" she asked.

He didn't answer or move, but his eyes were open.

"We're going to pull you across, professor," she said calmly. "But we can't do it without your help."

He squeezed his eyes shut for a few seconds, and then blinked several times. "What do I do?" he whispered.

"We're going to pull the rope tight against you and I need you to jump over to where I am." She stood up and nodded to Nash, Stone and Dieter who pulled the guide rope tight.

"Professor, I need you to unhook your d-ring and place it on the other side of that ice screw you're hanging on to."

"Okay," he gasped, but he didn't move.

"Professor," she said. "Please help us."

In one quick movement, he unhooked the d-ring, swung it around the screw and rehooked it. He grabbed back onto the screw and shut his eyes again.

"Okay," she said, hoping to calm the terrorized professor. "We're almost there. When I count to three, I need you to jump across the ledge." She backed up several steps. "Don't worry. The rope will keep you from falling."

He nodded his head quickly.

"Ready?" One ... Two ... Three!"

207

Professor Thomas opened his eyes, leaped across the opening, and stumbled into Kara's arms. She grabbed him and pulled his shaking body around hers. He stopped at the next ice screw and clutched it tightly.

"Now it's your turn, Karl." Kara stood up and took a step towards him. The ledge below her feet broke free sending her sailing toward the lake below.

The nylon rope screamed through the d-rings attached to the ice screws along the frozen wall, pulling hard on them as it went. As it did, Kara's weight popped them off the wall, one at a time.

Nash and Stone dug into the slippery ice as they fought hard to gain a secure footing. Nash was pulled off balance and he was flung forward, landing on his face. Stone slipped and fell backwards, stopping Nash from going over the edge.

"Nash!" Stone shouted dropping the nylon rope. "Untie the line."

Nash rolled over and untied himself just as the last two ice screws popped off the ledge. The nylon line ripped out of Stone's hands, streaked past Nash, and flew into the void below.

Nash crawled to the edge and looked over. Kara was dangling, feet first, tangled in the rope about six feet below him.

Dieter crouched down and peered at Kara. He grabbed the rope and started swinging her below him, slowly as first, then faster and faster building up the momentum—swinging her left and right.

Kara realized what he was doing and yelled, "No, Karl! Don't!"

"Get ready to grab the ledge," he shouted as he continued to swing her back and forth.

"Karl," she shouted. "It's not stable."

"Grab it now!" he shouted, swinging her harder.

Kara reached her hand toward the ledge and Nash grabbed for her but couldn't hold onto her. The next time she swung up, she and Nash grabbed each other's arms, and he pulled her back on top of him.

Dieter screamed as his ice screw tore out of the wall. He pitched forward, and fell, dragging Kara back down with him.

The rope started to cut into the rim of ice as they teetered back and forth.

"It won't hold us both," Dieter said, pulling himself up and grabbing his d-ring.

"No, Karl! It will hold," Kara pleaded.

Another chunk of ice broke off and the rope slipped about two feet lower.

"I'm sorry for everything," Dieter said gently. Then he unhooked his d-ring just as the next section of the ice broke away.

"Karl!" Kara cried as he plummeted into the frigid lake below.

Professor Thomas fell forward and vomited several times.

"Kara!" Nash yelled.

She did not respond.

"Kara?" Nash said gently.

"Please give me a minute," she managed between sobs.

The cold wind whistling eerily through the opening in the ice cave masked her crying.

"Okay," Kara called. "Pull me up."

Nash, Stone, and Professor Thomas pulled the rope hand over hand until they had her back on the ledge.

Nash pulled her into his arms and hugged her tightly.

"He gave his life for me," she sobbed.

Nash nodded and pulled her closer, allowing her to cry on his shoulder.

He held her for a while longer, then to Nash's surprise, she straightened up and, in a steeled voice said, "Let's get the fuck out of here."

Off To Atlantis

Exhausted and hungry, limbs numb from the cold, and in need of water, the group emerged from the ice cave as the sun was setting.

"Over there!" Stone pointed to a snow-covered hulk about three hundred yards to their right.

"It's one of the snow cats," Nash said, marveling at their good fortune.

"We must have gone in a circle underground and ended up where we started," Stone observed. He squinted in the low light and added, "Doesn't look like anyone is there."

They jogged toward the snow cat and stopped about fifty yards from it. They all knelt.

Stone looked around. "I don't see anyone."

"Where are Hoffer and his two goons?" Kara asked.

"They probably took the other one back to the helicopter," Nash guessed.

Satisfied, Stone stood up and said, "Let's go."

When they reached the snow cat, Stone climbed inside and started it. It roared to life, rattling and blowing smoke. He gave the others thumbs up signal, and they eagerly climbed inside.

There was a canteen lying on the floor of the passenger side. Professor Thomas picked it up and took several large gulps.

"They may have poisoned the water," Kara warned as he drank.

The professor spit the water still in his mouth all over the inside of the windshield.

Kara took the canteen from him. "I was only joking, professor." She took a large swallow of the water and handed it to Nash.

"What do we do now," Professor Thomas asked. "We can't go back to their base. They think we're dead."

"If this is the one I came in, the driver put the map in that glove box." Stone pointed to the dashboard in front of the professor.

He fumbled it open, pulled out the map and handed it to Stone. Stone unfolded it and began to study it."

"What are you looking for?" Nash watched him tracing a route with his finger.

"Some friends of mine have a research base near here." Stone looked from person to person. "Well, not exactly near here, but I think we can reach it."

"And if we can't?" Kara asked.

"Then we die trying," Stone reasoned with half a laugh. "In my opinion, that's better than dying just sitting here."

"What base and what friends?" Nash asked, hopefully.

"Some people I know who are hunting for Atlantis."

Nash rolled his eyes. "Are all of your friends as crazy as you?"

"And as dangerous?" Professor Thomas added. "I'm going to die out here because you lied to me about the scrolls."

"I'm serious," Stone said. "The legend states that the King of Atlantis built the capital city that consisted of defensive concentric rings, roofed over so they were subterranean. At the very center was the temple of Poseidon surrounded by a wall made of solid gold."

"More damned treasure hunters," Professor Thomas cried, annoyed.

"I'm sorry I lied to you, Professor, but you were on a treasure hunt of your own."

"I never..."

"Your scrolls may not have been made of gold, but they are a treasure...if they even exist at all."

"Oh, they exist," Professor Thomas snapped quickly.

"But Atlantis or Nazi treasure don't?" Stone asked.

"Okay," Nash said. "We see your point. It's just that the legend of Atlantis is a lot more far-fetched."

"My friends have aerial photographs that clearly show a circular structure or pyramid formation beneath the ice of Antarctica. They setup camp about the same time I started to organize this Nazi treasure trip. Otherwise, I'd probably be with them now."

"I'm willing to believe in fairies at this point if we can find someone to get us back to Europe and stop this thing," Kara said. "My father, my uncle, and Karl all died because of it."

"Do you think we can make it on the fuel we have in the tank?"

"We have just over half a tank left, so I'm pretty sure we can. Then again," Stone said with a wink, "that's our only option."

"Why not just alert the authorities to the Black Sun's plot?" Professor Thomas asked.

Stone shook his head. "No matter who we talk to, who will take the word of two fugitives, a fortune hunter, and a dusty old college professor against a multi-billion euro conglomerate?"

"Stone's right," Nash said. "We have to do it ourselves. We have less than a week to get back to Germany and figure out a way to stop Adler. The question is, how?"

"I can get us back into Germany," Stone replied,"but the rest is up to you."

"And how will you do that?" Kara asked.

"I have a vast network of contacts. For starters, my friend in charge of the Atlantis mission should be able to arrange transportation to South America and their support base there. From there we go to the Canary Islands."

"What about travel papers?" Nash asked.

"Leave that to me. Once we hit their support base, my contacts can smuggle us into the Canary Islands. And once there—"

"We're in the European Union," interrupted Kara, "And we can travel through the EU without passports to Germany."

"Exactly," Stone replied.

"We're forgetting one thing," Professor Thomas sighed. "We don't know where the Black Sun secret lab is. And even if we did, you said we'd never convince the authorities."

"Whatever we can do," Nash replied, "we'll first have to get to Stone's friends."

He nodded at Stone who dropped the snow cat into drive.

Anything For A Friend

"Wake up," Stone said. "We're here."

The sun was just beginning to rise, and Nash saw a small camp in the distance. A geodesic dome sat in the middle of a bleak icy white landscape. About twenty feet in diameter, it was surrounded by an assortment of small, colored nylon tents. There was an old C-47 transport plane next to the snow-covered camp.

"I'm freezing," Professor Thomas grumbled. "What happened to the heater?"

"I turned it off about two hours ago to conserve fuel. We're running on fumes now."

"I hope you're right about them helping us," Kara said, yawning and stretching.

"Trust me," Stone assured them. "Their leader and I are old friends. We go way back."

"That's quite a story." Diane Powers, the American leader of the multi-national *Atlantis Antarctica Search Expedition,* poured herself another glass of vodka and then slid the bottle across the table to Stone. He upended the bottle and took several large swallows.

She surveyed the motley crew of visitors as Stone filled her in on their exploits.

"You really believe what your friend told you?" Diane asked, swirling the drink in her glass. "That some crazy neo-Nazis are going to create a second holocaust to instigate a civil war in Europe?"

"He died helping us try to stop it," Nash said. He looked sympathetically at Kara. "Several people did, actually."

"That would be hard for the authorities to swallow. I can understand your dilemma. I wish I could help."

"You can," Nash said, leaning forward. "The ball's in our court, so we have to get back to Germany as soon as we can and figure a way to stop them."

"Where's your staging base?" Stone asked.

"In Tierra del Fuego."

"Perfect," Stone grinned. "We have a bit of luck there. Can you fly us in on your transport plane?"

"We'll fly you in. No problem," Diane replied, looking at Stone with a warm smile. "Anything for you." She leaned over and placed her hand on Stone's. "This man knows his stuff. His treasure hunting skills led to the recovery of priceless art stolen and hidden away by the Nazis after the war."

"And got paid a pretty commission for it, too, I bet," Professor Thomas scoffed.

"We're happy to be in the presence of such a great humanitarian," Kara cut in. "But how soon can we leave here?"

Diane shrugged and Stone motioned for her to drop the subject. "We're doing a supply run tomorrow. Get some rest and hot food. It isn't gourmet, but it's filling. You'll find some bunks in the next room. Feel free to use them."

"Good," Stone said gratefully. "Can you make arrangements with your contacts in Tierra del Fuego to fly us to the Canary Islands?"

"No problem. I'll just mention your name. I'm sure they know you."

"Christ, Stone," Professor Thomas sighed. "Is there anyone you *don't* know?"

"Well," Stone said, smiling. "I don't have a lot of friends at Interpol."

Diane laughed. "You know that's right."

"What do you mean *us*?" Nash asked.

"What?"

"You said 'fly us.'"

"I'm throwing in with you." Stone smiled at Nash and Kara. "You know. The great humanitarian?"

"I'm not sure that's a good idea," Nash said. "If you are a person of interest to Interpol, it might make traveling a little more difficult."

"Don't forget that I did my research on you before contacting the professor here," Stone said. "I'm not the only one Interpol would love to talk to."

"What does he mean by that, Jeremy?" Professor Thomas looked back and forth between the two men.

"It's nothing," Nash assured him. "Kara and I were mixed up in a—a misunderstanding of sorts."

"Then it's settled," Stone said firmly. "We're going Nazi hunting."

"If that's the case," Diane said, "you're gonna need more than just your dicks in your hand." She winked at Kara. "Present company excluded."

"You always did have a way with words." Stone laughed.

"I'll pull together some light arms and gear for you." Diane told him. "I trust everyone here knows how to handle a gun."

"You have guns?" Professor Thomas was shocked. "On an expedition?"

"Professor," Stone said. "If there's treasure here, I guarantee there are those who would steal it. Don't you think there are people who would do anything to get ahold of your precious scrolls if you had found them?"

Professor Thomas slowly nodded his head.

"Now get some rest and food," Diane said. "You leave for South America tomorrow." She turned to Stone and said, "I'll expect you in my room after dinner." She stepped forward and kissed him deeply.

After she left the room, Nash turned to Stone. "An old friend?"

"You got me," he said, laughing. "She's my ex-wife."

Countdown

Adler smiled as Hoffer told him about the expedition. "And they're all dead?"

"We just made it out of the inner chamber before the grenade went off."

"Thanks to you, the lab has more than enough material," Adler said. "Tomorrow at this time, we'll be witnessing the beginning of the new Reich."

Hoffer clicked his boots together and nodded his head.

"Has everything been checked?" Adler asked.

"And re-checked," Hoffer replied. "The lab sub-station is ready to go, and the Tower broadcast equipment has been re-calibrated for maximum range."

"Any problems with the administration?"

"None. Our license gives us full access to the tower and broadcast equipment. We're ready to cut into the broadcast from the lab when the time comes."

"Secondary back-up?"

"Installed and tested," Hoffer replied confidently.

"I'm sending Stobl there just in case." Adler stood and walked around his desk to Hoffer and grasped his shoulder. "You've done well." He looked at his watch. "Now go. I'll meet you at the lab."

A Note From The Grave

The cargo plane landed smoothly at the airport in Tierra del Fuego.

"Just follow my lead once we get to Customs," Stone told Nash, Kara, and Professor Thomas as they collected their belongings.

"Are you sure these papers will hold up?" Nash asked.

"They always do," Stone said. He held up his passport. "Do I look like a Jason Bartlett?"

"About as much as I look like a Peggy Sullivan," Kara said.

"What about the guns we have in our possession?" Professor Thomas asked. "I don't relish the thought of spending my twilight years trying to tunnel out of some third-world country prison."

"Trust me," Stone said laughing. "We'll have no problems."

They made their way into the terminal and to the Customs counter.

"We're with the Associated Press," Stone said, handing the man his passport. "We're returning home from covering the *Atlantis Antarctica Search Expedition.*

"Did you say Atlantis?"

"Yes, sir," Stone said and winked. "Next week it'll probably be Bigfoot, but it sells papers and news is news, right?"

The Customs agent shook his head and then motioned for the others to hand over their passports.

He stamped them all without even looking at them and then waved them through.

They boarded a private charter and landed at a small general aviation terminal at the Tenerife North Airport in the Canary Islands.

Once again, they breezed through Customs.

"Ever been to the Canary Islands?" Stone asked casually. "Great vacation place. Beautiful beaches, lush resorts, and mild sub-tropical weather year-round."

"Can the travel advisory," Professor Thomas retorted. "We're not here for a vacation. How do we get to Germany?"

Stone shrugged his shoulders and said, "There's a flight to Berlin departing in a few hours. I'm famished. Let's get something to eat while we wait."

They grabbed some sandwiches and drinks, taking seats by the windows of the snack bar. Kara plucked a discarded newspaper from her chair and began to read as Nash and Stone made idle chitchat. Professor Thomas stared out the window at the planes as they passed.

Kara flipped to the "Life" section of the paper and began to read the article about the Muslim Eid ul-Fitr, marking the end of the fasting month of Ramadan.

"We're running out of time," she said. "The end of Ramadan is today."

"We'll do all we can do," Nash said. "We've didn't come this far to give up now."

Kara reached into her pocket and pulled out a folded piece of paper.

"What's that," Stone asked.

"A note from my father."

"May I see it?" he asked.

"Why? She pulled it closer to her.

"The back," he said. "It looks like one of those tourist maps of underground Berlin."

She turned it over and looked on the back as Stone came around to her side of the table.

"I was right. This map shows the locations of where the Nazi government ministries existed—the nerve center of the Nazi party."

Nash looked questioningly at Stone.

"Hitler's chancellery, Goebbels propaganda ministry, and the foreign ministry of the Reich?"

"So?" Kara said.

"You said everything he left you was a clue that eventually led you to where we are now," Stone said. "What was the clue on this map?"

"There wasn't one," Kara said. "At least we never looked for one."

Nash joined them, and the three of them studied the map while Professor Thomas continued to stare out the window.

"What are these dots?" Nash asked. "My German isn't that great."

"It says that the blue dots are the locations to tunnels and the green dots show bunkers that are open to the public in the old Ministry area," Kara told him.

"Today, this section of East Berlin has been replaced with modern apartments," Stone added.

"What does the red dot represent?" Stone asked.

"What red dot?"

"Right there." He pointed to the lone red dot on the map.

Stone lifted the page closer to his face and studied it. "I'll be damned."

"What is it?" Kara asked.

"This dot was placed there by hand." He looked up at Kara. "By your father's hand, I'd be willing to bet."

"It could be another clue," Nash said.

"That dot is behind the old Traffic Ministry building of the Reich." Stone told them. "I think your father found an entrance to the Black Suns' secret underground lab."

"How did you jump to that conclusion?" Nash sat back down.

"I know underground Berlin. I studied the known tunnels and bunkers searching for the Reichstag gold, and this location is new to me." He paused a moment. "And it's near the Reichstag building complex. Near where the lost Nazi gold from the Reichsbank might be."

"What does that have to do with the Black Sun?

Stone straightened up in his chair as if he were going to give a lecture. "To begin with, the Nazis not only built bomb shelters for citizens, but they also built entire bunker cities with plans for highways connecting the buildings of the Nazi Ministry District in today's East Berlin."

"If you say this dot on the hand bill is unknown, why hasn't it been found before?" Kara asked.

"There are thousands of these bunkers throughout Berlin, but only a small percentage have been discovered. Most only recently. Many are privately owned and don't show up on tourist maps." He leaned back in his chair. "It's been reported that building in Hitler's time was a ratio of three to one: One building above and three below ground.

"Take the four-level bunker at Gesundbrunnen at Alexanderplatz in the center of the city. One enters the bunker from an inconspicuous door in the train station there. It just opened to the public and houses an exhibition by local artists."

"Art?" Kara asked.

"And museums and, in one case, a restaurant." Stone continued, "Many of the bunkers found are amazingly well-preserved. Those located in the suburban areas are surrounded now by apartment buildings and offices. Even today, they don't look out of place. You can walk past these bunkers every day, like the one at the old Ministry building your father's map points to, without giving them a passing glance. They have blended into Berlin's cityscape."

"That still doesn't explain why you think this is the Black Sun's lab."

"What else could it be?"

"You said there could be thousands of these bunkers in Berlin," Nash retorted impatiently.

"And an extensive network of underground tunnels," Stone replied, "with one running from the government sector in Mitte to the airport in Tempelhof. Goering could ride in his car the seven kilometers from his Luftwaffe building on Wilhelm Strasse to the airport, in total secrecy. Also connected to this tunnel was the famous Führerbunker."

"I'll buy into the fact that the Black Sun's lab is in one of the privately owned bunkers, but why this one?"

"Because it's the only thing left that we need to find," Stone said. "Kara's father led you to everything else you needed to stop this."

"I hope you're right," Kara said, hopefully.

"I guess we'll find out in Berlin," Nash said.

The Lost Bunker

Less than an hour after landing at the Schönefeld airport in old East Berlin, the group was on their way to the location marked on Professor Tillman's map.

They huddled together on the S-Bahn in silence.

Exiting the subway, Stone led them through the old Ministry district, now flanked by small apartment complexes.

"It's hard to believe that sixty years ago this area was the nerve center of the Nazi Party," Kara informed them. "Hitler's Chancellery, Goebbels Propaganda Ministry and the Foreign Ministry of the Reich all stood here."

They stopped in front of a ghost of a building, still bearing the scars made from several hundred bullets.

"This is it," Stone said. "The Traffic Ministry of the Third Reich. Let me see that map again."

Kara handed it to him, and he studied it for a moment. "It looks like the dot is in the back courtyard."

They made their way through the abandoned, graffiti-covered building and found a courtyard covered in weeds and debris.

"Look around for anything that looks like an entrance to a hole in the ground," Stone told them.

"Are you sure there's a bunker here?" Kara asked.

Stone surveyed the building and said, "The Traffic Ministry would have been a major target of Allied bombing. Hundreds of people worked here. I'd be willing to bet that there's a bunker here somewhere."

They split up, and after several minutes of searching, Professor Thomas shouted, "Over here!"

He was standing in front of a partially collapsed concrete archway.

Nash and Stone quickly went to work clearing the debris. After about twenty minutes, they had uncovered a hole large enough to climb through.

"It's your discovery, Raymond." Nash clapped the professor on the back. "Do you want the honor of being the first one in?"

Professor Thomas investigated the dark hole for several seconds. "I'm afraid this is where I get off." He put his hand on Nash's arm. "This trip has drained me, and I just can't do it anymore. You understand, old friend?"

Nash gave him a half-smile and nodded.

"I wish I could help you," Professor Thomas added, "but I'm almost seventy years old, and I'm way out of my element."

"You can still be of help," Stone said, handing him the tourist map. "Take this to the police and tell them what's going on. Bring them here."

"You said the authorities would never believe it."

"Tell them you know where Nash and Kara are," Stone replied. "That will get their interest." He looked over at them. "Agreed?"

Nash and Kara nodded.

"Good," Stone said giving him a thumb's up. "It's settled. Now get going."

Kara grabbed his arm. "Thank you for everything, Raymond." She kissed him on the cheek.

Professor Thomas blushed, then shuffled back into the building.

Behind him, Stone turned on his flashlight and led Nash and Kara into the tunnel.

"Be very careful," Stone warned. "This place looks like it hasn't been touched in sixty years."

Following Stone, Nash and Kara walked gingerly over the creaking floorboards spanning a shallow pit.

'You're right, Stone," Nash said. "No one's been here for years. This isn't the place."

Stone pointed to a door-sized opening several yards off to their left. "It's a corridor." He shone his flashlight into the darkness beyond. "I'm betting it will lead to a series of bunkers."

"How does that help us?" Nash sounded annoyed.

"Most of these bunkers were connected, remember? The lab could have been brought in from another entrance. I say we keep going." Stone moved ahead without waiting for an answer.

Nash and Kara retrieved their flashlights from their packs and followed Stone as he descended more than fifty feet under the Traffic Ministry's courtyard.

Stone followed the beam of his flashlight around the bunker. "We're no more than a hundred and fifty yards from where the Führer bunker stood."

"Do you think Hitler's bunker is connected to this one?" asked Kara.

"Doubt it," Stone replied. "If this is an entrance to the Black Sun lab, then I doubt they wouldn't be stupid enough to connect it to something as archeologically popular as the Führer bunker. No, this is new, and your father knew that." He paused. "But bunkers like this were part of a vast network of tunnels that connected subway stations."

"What are you talking about?" Nash asked.

"Ghost stations," Stone said. "Forgotten tunnels of the U-Eight subway line beneath the streets of East Berlin." His demeanor changed. "Let's move on."

For several minutes, they walked through the sixty room bunker that looked like it had been untouched since World War Two. Nash shivered as he imagined hundreds of fearful Germans shuffling in with battered suitcases, cooking pots for helmets and small stools to sit on, huddled in here as the *thump, thump, thump* of Allied bombs exploded above them.

Kara shrieked and waved her hand in front of her face. "What was that?"

"Bats," Stone replied. "They like it down here in the damp

coldness. These walls are made of concrete six feet thick with ten-foot-thick ceilings."

They walked further, exploring the bunker.

"It looks like a dead end," Nash desponded.

"Not exactly." Stone encouraged, pointing his flashlight at a small, three-foot by three-foot hole punched through the brick wall of the room at ground level.

Stone dropped down and disappeared through the hole in the wall.

"Come on over," he shouted.

They found themselves in a large bomb shelter complete with triple-bunk beds, exposed pipes, old egg-shaped lights with steel frames—even a kitchen. There were *Rauchen verboten!* signs painted on the walls and arrows pointing the way to the men's and women's toilets. Long narrow benches lined the walls.

Nash carefully explored the cavernous room and walked over to a desk in the corner. On it were air raid guidelines lying next to a 1943 edition of the Nazi party newspaper. Except for the layer of dust covering everything, the bunker looked like it had been used yesterday.

On the back wall, Nash discovered a large, rusted metal door. He grabbed the door handle and started to turn it.

"*Stop!*" Stone shouted. "Don't open that!"

Nash yanked his hand away from the door handle and jumped backwards. Stone rushed over and put his hand on the door. "Feel how much colder it is?"

Nash touched it. "Yeah, so?"

Stone pointed at the floor. "And see that water leaking under the door? There's probably more than a ton of water behind this door.

"What?" Nash replied. "How?"

"In nineteen forty-five, when the battle for Berlin raged above, the citizens went into the underground network to escape the street fighting. In response, the Russians blew up the Spree canal walls and flooded the bunker network. The flood killed thousands. Little is known of the bunkers we're snooping around in. They could be flooded." he warned. "Let's move on."

A few minutes later, passing through one of the exit doors in the bunker, they entered a room that opened and led to another heavy steel door. Stone touched the door in several places and finally pointed his flashlight beam at its threshold.

He grabbed the door handle and yanked it open. Nash and Kara anxiously jumped backwards.

The steel door opened to a tunnel only about four feet wide and five feet tall. They followed it to another, smaller metal door. Stone examined it, then pushed on the door handle. A blast of musky ionized air rushed in.

"It's a service tunnel," Stone observed as he moved his flashlight in and around the space ahead of them. As they approached the end of the tunnel, Stone shouted, "I see subway tracks!"

One by one, they climbed down from the service tunnel and onto the tracks.

"I'll bet this leads to the ghost station," Stone said excitedly, trotting quickly down the tracks.

"Stone, wait for us." Nash took Kara's hand and began to follow him.

"This has to be it." Stone turned and looked at them. "This must lead to the ghost station I was looking for. We're in the right area."

"Stone," Nash cautioned. "We're not here for the gold. We need to stop Hoffer."

"*You're* here to stop Hoffer," Stone heatedly replied. "*I'm* here for the gold." He turned around and ran down the subway tracks, disappearing into the darkness—the diminishing bobbing of his flashlight was all Nash and Kara could see.

"Damn it, Stone!" Nash ran after him. "Get back here!"

But Stone vanished into the subway tunnel, and soon not even his footsteps could be heard.

"Now what?" Kara asked.

"We go without him," Nash hissed. "I'm not following him on his loony treasure hunt." He waved his flashlight around the subway tunnel. "There's a ladder over there. Let's see where it leads."

The Tale

Professor Thomas half-ran, half-walked for two blocks before he saw a meter maid ticketing a car on the side of the street. He rushed over to her.

"I need you to call the police," he gasped, trying to catch his breath. "It's a matter of life and death."

"Whose life or death?" the woman asked.

"Thousands," he huffed. "No, tell them that I know the whereabouts of Jeremy Nash and Kara Ackerman."

"Sir, I—"

"Just call them! They are wanted for multiple murders."

Detective Schmidt raced to the location the meter maid had called in. His office had been monitoring the police scanners for anything to do with Nash.

Once he arrived, he listened as the professor explained the plot Nash had uncovered.

"You've got to send someone after them." He waved the map in front of him. "They're down there now, and they can't stop this themselves."

"Why am I supposed to believe any of this?" Schmidt replied sharply. "For all I know, you may be trying to get some publicity for your latest and greatest archeological discovery."

"So, you aren't even going to try to stop this?" Professor Thomas looked exasperated. "I'm telling you about a second holocaust."

"Professor," Schmidt replied, "by your own admission you were part and party to much of Nash's activities over the last few days. That makes you an accessory to his crimes. If this is true, we will have to hold you."

Thomas's face drained of all color. He didn't plan on this. Just tell the police the threat and he could go home. That's what he had bargained for.

But that wasn't going to happen.

He had to find a way out. But he also promised Nash he would get the authorities to take action.

He figured a way to do both.

An animated argument broke out between the meter maid and a motorist who had returned to his ticketed car. Detective Schmidt turned towards them. The professor reached into his belt, pulled out his flashlight and hit the detective over the head with it, dropping him to his knees.

The meter maid started to scream into her walkie-talkie as the professor ran back the way he came.

"Schmidt!" Heinrich shouted. "You idiot!"

Schmidt said nothing. He only stared down at the ground.

"That's twice *you* let someone involved in *my* case escape," Heinrich growled. "And why didn't you contact Interpol as soon as you knew where Nash was?"

Schmidt mumbled something incoherent and rubbed the back of his head. He held up the tourist map he had taken from Professor Thomas.

Heinrich unceremoniously snatched it from his hand and stared at it.

"The red dot," Schmidt said. "The old man said they were in a bunker marked by the red dot."

"Pull a team together. We're going in after them." He handed the map back to Schmidt. "Now!"

THE GHOST STATION

Breathing heavily and covered with sweat from his long run down the tunnel, Stone reached a brightly lit subway platform alight with modern halogen lights one would see at construction sites.

He hoisted himself up onto the platform and looked around.

There were dozens of boxes stacked around intermixed with a variety of construction materials.

"They've found it," he hissed. "Someone's found *my* treasure."

He ran to a small group of wooden boxes that were separated from the others. He tried to pry the lid off from one of them, but it was tightly sealed.

Frustrated and angry, he rushed across the platform towards the construction equipment. Finding a large crowbar, he hurried back to the first wooden box and quickly pried it open.

The box was filled with glass vials, beakers, test tube racks, centrifuges, and rubber tubing.

Distraught, he feverishly opened the other boxes and found similar laboratory equipment.

The sound of rushing wind that, within seconds, inundated his face with warm ionized air, was followed by the squealing wheels of an oncoming train.

Stone ducked down behind the boxes and watched as a modern looking, olive drab tram pulled into the station. The door opened and a tall man, leading a large, one-eyed Doberman Pinscher, stepped onto the platform. He was followed by one of the guides from the Antarctica expedition.

The dog perked his ears up and looked toward Stone's hiding place. The canine tugged on his leash, pulling the tall man towards the boxes. It sniffed around the ground and then began to bark excitedly.

The man dropped the leash, and the dog jumped on the top of one the boxes, looking down at Stone, bearing his white teeth and barking menacingly.

Stone drew his pistol.

"Halt!" The Antarctica guide had moved behind Stone and had a P-38 aimed at his head.

Stone slowly lifted both hands and dropped his pistol.

"Herr Stone!" he said. "I'm not at all happy to see you as you are supposed to be dead."

"Mr. Adler," Stone cautiously replied, slowly standing up. "I'm just as unhappy to see you."

Adler looked around the station platform. "If you're here..." One eyebrow went up, and he smiled. "Then I assume Herr Nash is here, too."

Death Replicated

"That bastard." Nash spat, looking down the tunnel where Stone disappeared.

"Let it go." Kara softly touched Nash's arm. "We don't have time for him. We need to keep moving."

They continued through the main tunnel, exploring each room as they went.

"Look," Kara said, pointing her flashlight at a new conduit running along the ceiling of one of the rooms. "It looks brand new."

"Recently been installed," Nash agreed. "We need to follow it."

They followed the conduit from room to room for about a hundred meters, where it made a sharp turn and headed up through the ceiling.

"Now what?" Kara asked.

There was a very large steel door to the left of where the conduit disappeared.

Nash pulled up on the handle and yanked the door open, but it only moved a few inches. "Help me with this."

Together they dislodged the door and entered a small bunker.

"Christ!" Nash exclaimed as they shined their flashlights around. The room was filled, almost floor to ceiling, with boxes of World War Two munitions. "There's artillery shells, grenades and small arms ammunition in here."

"This place is a disaster waiting to happen." Kara turned to leave.

Nash shined his light to the right and then above him. "Wait. The conduit goes through that door above us."

Below the door was a small staircase.

They carefully climbed the old staircase and went through a much smaller hatchway. In front of them, a set of well-worn steps ascended into the darkness.

"Hear that?" Nash asked.

Kara nodded. "It sounds like a generator."

They passed through another steel door and entered a hallway lit by amber lights hanging from the ceiling.

"I think we found what we're looking for," Nash whispered.

"Yes, you did."

Nash spun around. Hoffer was holding an automatic pistol to Kara's head.

Hoffer barked some orders into an intercom to his right and within moments, two guards showed up at his side. They were big, they were burly and-—they were the guides from Antarctica.

"Someone wants to meet you, Herr Nash," Hoffer said. He nodded curtly, and the two henchmen prodded Nash and Kara forward with their pistols.

They were led down the amber lit passageway, interspersed with security cameras, through a door that led to a small complex of rooms. A few moments later they were standing in a fully equipped laboratory that occupied a large, old air raid bunker.

Against one of the walls a bank of flat screen monitors, connected to various pieces of equipment, flashed numbers and chemical symbols.

In the center of the room, a large, drab-gray box had dozens of tubes running into it. They were connected to an array of vials of material suspended from racks above the machine. A single tube allowed an output of semi-green glowing material to flow into a holding tank below.

"What is that?" Kara asked.

Nash only shook his head.

"I should have known that you would make it out of Antarctica and end up here, Herr Nash." A tall man stepped out of the shadows. He was holding a chain link leash with a not-so-friendly black Doberman on the other end. The dog's ears pointed straight up, its one yellow eye fixated on Nash, and its muzzle raised in a tight snarl.

Nash instinctively backed up a step and shielded Kara from the dog. "I'm guessing you're Adler."

"Correct, Herr Nash. How did you find this lab? What led you here?"

"A note from the grave," Nash said. "Professor Tillman actually figured everything out and led us here."

"It seems I've underestimated the old Jew," Adler replied. "But I seriously doubt he figured *everything out,* as you say."

"We know enough."

Adler pulled up one of the lab chairs, sat down, and ordered his dog to do the same. "I'll give you a biology lesson." He motioned to Nash and Kara to sit near him.

They declined. Adler shrugged.

"Do you know what a nano-factory is, Herr Nash?"

"I've heard of them. They manufacture things on a nanoscale."

"Very good. And the beauty of a fabricator is its ability to build nano-factories that can build another and another, and so on and so on."

"You're using a nano-bot self-replicating process?" Kara asked. "That's deemed illegal by the EU!"

"Not illegal," Adler disagreed. "Just very tightly controlled."

Kara looked around the lab. "And I assume you haven't reported any of this to the EU authorities."

Adler just smiled. "Of course not. We wouldn't want them to look too closely at our activities. I'm sure they would frown on our endeavors here."

"Like creating a biological weapon?" Nash asked.

Adler's eyebrow went up.

"Combining biological material with inorganic components?" Nash added.

Kara jumped in. "If you lose control of the nano-factory process and the self-replicating gets out of control, you'll create gray goo. And if that gets into the environment it will devour all carbon-based objects on earth—including every living thing."

"There's no need for concern," Adler remarked confidently. "We have a set of multiple generators with backups below us that keeps power to the fabricator. There's no way we can lose control of the self-replicating process."

"We know all about your ethnic cleansing plot," Kara told him with disgust. "And your sick plan to start an ethnic civil war in Europe."

"We also know you're using the bacteria from the lake in Antarctica as a feedstock for your nano-factories, to create something to put into the food supply." Nash pointed at the drab-gray machine.

"It seems that I may have greatly underestimated Professor Tillman," Adler admitted. "The genetic foods branch of our corporation has created a nano-capsule that we have added to the ethnic foods we sell throughout Europe. Halal food, Kosher food, you name it."

"But that would leave evidence," Nash said, shaking his head. "The poison in the food would be easily traced back to your company."

"Not at all," Adler said. "The poison, as you call it, is encapsulated in the material—in this case, the bacteria in the lake—created by the nano-factories. The nano-capsules are easily absorbed by the body and attack it in ways that medical inspectors would not recognize."

"But German citizens eat ethnic foods, too," Kara protested. "Your plan to make it look like an ethnic derived plague would also infect many non-ethnic Germans."

"Not necessarily," Adler protested. "That's the beauty of the nano-capsules.

"Beauty?" Nash hissed.

"The nano-capsules," Adler went on, "deliver the bacterial

agent only when activated by temperature—similar to how tumors heat up when beamed with microwaves. The advantage of our nano-capsules is that we can contaminate as many people as we like, using our distribution system, and then selectively activate them for certain periods of time."

"And make it look like the spread of a real plague," Kara observed.

"And Professor Tillman discovered your plan—so you killed him!"

"I didn't kill him," Adler replied matter-of-factly. "That man who was hunting you two across half of Europe did. A loyal Knight of the Hoy Lance of our Black Sun Society. His name is Stoble."

"But why frame me for the murder? You could have easily killed Tillman without involving me. I was no threat to you. I knew nothing of this. And even if Tillman were able to tell me about this, I wouldn't have believed him."

"To be honest, Herr Nash, what we're doing here, and about to do, has very little to do with you."

"Then why?"

"I was just doing a favor for a friend," Adler said, smiling.

"What friend?" Nash asked. "The powerful enemy I keep hearing about?"

"That's not important, Herr Nash. All you need—"

A shuffle of footsteps was followed by Hoffer and two henchmen who were pulling a protesting and cursing Stone into the lab. They dragged him over to a nearby desk and unceremoniously dumped him into a chair.

Inundation

Professor Thomas looked back over his shoulder one last time before entering the Traffic Ministry building. Once inside, he bent forward, placed his hands on his knees and tried to slow his breathing. When he caught his breath, he moved quickly into the rear courtyard. He went straight to the dilapidated archway outside the bunker but hesitated nervously.

The sound of an approaching police siren forced his hand. He stepped inside and walked quickly across the wooden floorboards that led into the bunker.

Christ! he thought. *I'm a fugitive now.*

He moved farther into the bunker until it became too difficult to see. He snatched his flashlight from his belt and switched it on. Nothing. He switched it off and on several more times.

"Damn it!" he hissed, dropping it on the ground. "That detective's head was harder than I thought." He reached into his jacket pocket and pulled out his pipe, tobacco and lighter. He flicked the lighter on and held it out in front of him as he proceeded deeper into the tunnel.

He hoped wherever this led, he would wind up finding Nash and Kara—with the police on his tail.

In quick sequence, Thomas, used to ferreting around old tombs, found the small three by three hole punched through the brick wall of the large bunker.

He entered the bomb shelter, glanced at the bunk beds, the exposed pipes, the old lights, and the signs for the toilets. At the back of the bunker was a large, rusted door.

On the opposite side were three other smaller steel doors.

Which one? Well, you pay your money and you take your choice.

He pulled on the door handle of the large, rusted door and jerked it open.

He immediately regretted his decision.

Suddenly, a tidal wave of dirty, filthy, foul-smelling water poured into the large bunker, forcing him back against the far wall. He pushed his back against the rushing water and, with his heart hammering, felt his way along the wall to one of the other doors. He opened it, climbed through, and slammed it shut behind him.

The ugly roar of water threatened in the darkness behind it.

Stalling For Time

Keep talking, Nash thought. *Stall for time. Think of a way out of this.*

"How do you plan to activate the nano-capsules?" Nash asked.

Hoffer walked over to Adler and took a seat in a nearby chair. He looked at Adler, who smiled and nodded his head. "You're familiar with the Berlin Radio tower?"

"The Fernsehturm? Yes, but I don't see—"

Hoffer held up his hand. "We recently purchased a small, local radio station. Like all the other stations around Berlin, it broadcasts from the tower. We'll piggyback our microwave signal on a special Muslim Eid broadcast tonight." He looked at his watch and said, "In less than an hour, actually."

Nash glanced at Stone and gave him an almost imperceptible nod.

"Is this the transmitter?" Nash asked, stepping toward the large console that had more flashing lights than a Christmas tree.

Two of Hoffer's henchmen stepped closer to the console and raised their guns.

"Be careful, Herr Nash," Hoffer warned. "Don't have any foolish ideas."

Nash held up both hands and took a half-step backwards. "I didn't see any satellite dishes or wires except for the conduit that we followed to get here."

"That conduit was poorly concealed but necessary. It connects this console, with the powerful microwave transmission equipment we've installed, to the Berlin radio tower. From here, we can activate the nano-capsules in all of the ethnic food we have distributed around most of Germany."

"Our special celebration broadcast will open with the appropriate Arab music for the first five minutes or so," Adler added. "Then we start the microwave broadcast."

"And the children?" Kara asked, her voice almost pleading. "They didn't ask to be born Arab."

Adler shrugged his shoulders. "A total cleansing." He leaned forward and softly stroked the neck of the massive Doberman Pincher that sat between his feet.

"But some non-ethnic Germans will die in the process," Nash protested. "You can't prevent them from eating the contaminated ethnic food."

"If some Germans die, all the better," Adler said. "It will appear that they have contracted a highly contagious, deadly disease, and it has spread to the German population." He leaned back in his chair and said, almost nonchalantly, "There are unavoidable casualties in every war."

"Let me guess," Nash said. "The result will be widespread panic and a complete breakdown of law and order. The authorities will be unable to control the situation, so vigilante groups will start attacking the ethnic groups in an attempt to eliminate them and stop the spread of the disease. The resulting civil war will allow the Black Sun to take political advantage, and you will take control of Germany."

"Today Germany, tomorrow the world," Kara spat.

The corners of Adler's mouth turned up a little as he met Kara's hateful stare. He nodded his head slowly.

Kara balled her hands into fists and started towards Adler.

Nash grabbed her arm and pulled her back. "Kara, they—"

Stone mumbled something incoherent.

"You have something to add, Herr Stone?" Adler demanded, sarcastically.

"I said that you and your ugly dog have more than just that in common. You're both sons-of-bitches." Stone moved to his left and kicked a heavy metal trashcan at his feet toward the dog.

The large Doberman yelped in alarm and jumped backwards, his leash nearly pulling Adler off his chair.

Adler caught his balance and shouted, *"You bastard!"*

The thug closest to Stone grabbed his arm and spun him around. Stone jerked his knee up hard and fast, catching the man squarely in the crotch. The large man howled in pain and dropped to his knees, his gun falling to the ground beside him.

Stone scrambled for the weapon, but before he could grab it, the Doberman launched itself through the air and hit Stone in the back. Stone and the dog fell together to the ground.

Nash watched in awe as Stone fought with the enraged animal. Both man and animal issued guttural growls and yelps, and each one seemed to give as well as it took. The dog's teeth gnashed at Stone's face and throat as Stone tightened his grip on its throat and pummeled the beast's back and sides with his free fist.

One of the other guards stepped forward and aimed his gun at the sprawling mass of man and dog.

"Don't shoot!" ordered Adler. "You'll hit my dog!"

The man-dog thing rolled around the floor, knocking over chairs and lab equipment as they fought in front of the transmitter. The dog let out an unearthly scream of pain, and Stone spit what remained of its bloody ear onto the ground at Adler's feet.

"Stop him!" Adler screamed. "Stop him from hurting my dog!"

One of the henchmen maneuvered toward Stone and the howling dog. He tucked the gun into his waistband, reached down, grabbed the animal by its hindquarters and pulled.

Stone, seeing what was happening, let go of the dog. The guard and the dog fell backwards and landed on the ground with a loud thud. The Doberman instinctively turned and started attacking the guard. The guard pulled his gun out of his waistband, but the dog grabbed his forearm and bit deeply forcing the henchman to drop his gun.

Stone grabbed the gun and fired two quick shots. The first one took most of the dog's head off, and the second shot wounded the guard in the shoulder.

Hoffer drew his automatic pistol and aimed it at Stone.

Stone dropped down behind the wounded guard and used him as a shield. He forced the man to his feet by pressing the gun into his temple. Stone started walking backwards, keeping the large man's body in front of him.

Stone continued to back up until he was in front of the transmission console. He shouted, "Ladies and gentlemen. We interrupt this broadcast for a serious announcement. There will be no party today."

He pushed his man-shield at Hoffer, turned and emptied the automatic pistol into the console. Sparks erupted from the equipment, and the console caught fire.

Hoffer aimed his pistol at Stone and shot him through the back.

Stone grimaced and fell to his knees, dropping the gun to the ground.

Hoffer walked cautiously over to the console and put his gun to the back of Stone's head. He kicked Stone's gun out of reach and then turned and looked at Adler. Adler nodded and Hoffer pulled the trigger, splattering blood and brains across the smoking console.

Kara gasped and moved closer to Nash.

"That was for my dog," Adler told them as he knelt down over the animal's carcass and stroked its back.

"You're through!" Kara exploded. "You can't transmit, and the police are on their way."

"Police?" Alder yelled. "You don't expect me to believe..."

"We gave the map my father had of this place to a friend and told him to tell the police where we were going and what you were doing." Kara snarled. "They should be here soon."

Adler glared at her.

She lowered her voice. "Like I said, you're through."

He stroked the dog for a moment longer and then looked back at Kara.

"We're not though, Frauline. This location made it easier, but we can do it at the source." Adler stood and roughly grabbed Kara's arm.

Nash moved forward, but one of the henchmen jabbed a pistol into his stomach and then slammed it against the back of his head. Nash collapsed to the ground.

Adler pulled Kara closer to him and sneered. "If you're telling the truth about the police, I may need a hostage."

She tried to pull away, but he yanked her back and growled, "You're coming with me."

Adler turned to Hoffer and said, "I'll meet you at the tower." He motioned his gun toward Nash's crumpled body and added, "And eliminate *that* problem—for good."

"No!" Kara cried out and tried to pull away again. Adler grabbed a handful of her hair, pulled her head backwards and pushed his gun into her ribs. "Hostages work better when they're alive, but I'm in no mood to argue semantics with you." He forced her up the stairwell and through the heavy door.

Gray Goo

Professor Thomas pressed his back against the cold, damp wall and tried to catch his breath. When his heart rate returned to normal, he tried the lighter he still gripped tightly in his hand. To his surprise, it lit.

He walked down the long corridor, stopping every few minutes to relight his lighter.

When the tunnel crossed a much wider one, the professor paused in the intersection to look as far down each section as his dim light would allow.

He cocked his head to one side and listened.

Humming.

It was the hum of machinery, and it seemed to be coming from his left. He turned toward it when he heard another sound emanating from the way he had just come.

Oh Shit!

It was the sound of barreling water, and it was headed his way!

He ran down the wider tunnel toward the sound of the machinery, stumbling twice before dropping his lighter. He cursed, but continued to run, feeling his way along the walls of the tunnel while running as fast as he could without toppling over.

The cold, damp stink of the oncoming water filled his nostrils, and he knew it was getting close.

The humming sound increased and became louder than the roar of the oncoming water. He slammed into a metal door and fell backwards. Pushing himself to his feet, he fumbled for a handle, found it, and pushed hard through the entry way into artificial light.

He was staring down a set of metal stairs just as the water hit him in the back.

Nash opened his eyes and blinked several times. The fuzzy shapes he was seeing began to come back into focus, as did his memory. "Kara!" he shouted and tried to sit up. The pain in his head and the rush of dizziness made him fall back.

"She's gone, Herr Nash," Adler's henchman hissed. "And so are you." He raised his pistol and pointed it at Nash's head. Nash closed his eyes and took a deep breath.

There was a loud roaring sound, and when Nash reopened his eyes, Professor Thomas, levitated on what looked like a tidal wave of water, flushed down the stairwell. The flood washed over the goon, and he was thrust down the stairwell and back into the lab.

The water pushed Nash under one of the lab table. He grabbed one of the legs to stabilize himself just as Professor Thomas came rushing by. Nash reached out and grabbed for him, snagging the back of his jacket.

As he held the waterlogged professor tight, the foul-smelling water flowed into the lab's air return near the floor and poured into the utility room below.

When the water subsiding, Nash pulled the professor towards him. "Raymond, are you okay?" he anxiously asked his limp friend.

Professor Thomas pointed over Nash's shoulder. Adlar's henchman was sludging through the water towards them. He didn't appear to hold a weapon, but Nash knew from experience what the guy could do with his bare hands.

"Geez, this guy just won't quit," Nash moaned.

A horrible whining sound came from below them. The floor began to shake as the noise grew louder. The lights in the lab blinked twice and then went out. Within seconds, yellow emergency battery lamps lit up.

As the pitch of the whining increased, the floor below the goon exploded in an eruption of concrete and rebar, leaving a gaping hole in its place. When the smoke cleared, miraculously the goon was clinging to a piece of rebar.

He looked at Nash and pleaded, "Help," just before the rebar broke from the concrete, and the man vanished into the void.

"Mother of God!" Professor Thomas cried. A second explosion rocked the room.

"It's the generators," Nash shouted. "We've got to get out of here." He helped the professor to his feet, and they moved quickly to the staircase.

Nash stopped just long enough to grab one of the goon's automatic pistols lying at the foot of the staircase. He stuffed it into his belt and guided the professor up the steps.

Several strange noises made him look back. He squinted his eyes through the lingering dust of the explosion.

It was Hoffer. He returned standing in front of the nano-factory, yanking the feed tubes out. He turned to Nash and the professor. "You've got to help me," he shouted. "Without the generators…"

The machine bucked and shook. A gray cloud seemed to explode out of it.

Gray goo.

The goo quickly devoured the machine that birthed it and was spreading across the lab floor.

Professor Thomas took a step forward, but Nash grabbed his arm and pulled him back. "There's nothing we can do."

Hoffer started to scream. The goo, acting like a swarm of tiny nano-bots, now encased his legs and lower torso.

It emitted a hideous hiss and devoured everything in its path.

Nash and Thomas watched in shock as Hoffer's body was stripped of flesh and muscle, and his bones evaporated into a fine dust. Within seconds, he was entirely consumed in the gray swarm of nano-bots.

Nash and Professor Thomas bolted up the steps. About half-way up, the professor tripped and fell forward.

"My ankle," he cried. "I think it's sprained."

"You have to try and stand. On one leg—hop! We have to get the hell out of here."

Professor Thomas nodded bravely, and Nash helped him to his feet.

Nash paused in the doorway for a second, in awe, as the gray cloud swirled around, over and under everything in its path, dissolving everything it touched into a fine mist of self-replicating nano-bots.

Snap out of it! Get the hell out of here!

Once at the top and into the tunnel, they looked down the stairwell as the entire lab complex collapsed into the bunkers below.

"My God," Thomas cried, as he watched the lab disintegrate below him. He stood frozen in the doorway, staring at the total destruction.

"We gotta go." Nash yanked his arm hard.

They scrambled through the tunnel until they came to a large steel door. Nash turned the handle and pushed it open. They exited onto a parking garage.

A horn beeped and they jumped backwards. A woman gave them a dirty look as she passed by in her car.

"All of that was below this garage," Professor Thomas noted in a daze. "The second holocaust was being planned twenty feet below these people's everyday lives." He shook his head. "I can't believe it."

"Come on," Nash pushed.

They made their way out of the garage and into the bright sunlight of the street.

Nash looked around in every direction. "There," he said, pointing to a radio tower about a block away. "That's got to be the Berlin radio tower."

Professor Thomas looked where Nash was pointing.

"Find the police," Nash told him. "Tell them there's going to be a terrorist attack on the radio tower."

"Why don't we just try to get the tower evacuated?"

"It won't do any good," Nash told him. "I don't want to cause a panic."

Professor Thomas nodded, forgetting his ankle. "But where are you going?"

"After Kara. Adler took her to that radio tower. I have to find her and stop him."

The gray goo moved through the bunkers and tunnels under the lab. It consumed everything in its path as it spread.

The concrete walls of the arms bunker deteriorated into a fine dust as the gray cloud swept over them and covered the seventy-year-old boxes of ammunition, anti-aircraft shells, and bombs.

Terror At Alexander Platz

"Inspector?" The young officer stood in front of Heinrich who was talking on a walkie-talkie. He held up his hand, signaling the young officer to be quiet.

"Inspector, may I interrupt you?"

Heinrich turned his back and continued to speak into the walkie-talkie. After a moment, he turned back and said, "What is so damned important that it couldn't wait for thirty seconds?"

"Dispatch called. They said they're holding a man. He said he had to talk to you." The officer paused for a second. "He said it was a matter of life or death."

"Is his name Thomas?"

"Yes, sir. They're bringing him here."

"Why didn't you say so?" Inspector Heinrich pushed past the young officer.

A blue and white squad car turned a corner and came toward them. Heinrich walked up to the edge of the curb.

As soon as the vehicle came to a stop, Heinrich leaned forward and snatched open the backdoor. A very overwrought Professor Thomas screamed from the back seat, babbling almost incoherently about Nazis, secret bases, genetic weapons, tainted food, and terrorists.

"Slow down, professor," Heinrich ordered grabbing Thomas by both shoulders. "What terrorist?"

"They're going to blow up the Fernsenturm radio tower," Thomas gasped. "Jeremy Nash is there trying to stop them. We have very little time."

Heinrich pulled the walkie-talkie to his mouth and barked in some orders. When he was done, he turned to the professor. "You come with me and tell me everything you know."

Nash tucked his gun into his belt and pulled his jacket down over it. He half-jogged to the plaza of the Fernsehturm radio tower and then quickly mingled in with a large group of people standing before it.

"The tower is reported to be three-hundred and sixty-five meters high," a perky, young woman wearing a blue blazer said loudly. "This number was deliberately chosen by Walter Ulbricht, the Leader of the Sozialistische Einheitspartei Deutschlands, so that every child would be able to remember it, just like the days of the year."

She paused to allow the group to look up at the long tower pedestal. It had a large, round multilevel ball on top of it, and a soaring broadcast tower on top of that.

"It's really three-hundred and sixty-eight meters," she said, lowering her voice as if she was telling a secret. "But I won't tell if you don't."

Several people laughed. Nash began to slowly move forward through the crowd.

"The location of the tower was deliberately chosen so that it would impose on West Berlin's Reichstag building," the guide continued. "The tower was intended to show off Communist East Germany's strength."

Nash pushed forward again, this time bumping into a rather rotund woman who was holding a travel brochure. "Wait your turn like everyone else," she said in a nasally British accent. A tall, slender man to her left gave him an apologetic look.

"Now if everyone will please look at the ball," the guide pointed upwards. "You can see what appears to be the reflection of a giant cross. Berliners have dubbed this optical illusion of a luminous cross *Rache des Papstes*, or *the Pope's Revenge*. It's supposed to be

God's revenge on the secular socialist State for having removed crucifixes from churches."

Nash squeezed past the fat woman as she craned her head to see the cross.

"Today, the Fernsehturm tower's main clients are the radio, television, and digital television transmitters in the tower located above the sphere, but there is only one inside the tower's ball—its a digital radio station," the young guide continued. "We'll be taking the elevators, because the stairway leading to the observation level has almost a thousand steps." Nash yanked open the door and quickly entered the lobby.

Nash looked quickly around the lobby for a security guard. He saw an old man, wearing the tell-tale uniform, sitting at a desk on the far side of the room. Nash started towards him when he felt an ominous rumble beneath his feet. The vibration quickly grew in intensity, and the ground began to undulate wildly beneath his feet.

Someone shouted, "Earthquake," and people ran towards the exit.

Nash tried to hold his balance, but he ended up on the floor.

Suddenly, a huge explosion erupted from outside of the tower. Shards of concrete and blacktop flew through the plate glass windows of the lobby, impaling several people.

When the blast subsided, Nash jumped to his feet. People around him were screaming and crying. Some were lying face down, unmoving, while others were running in panic from the plaza—some clutching small children.

Through the broken windows, Nash saw several people in the street pointing up at the tower.

He pressed his way forward through the dilapidated visitor's center, fighting his way through a wave of panicked people, to the walkway to the tower.

The walkway led to a central staircase that went up four ways from the center of a high entry hall. He checked the visitor map and found the level with the digital radio station.

He climbed the stairs and followed the wood paneled hallway that rounded its way to the main elevators. He pushed the call button for the elevator several times, but the panel showed them still on the first floor.

"Damn," Nash swore. "They're shut down because of the explosion."

He went around the corner and entered the stairwell. He looked up at the immense staircase spiraling up from him and around the elevator shafts.

What was it she said? Almost a thousand steps to the observation level?

He took a deep breath and started his climb.

Step by step, breath by labored breath, he pushed himself to climb the spiral stairs inside the tower pedestal, dimly lit by emergency lights.

Finally, he reached a door, opened it, and entered the observation level. In front of him were angled windows that wrapped entirely around the deck, providing a panoramic view of Berlin. From there he found the open staircase leading to the restaurant one level up. He ran through the restaurant until he found the stairs to the tech levels and hurried up.

Adler led Kara down the hallway and into a large room filled with broadcasting equipment. Stobl was sitting in front of an audio console. He swiveled his chair around when the door opened.

"You!" Kara cried. "You killed my father?"

"No need to thank me, frauline." Stobl stood, clicked his heels together, and nodded his head curtly. "It was my pleasure, as was killing your uncle."

Kara shrieked wildly and charged the man, clawing at his face. He grabbed her arms and easily pinned them to her side. She kicked him in the crotch, making him expel a gust of air and bend over slightly. He resumed his posture and smiled at her. "Once we've finished here, killing you will also be my pleasure."

Kara turned to Adler. "You're mad!" She struggled against the large man's grip. "You're going to kill thousands of innocent people."

"Stobl," Adler hissed. "Shut that Hündin up!"

Stobl pushed her into the chair he had been sitting in and grabbed a roll of duct tape hanging from the pegboard above the console. In less than a minute, Kara was securely bound to the chair.

"Adler, I'm begging you."

Stobl tore off a piece of tape and plastered it across her mouth.

"Just a few more minutes and we will be ready to—" Adler grabbed the console with both hands as the room began to shimmer for several seconds and then began to shake violently.

Pieces of conduit, pipe and equipment came detached from the ceiling and walls. Several windows in the room cracked—some popped out of their sills.

Adler and Stobl hugged the broadcasting console to hold their balance. Kara careened across the floor in her chair.

"What the hell was that?" Adler asked when the shaking stopped.

"I think it—"

The floor beneath them started to tilt and the broadcast terminal slid out from the back wall.

Kara screamed into the duct tape covering her mouth, forcing a portion of it to tear away from her upper lip.

As the first rumble began to shake the police vehicle, Professor Thomas cried out, "What on earth?" and grabbed the back of the front seat.

The squad car was thrown several feet into the air and came crashing back down on its tires. It leaned at an odd angle.

"Get out!" Heinrich shouted. "We're under attack." He and the driver jumped out of the vehicle, leaving the alarmed professor locked in the backseat.

Panicked tourists were running in every direction. Heinrich

surveyed the situation before returning to the vehicle and opening the back door.

Professor Thomas climbed out. "It's the terrorists."

"Settle down, professor. It looks like an earthquake."

"Mein Gott!" The driver shouted. "Look at the tower!"

Heinrich and the professor turned around and stared up in horror.

The tower had tilted almost twenty-five degrees and threatened to tumble into the Alexanderplatz.

Fernsehturm Berlin

Once the tower tilt miraculously settled, Adler moved to the broadcast console and started adjusting the controls. He clicked the switch on and off several times before slamming his fist down on the console.

"*Scheisse!*"

"What's wrong?" asked Stobl.

"The console accepted the command codes, but nothing is happening." He furiously clicked the switch on and off again. "We can't broadcast until the circuit is closed. Help me check the connections."

Stobl stumbled up the incline of the floor and helped Adler pull the console back away from the wall. Three bare wires hung from a torn conduit. Stobl reached down and yanked them close to the console. "I can't see where they connect."

"It looks like they were pulled out from inside," Adler said. "We don't have the time or tools to do this here. You'll need to manually close the circuit at the tower itself."

Stobl nodded and left for the service stairs.

"Having a problem?" Kara mumbled through the loosening duct tape.

"I'd be more concerned with your own problem." Adler walked to her and firmly pressed the duct tape back over her mouth. "You will not live out this day."

In a wall at the back of the restaurant, directly below the broadcast tower, the wires that Stobl had yanked through the wall stretched to capacity and pulled free of their plastic housing. The bare wires touched together and began to spark. The insulation caught fire, spreading in both directions. With nowhere else to go, it stopped at the side wall and the elevator shaft.

Starved for adequate oxygen, it smoldered hotter and hotter.

Between A Rock And A Hot Space

Nash entered the lower tech level and drew his pistol from his belt. He quickly and quietly went from office to office, working his way across the platform.

Halfway down the corridor, he heard voices coming from one of the rooms ahead of him. He started toward the sounds when a door up ahead on the right suddenly opened and Stobl stepped out into the hallway. Nash instinctively ducked into the open door beside him and crouched down. He leveled his pistol at the doorway and waited.

Stobl ran past him without even glancing his way. Nash heard a door open and close, then heard Stobl's footsteps on the stairs.

Breathing a sigh of relief, Nash went back into the hallway and carefully made his way towards the door Stobl had come out of.

Looking through a large office window next to the door, Nash saw Adler sitting at a console, working feverishly on its controls. Kara was bound to a chair that was leaning against the far wall.

Nash slowly turned the doorknob and stepped inside.

"That was fast." Adler turned toward him. "Did you—"

Nash had his pistol pointed at Adler's chest. "Game over, asshole."

Adler smiled and shook his head. "Your resourcefulness amazes me, Herr Nash."

"So I've been told. Now untie Kara."

"I can't do that, Herr Nash. As you can see, I have a radio show to broadcast."

"Not in this lifetime. Now untie her or I'll shoot you, then untie her myself."

Kara stomped her feet and jumped in her chair, mumbling something through her taped mouth and nodding towards the door.

Nash turned and immediately felt a heavy blow across his face. He stumbled back, pointing his gun blindly in the direction of the blow. A pair of strong hands grabbed his arms and turned him around slamming him against the wall, the impact flinging the gun from his hand.

The air burst from his lungs, and he slipped to the floor in a daze.

Stobl kicked the pistol aside.

"Perfect timing." Adler smiled. "Did you close the circuit?"

Stobl nodded his head, still glaring at Nash.

Adler turned the switch on the console again and Arabic music began to play through the booth's speakers.

Adler walked over to Nash, bent down, and grabbed him by his hair, yanking his neck backwards.

"How did you say? Game over?" Adler sneered. "It is. For both of you—and the ethnic scum of Germany."

"It's scum like you that give terrorists a bad name," Nash croaked.

Adler spit in his face and then stood back up. "You've been lucky twice before, Herr Nash. But I can assure you that there won't be a third time." He looked at Stobl and said, "Kill them. Now."

Adler gave a mock good-bye wave and walked out of the office.

"Kara," Nash moaned, turning his head towards her.

"Don't worry. I'm going to let her watch you die and then kill her, too."

Stobl cocked his P38 and aimed it at Nash, but before he could pull the trigger, Adler began to scream from the other end of the hallway. Stobl turned and ran out towards him.

Adler inserted the master key into the elevator lock and turned it to the right. He pushed the call button and waited as the elevator began to make its ascent.

The doors opened and the air from the hallway was sucked inside, feeding the oxygen-starved fire smoldering in the lower levels of the elevator shaft. A blast of orange flame exploded from inside of the elevator completely engulfing Adler. As the elevator doors were sliding shut, his body was thrown like a ragdoll twenty feet down the hallway. He screamed and rolled around on the floor trying to put out the fire.

Stobl ran towards him and started to beat out the flames with his hands. "What happened?" he asked.

Adler only moaned.

Stobl lifted him in his arms. He ran to the elevator and pushed the call button several times.

Adler moaned again and tried to say something.

"It's okay," Stobl said. "The broadcast has begun, and I'll get you to a hospital."

Adler breathed something incoherent.

Stobl leaned his head closer to Adler and listened. "No. The elevator..."

The *bing* signaling the arrival of the elevator was followed by a deafening roar.

Nash crab-walked quickly across the floor and hurled himself towards Kara. His body knocked the chair over. He pulled her down just as a large ball of fire passed over their heads, the heat searing their backs.

Adler's body was blown through the plate glass window of the broadcast booth, his lifeless body bounced onto of the console.

Stobl was lying in the doorway, his clothes aflame.

Nash tried to cover Kara's face, but she shook her head violently, refusing to let him. He carefully pulled the tape from her mouth.

"I need to see this," she sobbed, taking in the gruesome sight before her. "They killed my father."

"We've got to get out of here," he told her. "This whole place is on fire."

Nash grabbed a large piece of the broken plate glass window and began to rip through the duct tape still binding her to the chair.

By the time he had freed her, the flames had licked their way up the walls and across the drop-down ceiling. Electronic equipment began to hiss around them as it sizzled in the intense heat.

Staying low to the floor and gulping what oxygen there was, they made their way towards the door. Nash reached down and scooped up his pistol from where Stobl had kicked it earlier.

Stobl's smoking body blocked the doorway. The stepped over it and ran down the hallway.

"Over there," Nash pointed. "The stairs."

They quickly crawled to the exit door Nash had come through earlier, and he pushed the door open. Smoke and intense heat billowed up from below.

"We've got to go up," Nash said, taking her hand and pulling her up the stairs.

Kara nodded, and they hurried up the stairs through each level, coughing as the smoke followed them. Within a few minutes they reached the top level of the ball.

"Now what?" Kara gasped.

"The map in the lobby showed two rescue platforms down below," he remembered.

"How far below?"

"Below the ball," he said sullenly. "Below the fire."

"Oh, God."

The smoke and heat were getting worse in the confined space. They could hear the roar of the fire as it consumed the levels below them. There was an explosion below their feet. The whole ball seemed to sway and shiver.

"By now Fire and Rescue should be here," Nash hoped. "We've got to make it to the roof. Maybe we can signal someone from there."

They continued to climb until they came to a locked door at the top of the steps. Nash hit the door several times with his shoulder, but it wouldn't budge.

"Climb back down about ten steps," he told her.

Once she was well below the door, he took out his pistol and aimed it at the doorknob. He pulled the trigger and was thrown back by the recoil.

"Did it work?" Kara called up to him.

Nash looked at the doorknob. It was still intact. "I'm afraid I missed it completely. I haven't had much practice with one of these."

Kara rushed back up the stair and took the pistol from him. "Turn around and squat down."

She expertly fired two shots at the doorknob and the door swung open.

They stepped out onto the roof and took several deep breaths, allowing the fresh, cool air to clear their stinging lungs.

Nash looked over the railing. He began to wave his hands and shout. Kara joined him and did the same thing.

"It's no use," he sighed. "We're too high up and there's too much noise and confusion down there. No one is paying any attention to us."

Kara ran to the other side and looked over. "Jeremy," she called excitedly. "I've found our way down."

The Descent

Nash looked over the edge and cringed as he stared at the suspended scaffolding hanging about four feet below the edge of the railing. "You want us to go down to the rescue platform using a window cleaning rig?"

"It's between this and a fiery death," Kara flared. "Do you want to flip a coin for it?"

A strong gust of wind flapped their clothes against their bodies.

"We're three hundred meters above the ground," Nash stated. "And it's pretty windy up here. Do they even wash windows in the wind?"

"Probably not," Kara said, climbing over the railing. "This rig is attached to these metal rails, so I'm guessing it'll be safe."

Nash took a deep breath and followed her. He grabbed the safety harness and buckled himself in as Kara removed the control wand that was hanging on a hook.

As she studied the controls, Nash was about to tell her to buckle herself in when there was a thunderous rumble from below. It was followed by a deafening explosion and the windows from one level below them exploded, showering glass shards out into the air.

The rig lifted several feet and banged back down, throwing Kara backwards. Nash grabbed her arm before she tumbled out. They held each other as the tower swayed sickeningly, leaning even further towards the plaza below.

"This tower is not stable," Kara cried.

"Tell me something I *don't* know."

Kara gave a quick glance around the rig to verify that there was no damage and then pushed a button on the control wand.

The rig started a slow descent.

Even in the high winds, and at the unusual angle, fortunately the rig was steady as a rock. It made its way slowly and securely over the outside circumference of the glass ball.

As the rig passed over the midway point of the ball, Nash looked down and could see the first of the two rescue platforms that circumnavigated the tower. He let out a sigh of relief.

When they reached the restaurant level, something flashed through the smoky window. Nash leaned forward and peered through the glass.

The window exploded outward, and a small dining table soared past Nash's face and hit the side of the rig. It hung by one of its legs for a few seconds before tumbling to the platform below.

It was followed by Kara's scream.

The hideously burned body of Stobl jumped through the shattered window towards her. Most of the hair was burned off his charred-black head. His arms were black with scraps of burnt clothing hanging from them. His mouth was twisted into a bizarre vicious grin.

Stobl slammed his fist into Kara's forehead, dropping her to her knees. He spun around and grabbed Nash around the throat and started to choke him.

Nash grabbed his forearms and tried to push him away, but the flesh peeled off in his hands. Stobl didn't even twitch.

What kind of animal is this man?

Another explosion rocked the tower from the level below them. It blew a huge hole in the outside of the ball's structure and nearly blew the window washing rig off from its side rails.

Kara lost her balance and was thrown over the side. She held on with one arm as the rig continued its slow descent on one rail, spitting sparks as it jerked back and forth in the wind.

Nash pushed Stobl backwards.

"Kara!" he gasped, dropping to his knees, and grabbing her arm with both hands.

Stobl jumped on him and flipped him over. Nash lost his grip on Kara's arm, and she disappeared below.

"No!" was all he could cry out.

The rig dropped several feet, throwing Stobl backwards and then onto Nash's chest with his full weight.

Nash clawed at his face trying to reach anything vulnerable that would force the madman back and off him.

The rig dropped again and was now directly under the ball, hanging and swaying above the first rescue platform.

"*You killed her, you son-of-a-bitch!*" Nash screamed.

Stobl squeezed Nash's throat and pressed his full weight on his Nash's chest.

"Now you will die, too," Stobl sneered.

As an inky blackness crept in from the outer edges of his consciousness, Nash's eyes went dim, and he closed them against the growing darkness.

Seeing Kara fall in his mind, Nash grabbed Stobl's arms in a last-ditch effort and pushed. To his surprise, Stobl's grip loosened, and his hands fell away.

Nash opened his eyes and, through blurred vision, saw a red spot slowly growing bigger on Stobl's forehead. Stobl slipped back and fell off Nash's body.

Nash took several shallow breaths and rubbed his throat. *How? Who?*

Nash pulled himself up on shaky legs and turned to see a well-dressed, stocky, middle-aged man with a closely cropped salt and pepper beard supporting himself on an ornate steel cane. He was holding a government issue pistol.

"Are you alright, Herr Nash?" he asked.

Nash stared at him without speaking.

"I asked if you were okay," Heinrich repeated. He pointed at his feet. "Frauline Ackerman was worried that I'd be too late."

"Kara?" Nash croaked out the words and looked down.

Kara was standing on the level about six feet below the

window washing rig. She was standing on one leg and clutching her left arm with her right hand.

Nash leaped out of the rig and threw his arms around her.

"Well, I guess you're none the worse for wear," Heinrich said smiling.

Reprieve

Nash and Kara were sitting side by side having their wounds cared for in a makeshift emergency tent that had been set up a few blocks from the tower. They joined the other tourists and tower workers who were hurt in the incident.

Nash heard one of the emergency personnel say there were only two fatalities in the fire. He was grateful that no one else had been killed.

Detective Heinrich and Professor Thomas walked up to them.

"Your friend filled me in on everything," Heinrich said, slapping the professor on the back. "Interpol didn't know if you were a co-conspirator in the terror attacks or just a lead to them."

"I trust they've made the right choice," Nash commented.

"Trailing you two worked out to our advantage," Heinrich replied.

"What happens now?" Kara asked.

"We'll debrief you at HQ, then you can be on your way." He motioned to Professor Thomas. "And the professor can go back to his stodgy old tablets."

"Not so fast," Professor Thomas said. "There is the matter of the missing scrolls and the existence of that Nazi base at the bottom of the world."

Nash raised an eyebrow. "Raymond. You're not telling me you still believe there are ancient scrolls there?"

Thomas smiled.

"You're trading the hunt in dust and heat for ice and cold, huh?"

"And I want you to help me," pleaded the Professor.

"Oh, no. I'm through with Nazis. I'll leave that up to you and

Indiana Jones." He looked at Kara and squeezed her hand. "Right now, I'm more interested in enjoying the sights and sounds of Berlin."

Kara squeezed his hand back and gave him a devilish encouraging smile.

"Wasn't that a delightful introduction to the sights and sounds of Berlin?" Kara sighed, watching Nash finish a hot shower. "A candlelight dinner and that lovely trio playing my favorite Cole Porter," she sighed once again.

And with that she slipped between the silken sheets of the large luxurious bed of their hotel room. Barely audible she whispered, "If I were a pussy cat I would be purring."

Then she added a little louder, stretching under the sheets, "What do *tom* cats do?"

Nash walked into the room drying himself off briskly. He stood over the bed, tossed the towel quickly aside, and growled, "They pounce!"

And he did.

Epilogue

The hotel phone rang, startling them awake. Nash fumbled with the nightstand and knocked the phone over. Rising on one elbow, he picked up the receiver and held it to his ear. "Hello."

"Nash, we still need to talk."

"Who is this," Nash questioned groggily.

"It's Marsh. Remember what I told you? We need to talk."

"It's not the best time right now," Nash said, annoyed.

"I'll meet you at the Lufthansa ticket counter at Tempelhof in an hour." Then he added, "You owe me. Remember?"

Before Nash could object, Marsh hung up.

Christ. Now what?

Nash slammed the phone down and rolled over.

Kara kissed him on the forehead. "Marsh?"

"Yep," he said, kissing the nape of her neck. "I'm meeting him at the Tempelhof in an hour."

"Do you have to go?" she purred.

"He said that I have a very powerful enemy and that my life is still in danger." He kissed down her shoulder to her breast. "I need to get some answers."

"So maybe you'll be a little late." He wrapped her legs around him and kissed her deeply.

"Now, what is this all about?" Nash grumbled as he took the seat next to Marsh in a corner near the Lufthansa ticket counter. "I don't have the patience for spy games at this point. Not after what I've been through."

He looked Marsh straight in the eye. "Now tell me. Who's this powerful enemy I've made."

"First tell me, did you receive something from your uncle recently?"

"What uncle?"

"Gordon Nash?"

That was probably the last relative he ever wanted to hear from. Gordon Nash was his father's brother. He was a Congressman from New Mexico and the sleaziest of political hacks. Through the years, he convinced Nash to give him the names of conspiracy nuts, New Age kooks, and urban legend believers. He then proceeded to shake them down for campaign contributions. He used them—and their money—to line his campaign coffers, promising to hold Congressional investigations into their pet beliefs—UFOs, Big Foot, 9-11, the Kennedy assassination, and other crazy and bizarre conspiracies they dreamed up.

Nash was disgusted with his uncle's political advancement at the expense of fanatics and refused to even talk to him.

"No," Nash said, firmly. "I really want nothing to do with that sleaze ball. If I did receive anything from him, I would have trashed it immediately." He paused for a second. "How do you know about my uncle?"

"I was doing research for him. A major contributor to his last campaign wanted him to look into something called the Committee. That's how I discovered that someone called the Chairman wanted you dead."

"Enough of this." Nash was growing impatient. "Tell me about this Chairman."

Marsh looked around to make sure no one there was interested in their conversation then he pulled out a tattered black notebook— the kind reporters use to take notes. "It's all in here," he said.

"What's all in there?"

"Pieces to a puzzle," Marsh said, slapping the notebook against the palm of his hand.

Nash reached for the small notebook, but Marsh pulled it way and stuck it back in his jacket.

"Damn it, Marsh! Stop playing games. Tell me what I want to know, or I'm out of here."

"And how far do you think you would get? They'll hunt you down, Nash. Believe me. I've seen what they can do."

"Okay," Nash sighed condescendedly. "Go on."

Marsh moved his face closer to Nash. "There is an organization. A global organization called the Committee."

"You told me that. So what?"

Marsh lowered his voice. "Have you ever heard of Humanity's Tombstone? Or the Ten Commandments of the anti-Christ?"

Nash shook his head. "This secret committee is a bunch of Satan worshipers?"

"If only it was that simple," Marsh replied. "They want to create a New World Order."

"Yeah. Yeah. I've heard this one before. They want to get filthy rich and gain political control of the world."

Marsh's attitude stiffened. "You know *nothing* about the New World Order. The members of the committee are not after money. They have all they'd ever want. They are not after political power either. To the committee, the masses are a nuisance and a hindrance to their goals."

"So, what are they after?"

Marsh became deadly serious. "You've seen pieces of their plan yourself. The energy project in Arizona and the ethnic cleansing attempt here in Germany."

"If they're not after money and political power, what do they want?"

"Utopian divinity—one only for themselves."

"What? How?"

Marsh patted the notebook in his jacket pocket. "The answer is somewhere in here."

"It's too early for this," Nash said. "I need a cup of coffee."

"You can probably get one in that Sports Bar," Marsh offered. "Go ahead."

"Can I get you one?"

"Sure. Two sugars."

Nash walked to the counter and ordered the two coffees. As they were being prepared, he wondered what his uncle might have sent him. Maybe he was too hasty in his response to the question from Marsh. Against his better judgment he was going to bring it up.

He returned to where Marsh was sitting, sat down next to him, and held out his cup of coffee.

Marsh didn't move. He looked asleep.

"Marsh," Nash said.

Marsh's head leaned back, and white foam drooled from the corner of his mouth. Nash saw a small dart protruding from his neck.

Marsh was dead.

Nash quickly looked around. No one was paying any attention to them. He stood up to leave, but then hesitated. He gently withdrew the notebook from Marsh's jacket, propped Marsh's body upright and quickly left the terminal.

Outside and alone, Nash opened the notebook. The book was filled with quotes and strange notations.

But one quote, circled, caught his eye. It read:

"We are on the verge of a global transformation. All we need is the right major crisis and the nations will accept the New World Order."

~David Rockefeller

About the Author

F rank F. Fiore is a five-star rated author of novels in multiple genres including Contemporary Fiction, Tecno-Thrillers, Action/ Adventures, Sci-Fi, Historical Fiction, and Westerns. He lives in Arizona with his fetching wife, Lynne.

Connect with Frank online at:

www.frankfiore.com

Also Available From
WordCrafts Press

Wiggle Room
Darden North

A Pale Horse
Michelle A. Sullivan

Demimonde
James E. Cressler

Ill Gotten Gain
Ralph E. Jarrells

Plague
Marian Rizzo

www.wordcrafts.net